the
american
savior

A NOVEL BY

EVERETT HEATH

Reader House Publishing
The American Savior©
Cover Design: Kustom Creative

Everett Heath

The oldest of child of a career intelligence officer, Everett was born in Texas and months later his parents moved to England. He spent much of his childhood in Europe before returning to the United States. Everett flew fighter jets for most of his Air Force career. Writing fiction evolved from being a life long songwriter —he has played in numerous bands over the years. After living in Alaska for some time, Everett relocated to Hawaii. His favorite surf spot is a secret.

The American Savior

For
Mother and Father

Chapter 1

Everyone came home late but Abby. She was then a stay at home Mom. Earl dumped his shoulder pads on top of his muddy football pants on the back patio and abandoned his muddy cleats next to the doormat. If she was not in the kitchen Earl bolted for the fridge to gulp cold grape Kool-Aid from the pitcher. He finally remembered to wipe the purple mustache off his mouth in case he ran into Mom on the way to the shower.

Car headlights illuminated four boys, some still wearing their helmets, returning home from practice. The walk home was at early night, but only a half-mile from school. They'd walk line abreast, the tallest of the lot and their only true tight end walking on the street and hopping up onto the sidewalk when an oncoming car approached. Not much was said going home. They were tired and sore and starving. The end of practice wind sprints wiped them out. Earl lived the farthest away and for a hundred yards he walked alone. He loved the feel and smell of the crisp fall air. He thought maybe he smelled the dying leaves on the sycamores that lined his street. Maybe he smelled all the leaves of trees and plants, all dying to get on with winter. But he hoped not. He imagined the cool air delivered scents from faraway places he had yet to visit. Strange and exciting places, like Hawaii and the Grand Canyon, maybe Singapore. He walked in all the front lawns so his cleats would not clatter on the sidewalk. Thirteen-year-old boys played football in the Pop Warner leagues. Earl Neuhaus played quarterback and defensive end for the Yasby Rattlers.

The kitchen was empty and the Kool-Aid was guaranteed cold. Amy must be sequestered in her bedroom as usual, thought Earl. He leapt up in the air upon seeing no dinner in the oven or water boiling on the stovetop. No salad in the fridge. This could mean only one thing…takeout. Earl held his clasped hands over his head, closed his eyes and prayed, "Please, please make it fried chicken." In dirty white knee socks, boxers and sweaty t-shirt, he leaned close to his sister's bedroom door.

"Hey Amy, Mom go out for fried chicken?"

"Get creamed today in practice?" asked his sister, not bothering to let him in.

"C'mon Amy, you know I don't get creamed at practice."

"Oh yeah-- just during the games when everyone's watching." Since nine years old, Amy has been a first rate smart aleck.

"Fried chicken tonight or what?" Earl asked again, twisting the locked doorknob back and forth.

"I guess we're having 'or what'."

"Dad home yet?"

"Whatta you think?" Earl knew his father was not home but it was an irritating ritual he and Amy developed. Seeing the phone cord from the hallway table pass under her locked door was the norm. She was turning seventeen and thought she was hotter than the hottest starlet in Hollywood. At least most of the high school football players thought so. But she had big lips and a big mouth. And toothy, thought Earl. Model straight teeth--flashing all over the place like a toothpaste commercial.

Hands behind his head, lying slant ways across a Dallas Cowboys bed spread, Earl's stomach spoke. It was as if his stomach gurgling were actual voices, voices crying out for the want of food, hot crispy fried chicken to be exact. He imagined the voices saying, "Need fried chicken", in a distorted drawn out manner. The voices trailed off into an incoherent rumble, pausing in silence, and then increasing in volume, almost snapping out the demand--"Fried Chicken." He drifted off, falling quickly into a deep sleep. No one woke him for dinner because that night no dinner was served. His mother never returned home. Abby was no longer a stay at home Mom.

Chapter 2

Hot dusty air was in a tilted swirl amongst the bucket seats. Streams of white fuzz formed counter clockwise circles on the road and some accumulated on the windshield wipers before being whisked up and away. The cassette slurred to a stop hours ago. The FM radio played white noise. The baked road top was blanketed with tar filled cracks. The only music was the monotonous rhythm generated by worn tires. Clump-clump, clump-clump, ricocheting against the bottom of the BMW pressing against 80 mph, hustling towards Lubbock.

It was mid-August and Lt. Earl Neuhaus drove with windows down. Eighteen wheelers blasting by in the other direction created a bow wave of air that shoved the car sideways, increasing the ambient pressure inside the car, leaving his ears ringing with a stubborn sound—ssschhhhoom—the blast rising in pitch but dissipating in volume as the truck passed. Of course air conditioning changed the world, he mused, picking cotton fuzz from his top left incisor. Wished mine worked, he thought. If not for the searing heat distorting the air, the cotton gins could be seen almost 30 miles away. Not an inch of elevation change was visible looking across the miles of furrows of cotton. Other than being pushed around by fellow travelers on Highway 87, the outside air was still, as evidenced by the lonesome narrow column of black smoke standing in the distance just west of Reese Air Force Base.

Chapter 3

Earl checked in at 0700 hours at the dusty one story building known as the Student Center. All the buildings on base were plain sand colored one-story buildings, except the parachute shop. The cheap, deep blue stucco chute shop had attached to its own one story building a three story high square wooden silo with no windows above the first floor. This is where the parachutes were refurbished, checked over, and packed. Unlike the newer fighters, the T-37 and T-38 trainer jets required pilots to wear parachutes.

Earl picked up all his books and academic schedule, located his flight room, and filled out two hours worth of in-processing paperwork. Orientation started the next day. Completed just two months prior, Air Force Officer Training School taught him a few lessons he was to find very useful in his new profession. Keep your mouth shut, don't stand out other than in high achievement, and develop a reputation as a rule follower and team player. And, avoid volunteering for anything. For example, avoid telling anyone you graduated from Harvard with a degree in Religious History. Or that you had been accepted into Harvard Law School and had been granted a deferment but Harvard was unaware that you had also applied to OTS and Undergraduate Pilot Training and were accepted. And your father was not aware either because you informed him you were taking a year to go to Rome to study Early Catholic Leaders at University of Roma. You could care less what your mother thought of your decisions. Earl knew full well everyone, family or no, would eventually find out sometime. But he certainly was not going to be volunteering any information.

*****

OTS was mind numbing. There was plenty of dark morning PT, as if the Drill Instructors did not have enough actual material to teach the cadets. The Air Force was barely fifty years old. Marching, parading, and singing songs ripped off from the Army Airborne cadre to keep cadence while double timing in formation around the base. Wondering when the stubble of hair on his head would grow back. Folding tighty whitey underwear into neat squares alongside curled black socks, smiley face up. Memorizing the history of how the Air Force came into being. The names of the current four-star generals in charge. Plus the Secretary of Defense and Air Force. The basic elements of the Uniformed Code of Military Justice. Conduct unbecoming an officer appeared to be a very wide catch-all for anything the Air Force deemed inappropriate or potentially embarrassing to the high muckety-mucks. Shining shoes and polishing belt buckles and U.S. lapel insignia. And then back to shuffling around in formation singing Airborne chants, the fill-in-the-blank kind of song where the creative quip artists could try their verses out and if the Drill Instructors approved, five minutes of shuffling around the asphalt streets around the barracks were lopped off the run. If they disapproved then the shuffle drags on for an extra five minutes. Most times it was worth the risk because of Bartholomew James, who defended his name by proclaiming in a smooth drawl, "Listen, I'd rather have two first names than two last names—rather be first than last any day of the God-given week."

James was a natural in all things natural. He could move you to tears singing Leonard Cohen's *Alleluia*, recite snips of Yeats, Blake and Eliot, throw a football seventy five yards in a tight spiral, and make up some of the raunchiest ditties ever composed for marching. The DIs would not let him start singing until the formation was running along the perimeter fence behind the old corrugated warehouses, for fear of some Air Force officer's wife or righteous Colonel driving along with the windows rolled down overhearing the rest of the formation repeating the lines of Bartholomew James. It made the afternoon shuffle almost worth anticipating. Everyone knew they were in for a doozy when Bartholomew started out with the bluest of limericks that made even the DIs turned their heads in disbelief.

Bartholomew was large, which amplified his already large earthly presence. He measures six foot four but you'd swear he was near six ten. He keeps his thick brown hair flattop tight which accentuates his pronounced widow's peak that serves as a pointer for anyone needing directions to the rest of his striking physique. Lacquer green eyes are set wide in his face, above flat, dimple free cheekbones that frame his Bob Hope slender nose and extending narrow chin. He possesses wide shoulders and melon sized calves. Long fingers are set in wide palms. His midsection is not a bodybuilder's dream, but a beer lover's reality.

He seemed older than all the other candidates. He claimed he worked around the country before college but didn't mention what kind of work. Earl wasn't so sure about all of his

10

stories. But Earl certainly remembered him. Bartholomew played on the football team all four years. Earl graduated from the same college as Bartholomew. But Earl told no one. He did not know Bartholomew at college. The fact their small Division team did not rate regular national news coverage did not mean it was a big deal locally. He was a big deal. Especially since Bartholomew was not a local boy by any stretch. He was a big deal because he caught any pass he could touch and made every effort to punish any potential tackler by lowering his helmet into their solar plexus. Bartholomew was not extraordinarily fast but his hips lulled you one way as he galloped the other way--his balance was noteworthy. He never expected to beat any defender in open field running. However, he wanted to remind any tackler that taking him down came at a cost. He was a big deal because the rabid sports fanatics of Harvard's entrenched uber wealthy, power-player alumni, were thrilled. They were titillated. Maybe it is because sport talent is wealth and power neutral. No amount of stock options or U.S. Senate influence creates a talented athlete. Bartholomew sensed the Harvard power players viewed any endeavor other than acquiring power and influence as an occasional diversion from the serious matters at hand. After all, athleticism is fleeting. And also, after all, their world shapes *the* world and world shaping is the most serious of pursuits. If that is not entirely accurate how the tip of the power pyramid viewed their role, it did not matter because it was certainly how Bartholomew, who was not born into the existing power structure, viewed them. Bartholomew believed perception was damn near reality and damn near anything was typically good enough for most pursuits. However, it was the mark of a very special man who recognizes when perception was not good enough. Those men deserved close study. When Bartholomew found them, he studied them. But he knew what almost all men ultimately do. They habituate imitation. Men employ vicarious tentacles to feed their illusions. Bartholomew knew that imitation must cease early on and only reoccur to substitute good habits for bad. He had tentacles too, and illusions. But Bartholomew did not desire to imitate, he yearned to follow no path worn by another man.

"Where did you learn that song?" An eager beaver OTS cadet kept pestering Bartholomew on his formation songs. Cadet Eager Beaver was completely spellbound by the big man.

"Told ya, Eager, they come from a secret book of songs. You know that book has to be secret right?" The lyrics, Eager—the lyrics aren't for everyone's ears."

"Can I see the book? C'mon Bartholomew, let me see it."

Bartholomew made sure everyone called him by his full first name. He couldn't control the OTS cadre and he accepted that temporary condition. Their intent was to test him and everyone else for the next three months. Test their patience, physical limits, and mental toughness. It was a joke. The cadre knew it was just a game, and any OTS cadet with any sense would know also. But not every cadet knew it was a game. Many chose to take it personal. Some chose to become offended. They were weak, Bartholomew concluded. Maybe they'd shape up later in their lives, maybe not. He was convinced that if weakness was evident in a twenty one year old, weakness remains. Their only hope, he thought, was they have to realize their weakness. Now, weakness and the awareness of weakness itself were different matters, connected obviously, but within the space of difference lay the all essential—the all-essential Opportunity. That is, the opportunity to avoid any action in which weakness could wreck the success of any endeavor, large or small, crowd grabbing grandiose or anonymously humble. Opportunity was Bartholomew's touchstone.

Unlike Bartholomew James, dull nights at OTS did not tempt Earl Neuhaus to fully engage in gab sessions with fellow cadets. Earl lived in a different dorm than Bartholomew and stuck to small talk around the blank metal bunk beds lining the big open room. Yet he helped out his bunkmate and guys next to him making their hospital corners crisp, and how to keep cheap grey wool blankets taut against the squeaky bed frames. He was skillful in deflecting any innocuous probes of his background, almost always turning the conversation around to let the inquisitive cadet spill his guts about himself. Earl was convincing that he was interested in all the typical subjects strangers steer towards in an effort to fill the silence or reach out in attempts to wave off loneliness. Sports, cars, girls--any kind of man hobby. Earl was a natural born student of human behavior; he was fascinated by what prompted human activity. His mother brought that realization to the surface long ago. He could thank his Mom for at least something. Earl was to learn Bartholomew was also a keen observer.

Earl was aware of Bartholomew, his presence and effect on fellow cadets and cadre. But Earl's effect was subtle, barely noticeable unless you looked for it. Bartholomew found it early on, even though they were in different squadrons and dorms. Nearly as tall but slight, Earl parted his short sandy hair to the side, just like all up and coming professionals, careful not to attract attention with a flat top or comb back style. Earl was lean but borderline skinny. If beer drinking was a habit, it did not show itself around his short waist. His legs were not quite bird legs and were in full proportion. Earl carried himself without concern, for he was not aware of any concerns that he felt obligated to carry. It was in his gait and in his stance--alone or in a crowd. He seemed to exist without the bending weight of the human condition. It showed on his long face and color changing eyes. As if he was a special mirror—reflecting select expressions of others, or even more mysterious, reflecting their deep inward musings or contemplations unable to be articulated. A short squatty female cadet could swear she noticed his eyes change color—from ocean blue to ocean green. She told Earl, and yet her flirtatious observation did not change his demeanor. Bartholomew watched her fleeting interaction with Earl. It caught Bartholomew's attention.

With extensive practice, Bartholomew considered himself a master in concealing any hint of concerns he felt burdened to carry. With Earl however, he apparently either had no concerns or was more masterful than himself. That irked Bartholomew. Either way, Bartholomew thought, Earl was someone to watch, maybe even get to know. The list of people changed, depending on the psychological dependencies of the moment. Sizing oneself up against another was a dependency. If he ran into him again then Earl was definitely someone to get to know.

*****

Six thirty am, in formation outside the 416th Flying Training Squadron building, in the empty yellow striped parking lot, the smell of newly paved asphalt increasing the discomfort of being locked at attention--hung-over--tequila sweat pitting his short sleeve uniform. At least Bartholomew James was not going to catch hell for his hair. Crew tops were still a few years away from returning to style.

"Damn Lt. James, it's 630 in the morning and actually not too damn hot out this fine Lubbock Air Force Base day and you're sweating like you had a late night—or maybe an early morning. Which was it?"

"Both, sir."

"Honesty gets you no points in the parking lot with me, Lieutenant. Can you function today, mister? Nice tight wig, by the way."

"Yessir."

"You haven't started pilot training yet and you're already lookin' like a ham fist."

"Lose the after shave."

"Yessir."

Captain Pershing was a scrawny, pimply, red haired asshole. A B-52 pilot, he volunteered to return to Training Command for a softer tour than the strict, black and white, void-of-humor world of nukes. Definitely no sense of humor working around nukes. Plenty of strange characters amongst the bomber world, for reasons that Bartholomew could not figure. This proved to be the topic that introduced Bartholomew to Earl. Others jabbered away about the T-37 solo student packing it in on the first day of their pilot training class. The rising black smoke Earl saw driving in to Lubbock. Dying seemed to be part of flying. That fact didn't disturb Earl.

Chapter 4

Amy Neuhaus rang the doorbell at 830pm on a football Monday night and stayed two months. But it did not take two months for Earl to know what he knew about his sister. It took one long Monday night to confirm what he had surmised a few years back. He lugged in the case of white wine from her big black Chevrolet pickup. She carried the half-pound of dope in on her own. She emptied the contents of her drawstring shoulder bag onto the butterscotch laminated kitchen counter while spending no more than ten seconds surveying the kitchen, dining area and living room. The apartment barely required ten seconds to survey.

"I know there's not a drop of good wine in Lubbock. Can't be sure about weed, though. Never know when a flat-ass town has at least one supplier or even cultivator of herb. Just that sometimes it takes too long to find him. So I came prepared."

"I'll sleep on the floor, you sleep in my room and tomorrow I'll go out and buy you a pullout sofa. It's the least I can do." Next to the twelve-inch TV and expensive stereo, Earl's two low back cushion chairs were the only pieces of furniture in the living room. He never spent much time in his apartment. Why decorate much further?

Exiting the bathroom she declared, "Earl, your bathroom's too clean for a bachelor. You have a cleaning service or something?" Her skinny smile relaxed her eyebrows and almost made her face look as young as she was.

"Never know when I'll have a guest of your persuasion stop by."

"Surprised they're not camped at your door Earl. You got what they're after, handsome boy. Trust me on that score. Not enough mirrors though--you need mirrors."

"I'll keep that in mind when I re-decorate."

Amy changed into sweat pants and a wrinkled red t-shirt sporting a popular rock band's black star logo. She removed a bottle of wine she had put in the freezer, uncorked the bottle, grabbed a water glass from the cupboard and filled it. So began the evening.

Earl never asked about where she had come from. It just didn't matter--neither to him, nor to her. He listened and left his wine she poured him in the glass. Half-way through the second bottle Amy said, "Earl, I'm drinking alone again, aren't I?"

"I have a test in three hours. Can I call it a night and get some sleep?"
She drained her glass and swapped her empty with his full.

"For God's sake go to bed. I'll sleep on the chair cushions." She shooed him off to the bedroom with a slurry hand wave.

"Good night then..."

"Nite, nite Early Earl," she said toasting his departure.

"Don't smoke in the apartment Amy."

"Promise," crossing her heart with a drunken she-devil's grin. Watching his sister get drunk planted an ache inside him. He listened mostly, answering in short sentences when she asked about pilot training or what there was to do in a town like Lubbock, or if the coeds at Texas Tech were as hot as everyone claimed. It didn't matter much what he said unless he talked about women, which for some reason Amy seemed to perk up and pay attention. Earl thought Amy thought he was

18

homosexual. He thought, I don't dislike girls; I just don't have much interest. Pilot training's keeping me busy along with all the other thoughts that ramble through my mind.

To her he just said, "I'm not homosexual Amy, get off it."

"Hell, I know you're not a fag, Early boy. But I do think you got parts in you that aren't quite fully connected,"

"Maybe so, but at least the condition's not painful." His warm smirk matched hers.

"I got a settlement from my ex's old man. Unbelievable bastard wired me 500 grand. Can you believe that? Now, here's what I know you're not gonna believe—I set up the account to where I only can tap twenty five hundred a month unless I get someone in my family to send a goddamn letter to the bank saying it's some kind of emergency and I need the money!" Amy stared at Earl looking for a reaction. Earl scrunched his lips, preventing any possible reply. He had none to offer other than to nod his head a couple times.

"I knew you wouldn't believe me. Actually, the old man had some finance person of his set the whole thing up so I wouldn't go crazy with the money. Not that I would…"

Again, Earl scrunched his lips, this time uttering, "Hmm," under his breath.

"I heard that Earl."

"What?"

"That 'hmm'. I heard it. The whole story is true."

"Sure?"

"Positive." Waving her drink hand towards the door she shouted, "How do you think I got that shiny new Chevy in the parking lot? That was paid for in cash Earl."

19

"So the ex-father-in-law could guarantee you'd leave. Right?"

"Absolutely correct, smart guy." She was drunk loud and her voice went mean.

He got up from the chair, walked over and rested his hand on her shoulder. He leaned to her ear and whispered, "You can stay for awhile Amy, and you're welcome here, but not as a constant pissed-off drunk."

Turning her face towards his, she replied softly, "What about an occasional pissed-off drunk?" They exchanged weak smiles, but hers leaked sorrow.

"Good luck on your test. Sorry I robbed you of study time."

"It's only a weather test."

"The tall and majestic clouds, the thick puffy white ones—what are they called?"

"Cumulonimbus. Beautiful, but bad news for airplanes."

"Why's that?"

"The down draft. Serious air movement in those nasties." She said, "Mom gets into those type of clouds, doesn't she?"

"For the last time, goodnight. Let me go to bed." Amy did not want to be alone. She convinced herself he fell asleep as soon as he fell into bed. Amy double-checked before lighting up a half-smoked joint. But sleep did not come easy that early morning for either of them.

Earl doubled majored, knowing full well that he would need an advanced degree in something like business or finance in order to make a living above entry level. But he diverted off the academic track and joined the Air Force. He justified his decision because it served as motivation towards going in a direction his father would never have even remotely considered. His mother's input was absent. He knew his older sister was already on the comfortably numb track, absorbing glasses upon glasses of Sauvignon Blanc and boutique weed. You can retain your good looks only for a stretch of time living off wine and weed, plus an occasional greasy full stuffed omelet or a half-pound bleu cheese burger and steak fries. But crinkles on the face and cracked dry palms begin to tell the tale. The mind and body are being robbed of necessary elements. Amy was robbing her own body to feel extraordinary. The essence of extraordinariness is the feeling of being a total unique entity in the cosmos. Those wholly allured to extraordinariness think in cosmic terms, not mere earthly--far too parochial. Their dreams are individualistic in the extreme, yet look to fill a void by hoping someone would rescue them in the anonymous and unimaginable expanse of the cosmos. Small wonder the wine bottle never can go dry or bag of marijuana go empty. The need never fills the void because they search far out in the distance. They've convinced themselves their rescue awaits them far out *there*. Too far out. It kills them often and early, leaving the void ready, like a trap, to await the next victim's choice. The void requires nothing more than the attraction to delusion. Since freedom is permeated by fear and salving fear is human, as well as habit forming, becoming comfortable in numbness is one choice. Earl thought these kinds of things and knew that was Amy's choice.

Amy married and divorced at twenty-three. Her litheness, high cheekbones and lush eyelashes protecting speckled blue eyes caught the attention of all men who look—but she only gawked at the wealthy ones. The marriage was a disaster from the beginning but with ex-Daddy's-in law's ultimatum to her to disappear or else, she managed to secure for herself five hundred grand to do just that—which is precisely what she continues to do--and probably is her best attribute. She wanted no part of compromise in building a relationship. She didn't consider herself one who fostered anything, much less love. Amy called love an alien concept. Earl wanted to convince himself he knew better when Helen came to mind. He had not thought about Helen lately.

After their mother left; that's when Earl became quiet. And stopped wondering why he seemed to be able to sense the motivational essence of people—about how people ticked and tocked, about what drove someone to make a decision, or make one by not making a decision. He simply accepted his perceptive ability and so began his fascination with the variegated peculiarities that constitute human behavior. He began paying closer attention to those around him. Earl watched his classmates; how they talked, what expressions they made, the frustrations attaining verbal clarity, and inflections, pitch and volume variations of their speech. They were so transparent, so predictable. In the beginning he was too obvious—classmates he watched became self-conscious and ostracized him.

He discovered adults were not that difficult to see through either. He figured out everyone has vanities and most want to show you theirs. Everyone turns everyone else into an object and then envies what they do not believe they possess. Everyone copies whom they envy. Was Earl walking amongst anyone who did not mimic? He thought of his father and mother—two examples of unbound envy. He intuited fear came from threatened vanities. It was not fear itself Earl was attracted to, but the construction and the curious fragments of thoughts that induce fear. Not the instinct-to-survive kind of fear, but the fear of bruising pride.

His father and mother never made them attend religious services even though both were raised Catholic. He and Amy were not baptized. His mother never spoke of God or faith or church. When he was ten, his father answered his question. "We spend our Sundays together as family because that is what families are supposed to do. And we spend it at home." Earl never again raised the subject of God or church after he was a small boy.

His mother left home the week after Thanksgiving, but she left tending to the small particulars in his life a few years prior. Earl was fond of remembering her welcoming him home every day during his first years in school, calling him in for Saturday lunch after a hard morning's adventure in the big backyard of the fat neighbors that lived catty-corner to their house. Letting him stay in his pajamas on cold and rainy Saturdays and watch cartoons until lunchtime. Making him turn off the light and go to bed after hours hunched over his models, assembling and gluing Messerschmitt's, Hurricanes and Spitfires to hang above his bed from the fishing line tacked to the ceilings, recreating the Battle of Britain over him. He glued billowed cotton balls stained with streaks of orange markers to the aft section of the doomed Henkel bomber as his prized model Spitfire blasted off the bomber's tail--scoring another aerial victory. Earl did not realize his mother withdrawing from mothering until after she was gone. It made the last Thanksgiving as a family seem like a complete sham. She worked the full day and evening prior, plus the early morning, preparing the dinner. It was the best dinner she ever prepared. She was in a happy mood that day and through the weekend. He and his sister were in complete disbelief for days after. He thought that all his ruminations were because of his mother. Earl forced himself to stop wondering about that too.

It was the freshman course on Religions of the World that led Earl, for the first time in his life, to serious thinking about life after death. From then on he concentrated on the History of Christianity. This is when he discovered his founding principle, declaring to himself, "It is absurd to believe I am born from no first cause. Therefore I am born from a first cause. I acknowledge God to be the first cause." He was baptized while at Harvard. Death didn't seem worrisome so much anymore.

Chapter 5

"Hey Neuhaus, you got any civilian flying time?" Earl never looked up replying, "Not a minute." Lt. Bartholomew James grabbed the seat next to him in the squadron snack bar. "Heard you majored in religious engineering."

"How'd you know?" Earl finally turned toward him to see the big man's head appear to bounce off an invisible wall as a wide grin formed on his thick lips.

"Because our superior leader Captain Dickhead Pershing gave me shit for being a Divinity Studies major and threw your name out being a Philosophy major."

"Religious History *and* Philosophy."

"OK, Divinity Studies *and* Latin."
They looked each other in the eye for maybe four seconds before Bartholomew's head lurched back as he cracked up laughing.

"Called us a couple of fuzzy craniums or some bullshit." Earl viewed him with a flash of suspicion before joining him in a hard laugh that turned all the heads in the snack bar.

Earl deadpanned, "Let him forever be known as Richard Cranium." That sent Bartholomew crashing to the floor in big bellowing laughing spasms. The rest of the students turned to each other and looked at the other tables for some reassurance that *they* were the sane ones in the room. Earl was taken aback by his pratfall.

"It wasn't that funny, honestly..." Sitting up on the floor Bartholomew shot back, "The hell you say Neuhuas. *That* was good!"

Addressing the rest of the students, he said, "You all hear Capt Pershing's new nickname?" Earl leaned over and offered his hand. Bartholomew accepted and Earl pulled him up off the floor.

"I'm Bartholomew."

"I'm Earl. I remember, not Bart?"

"That's right. Not Bart. Bar-thol-o-mew," he replied, as if trying to get a Korean farmer's daughter to understand slow-speed English.

"OTS, right?" said Bartholomew.

"Right. And Harvard," said Earl.

Leaning in and whispering Bartholomew said, "No shit?" Earl nodded.

"Well, no shit," said Bartholomew, chuckling. "Damn."

"Never see you at the O'Club on Fridays. You a non-drinker or what"?

Earl said, "Not a bar type guy, I guess."

"You drink Jack Daniels, beer, what…?"

"Beer mostly."

"Stop by this Friday and I'll buy you a beer."

"Alright, sounds good." It did sound good to Earl, although, as Bartholomew was realizing, he just didn't have occasion to display how good a Friday beer really is. Nor much occasion to display any emotion. Earl seemed to be a human form extending out from the off-white paint covering the mason brick walls of the snack bar and the rest of the flying squadron. The building was built in the mid-fifties and little refurbishment had been done since. It had no visible character, no vibe, no comfort, which confused Bartholomew in a way. Earl hid behind his face, like the paint hid the drab mason walls. The tired building housed the lives of instructors and student pilots, withstood the daily jet engine blasts of training jets taking off and engine spool ups after performing endless touch and go's. It housed the elation and fear of flying jets. And the presence of death. Bartholomew knew it was just a matter of time before the real Earl peeked out from his covered demeanor. Then he would pounce on him. Bartholomew knew he knew much about people and had a few beer soaked theories as to why but he'd just as soon not think too deep about it. He was never in any hurry to self analyze and stir up apprehension. After all, performing well enough in pilot training to warrant a fighter was plenty effective agitating the insides.

Chapter 6

Today, the thumb worn checklist was not necessary.
Earl's preflight walk around the T-37 required no referral to
anything other than what he had committed to memory. The
exterior of the stubby and squatty white jet trainer did not have
that much to inspect. Pitot static ports clear, no flat tires, no red
(hydraulic) or black (engine oil) fluid pooling anywhere under
the airframe, clean canopy, no missing panels, engine intakes
clear, all red covers and streamers removed and placed in a
green canvas bag near the fire extinguisher. That was about it.
He referred to the checklist anyway; more to give comfort to the
crew chief whose eyes never left Earl as he conducted his jet
pre-flight for his first solo flight to the Military Operating Areas
or MOAs as they were called. His very first solo was a pattern
only flight. He flew around the airport-controlled airspace under
constant binocular surveillance by the air traffic controllers in
the tower as well as his instructor pilot who was out in a small
red and white observation building next to the runway. This
time Earl was leaving the nest and flying out of visual range of
the airport control tower--sixty miles west of the base to perform
acrobatics--Chandelles, loops and all manner of upside down
flying. It was two thirty in the afternoon at the end of July. The
tarmac was soaked in heat and the skin of the T-37 was skillet
hot. There were plenty of cumulus around but not enough to
threaten rainfall or develop into a cloud ceiling. Earl was only
cleared to fly in clear air, he was not checked out in instrument
flying. He hoped to swoop in, out and around some puffy
cumulous clouds in the area. Not that he would ever admit that
to a soul. There was not a stitch of a breeze on the flight line.

His tight weaved nomex flight suit did not breathe and his shoulders and back were soaked in sweat. The twenty-five pound parachute strapped around him gouged his shoulders and only added to the weight of the Texas Panhandle heat. All the more reason to get airborne ASAP so he could open the cockpit vents and let the freezing air at ten thousand feet blow over him.

The T-37's J-69 turbo jet engines emitted an extremely high and obnoxious squeal. With up to a dozen Tweets running at any one time, Earl learned quickly double ear protection was required unless you looked forward to a life of tinnitus. Like most everyone else on the flight line, he had lemon yellow foam ear plugs stuffed into his ears and wore the goofy looking blue cup ear protectors issued by the USAF.

It was very important to perform the engine starts, flight control checks, and brake check mistake free. The communication with the crew chief monitoring the start and overseeing the ground checks was by hand signals. If a crew chief was not in sight, the pilot's hands must be placed on the dash and knees flexed apart so as not to move the flight control stick and deflect an aileron or rudder and bang the crew chief or trap his fingers between the control surface and the fuselage.

Next important step was to make all radio calls concise and without a hint of hesitation. Keep emotion out of the voice, declare your intentions, and for God's sake acknowledge every radio call made to your callsign. Everyone knew who you were by your callsign—ground, tower, departure control, the regional air traffic control agencies, and every pilot on the same frequency. With the callsign Solo 41, everyone knows you are a solo student. His first radio call, requesting permission to start engines, was delivered with authority. Practicing the radio call to himself fifteen times during the preflight check helped. No one could hear him reciting aloud radio calls. The ramp was saturated in engine noise. Earl had not completed after engine start checks when thoughts of taxiing to the correct runway were forming in his mind.

"One step at a time." He repeated this five times to himself as his number two engine began to squeal during startup. RPM and oil pressure were in the normal ranges. Completing the rest of his checks he directed the crew chief with hand signals—bumping and then motioning clenched hands away with thumbs pointing left and right. The crew chief acknowledged by nodding his head and raising his arms showing the palms of gloved hands, a signal for Earl to place his hands on the dash while the crew chief bent underneath the low-slung jet trainer to kick the chalks clear of the main landing gear. The jet now belonged to Earl.

He finally noticed the ground control frequency was abuzz in airport chatter, so much so he could not squeeze his radio call in to obtain permission to taxi. His anxiousness to get the jet moving led his eyes to the fuel gauges. He thought, "I'm burning up fuel just sitting here on this damned hot ramp." He became worried he would not have enough fuel for the mission. Then he scolded himself for slipping into the irrational.

"I can't get a word in on ground," Earl said out loud and into his rubber oxygen mask that had become slippery with sweat streaming down his face. He thought, "Is this what the instructors mean by compartmentalizing thoughts and focus on the immediate task?" His crew chief was standing at parade rest ten feet off to the left side of his jet waiting in the standing heat for the damned Lieutenant to give the taxi signal. He had an urgent and irritable need for a Coke and a smoke.

"About damned time," they both said out loud to themselves as Earl gave the signal to taxi. He finally was able to wedge in a call to ground control to taxi. The crew chief motioned him to begin taxi and once Earl started forward the crew chief abruptly crossed both arms in front of his face. Earl hit the brakes, dipping the flat nose of the Tweet downward as if offering a slight bow to dignity. Tire check. The idea was to taxi forward just enough to roll the underside of the tires over so the crew chief could inspect for wear and tear on the section of the tire pressed against the tarmac. He sprang out from underneath the straight wings, looked left and right to check for other jets taxiing, gave the signal motion to rev the engines and taxi, and popped a crisp salute and wave to Earl as he turned left out of the parking spot. There were three T-37s and two T-38s on the main taxiway to ease Earl's mind as to which direction to taxi to the active runway. His canopy remained open as he taxied to "last chance." Last chance was the holding area next to the approach end of the runway where another set of ground crew gave the jets a once over—primarily checking for hydraulic, oil, and fuel leaks—before the pilots launched. The overhead was busy with students practicing landings. Sequencing takeoffs, touch and gos, and full stops is an art form. The tower controller was locked in a verbal rhythm like an auctioneer at the antique shows just south of town, and Earl began to mentally absorb the tempo of the radio transmissions in order to get his ready-for-takeoff request in without disrupting the cadence of directions that were being barked out by the

enlisted man in the tower behind the mike. Last thing Earl
needed was to piss him off.

"Solo 41, you ready for takeoff?" Startled, Earl fired off
the call, "Solo 41, affirmative."
"Cleared for immediate takeoff--once airborne contact approach
279. 5." As he taxied on the runway Earl remembered to close
and lock his canopy. The details of aviation instinct were taking
hold. That was it. Earl was unleashed upon the Panhandle skies.

Chapter 7

"Yo, Earl, over here!" Earl walked, sliding the toes of his black flight boots along the floor until he realized he was on a wood floor. He followed Bartholomew's voice until he recognized the bulking frame leaning on the long bar with one boot propped up on the foot railing. "It's Lubbock for God's sake. You would think the jukebox guy would stock the thing with at least country music." Bartholomew claimed he submitted a written complaint every time he came to the Officers Club bar. "Dammit, the O'Club management better pay attention to the regulars." Earl believed him, but he was probably the only one in the bar who paid no attention to the music. It took almost two minutes before their eyes became accustomed to the dark bar. He walked in the side door from the parking lot and Earl had to stop after the door slammed closed. He could not see and was unfamiliar with the layout.

"I can't see either when I first step in," he laughed motioning to the bartender for another beer, "I memorized the steps to the bar. Thirteen, by the way." Earl's beer arrived and Bartholomew picked it up and handed it over. When Earl grabbed the beer Bartholomew clinked his beer neck against Earl's. "Here's to Lubbock by the sea. Must have been an ocean here at some time eh, Earl?" Their eyes adjusted to the darkness.

"Not as crowded as I figured it'd be," said Earl looking over his shoulder at the rest of the bar.

"You're right," said Bartholomew banging his empty beer bottle down on the bar, "Must be a rodeo in town." Earl chuckled. He knew that one. If a place is dead, everyone said, "Must be a rodeo in town."

The Officers Club was dead for a Friday. The bar
usually had plenty of Lieutenants standing around tipping back
beers and complaining about instructor pilots. The few older
IPs that would stop by for a drink were tucked in booths
bitching about their clueless students. Everyone had to put up
with the lame music coming from the jukebox. It was filled
with fluffy AM radio top forty tunes and most, if not all of the
patrons listened to rock and roll or country music.

"Did you find it today?" asked Bartholomew.

"Find what?"

"The hole," said Bartholomew. Earl looked at him with a
scrunched brow.

"Where that student took it in the day we started pilot
training," said Bartholomew.

"I wasn't looking down too much out there," said Earl.
He did, however, remember seeing the black smoke column
driving into Lubbock on his first day. Smoke from the crash.
Now he wished he looked for the hole in the Texas Panhandle
floor. To see if death was still lingering about.

"The boomers must've been up to sixty thousand feet. I
felt like I was flying around a cloud city that had three of the
tallest cloud skyscrapers I'd ever seen. I could actually see the
clouds rolling higher in the updrafts. "

"Yeah, and could you imagine the little piece of shit
Tweet flying inside those monsters? It would rip the damn
wings right off," said Bartholomew.

"Believe me, I was thinking exactly that flying past them
today," said Earl.

What surprised Earl was what Bartholomew did not ask.
He did not ask him about what he was feeling when he pushed

up the throttles to full power and released the brakes, when he
rotated his nose wheel off the runway and felt the mains release
their grip of the earth, the feeling when he realized all of his
maneuverings were decided by him alone—pulling the stick into
his lap and the rush of G onset pressing his back into the steel
seat, looking through the rear view mirrors at the brown Texan
dirt fade from detail as he kept the nose of his T-37 pointed
straight upward. No, Bartholomew did not ask him anything
about those experiences. Solo flight was to be savored by one's
self, Earl thought. They are shared only by the few who solo in
jets. Guys talked more about the feelings of sex than the
exhilarations of flight. The intimacy of flying solo was too
precious to share aloud—even in the unshackled, intoxicating
realm of a pilot bar. Getting laid was the thrill of the conquest,
where orgasm is the mega bonus. Flying solo is an intimate
endeavor, also earned by one's ability, but with full realization
that if not for the gift of vision, flying would be just another
sensual push and pull exertion deemed a thrill. Flying is a love
affair--which is why many a woman recognizes the action of
flight as a serious threat to segments of their self worth.

Chapter 8

It was not a day that changed Lubbock. That day had already occurred in 1971. But it was still a day to remember. It was not necessarily a hot day. Just as in '71, the day prior had been beautiful, not a cloud in the sky, no dusty wind, just sunny and an outside temperature that was just right. On this day the morning was cool and clear. Upon recall, everyone seemed to remember that the bright white puffy clouds appeared to roll in, maybe from the North. Just past noon the sky began to grow mottled grey. The underbelly of the clouds appeared to be churning, like the image of a drunkard's upset and gurgling stomach. The swath of cloud cover was vast and darkness arrived much too early—about 117pm.

At Reese AFB, a weather recall was announced to get all the training jets back on the ground and tethered down for the anticipated ripping wind gusts. By circumstance, Lt. Karl Bergsten was the last T-37 in the cue to return to base. Not five minutes into the training airspace, while floating over the top of his first solo loop, he had difficulty keeping his wings level with the horizon because the northern horizon was becoming completely obscured by the arriving storm. He was so focused on performing his acrobatic routine Lt. Bergsten was slow to bring the dark storm into his crosscheck. After the G-loading decreased rounding out the bottom of his first loop, Karl rolled out wings level to accelerate and yanked the stick hard left to set up for another loop—this time an east west loop. The just completed North South loop was made more difficult because of the impending storm from the North obscured the horizon, his primary reference in keeping wings level over the top of the

36

loop. Already an aviation instinct was forming. The turn east was reflexive. The east and west horizons were clear of weather. His subconscious solved the horizon obscuration problem. As Lt. Bergsten pulled up for the start of the second loop, he heard the barking announcement from his UHF radio, "All Reese Air Force Base aircraft return to base, Repeat, all Reese Air Force Base aircraft return to base." The directive registered, and he relegated the radio call to the back bin of his conscious. Under the strain of four Gs, he forced aloud to himself his frustration with the return to base directive, "I'm finishing my acro, and the supervisor of flying can just wait two and half more minutes." Then immediately into the Cuban Eight Bergsten loved performing. The maneuver—two semi-loops connected by crisp aileron rolls. Acro is all about symmetry from precise maneuvering and exact airspeeds at different phases of each maneuver. The stick, which controls ailerons and the vertical stabilator, and rudder control, plus constant awareness of airspeed, which goes back to stick and rudder—and engine throttle control. Hands, feet and eyeballs are operating in symphonic precision—just the right amount of aileron deflection, a slow push on the right rudder pedal, all the while constantly peeking at the airspeed indicator and glancing outside the cockpit to cross reference God's big horizontal indicator.

"Solo 42, acknowledge this radio call."

"Somebody's pissed off," he said to himself, as he pulled the T-37 to level flight. Glancing northeast, Bergsten remembered the coming storm. Clouds had turned gray black since last time he bothered to check.

"Solo 42, copies, returning to base."

"That's affirmative, Solo 42, return to base *now*." The flying supervisor was no doubt pissed off. "What fuel state?" barked the voice.

"Solo 42 is Joker plus 2," replied Bergsten. He flicked the radio channel switch to the FAA frequency and waited for a break in the excited chatter of the air traffic controllers. He was riled by the Supe's admonishing radio calls, and fought against his impulse to get into a further lather over the fact he let the radio calls rile him in the first place.

The air base flight line was flooded with blue uniformed airmen running from jet to jet tying down the T-37s and T-38s. The darkened sky looked lethal. Lightening was still 20 plus miles away but no one hustling on the exposed flight line believed that the thick, cruelly jagged white bursts of electric anger were that far away. They cocked an ear awaiting the loudspeaker to clear the flight line due to lightening within 3 miles.

The student pilots were released early to go home. The base commander did not need any personnel not living on base scurrying around for shelter as the storm hit. The flying squadron commanders ordered those who rode motorcycles to work to hitch a ride home with someone who drove a car or truck. This irritated Bartholomew to no end. It was bad enough he had to endure a mandatory military motorcycle safety course, be on the Commander's "motor cycle" list, and wear a helmet and orange clown vest while driving on base. Now he's prohibited from riding his motorcycle during bad weather.

"Well, no shit I hate riding in rain, and also shitting in my drawers, that's why I use a toilet" he muttered aloud passing by the operations desk.

"Say again Lieutenant?" asked the airman behind the desk.

"Wasn't bitching at you Elvis," replied Bartholomew. His long black flaring sideburns and square chin earned the airman that righteous nickname. Plus he was also from Memphis and played guitar. It was the airman's destiny to be nicknamed after *The Man*.

"Got it, sir," he said.

"Everybody on the deck yet?" asked Bartholomew.

"Bergsten's the last one up. The Ops O's pinging through the hallways going on about Bergsten," said Lt. Earl, coming out of a briefing room.

"Mind giving me a ride to my place? Commander's afraid all us bikers will become hood ornaments on trucks in the rain," said Bartholomew.

"No problem."

"Thanks Earl. We'll have to catch up with Tornado boy Bergsten later."

"Tornado?" asked Earl.

"That Swedish boy is always last minute this, late to that. Should call him Glacier."

"They have glaciers in Sweden?" asked Earl. Elvis just shrugged.

"Norway, Sweden, you know, up north, butt ass cold, fjords, glaciers…You get the point." Earl and Elvis got it that Lt. James was just talking out his butt—again.

"Hey James, not a bad callsign name for Bergsten," said Lt Col Schindle, their Operations Officer, who showed up out of nowhere at the Ops counter. "Now, you two go home. James, you're a cycle rider, correct?"

"I'm giving him a ride, sir," said Earl.

"Good. Go…Now."

"Yes sir," they both replied in unison.

"Hog rider," muttered Bartholomew, grabbing his books and jacket from his locker. Earl gave him a questioning look.

"I don't ride a cycle, I ride a Hog…A Harley Davidson…A Fatboy," said Bartholomew.

"Let's go then, Fatboy," said Earl, thinking that may be a good callsign for one each Lt Bartholomew James.

Chapter 9

Tornados are easy to avoid by car, provided you can see the tornado and have options as to which road to choose. Over a town, tornados appear like a slow heavy-handed scrawl, carving a scarring obscenity across a neighborhood. Bartholomew pointed at the descending funnel, guessing it was 5-8 miles away. Earl saw it. The stoplight was swinging up to horizontal with the road. Earl's BMW shuddered in the gusts. Traffic seemed normal, but it was the seemingly random flashing brake lights of the cars and pickup trucks that hinted other drivers also saw the funnel and their brake lights telegraphed they were in a quandary as to what do or where to go. Others appeared oblivious.

"My apartment's straight ahead three miles," said Earl.

"Mine's up a little further ahead, off Frankford," said Bartholomew.

"Not sure we'll make it to your place. I'm going to get my sister out of the apartment." Bartholomew turned his quizzed look towards Earl, who was very focused on the road ahead.

"I know she's decided to stay in that apartment and take her chances. I'm not going to let her do that."

"And after we pick-up your sister we're going in the opposite direction of that black mass of weather goo, right?" said Bartholomew pointing at the storm front.

"She'll want us to find an underground bar," said Earl.

"Oh, my my," said a grinning Bartholomew pounding on the dashboard, "Your sister, you say? Never mentioned her before." Earl shook his head and cut sharply into the parking lot, noticing his sister's truck was still there. Pulling up the emergency brake handle, he swung open the door with the car still running.

"Start honking after a couple minutes," directed Earl, as he ran into the apartment entrance.

The sky was dark, and in the calm air the humidity was noticeable and rare for Lubbock. A young woman with a green plastic laundry basket crunched under her arm walked through a corridor from the middle of the apartment complex. She stared at the running BMW, walked over and bent down to see who was in the car.

"Earl?" she asked.

"I'm not Earl but he wants you in the car now. Bad weather's coming," said Bartholomew.

"Who the hell are you tough guy, and where the hell's Earl?" she demanded, walking back towards the apartment complex. Bartholomew reached over and pressed the car horn and let it sound off for five seconds. Earl exited the apartment as Amy was entering, bumping into him. They exchanged quick words before she brushed past, running inside. Bartholomew knew she was asking Earl who the hell that asshole was in his BMW.

"She's on her way back down. Great first impression," said Earl as he slipped back into the driver's seat. I knew it, grinned Bartholomew.

"So then, you know what I'm thinking, right?" said Amy, after she placed a large canvas bag in the backseat next to her. Bartholomew nodded with a poker face, looking straight into her dark dry eyes. He turned back around and said to Earl, "Let's find a clear road in any direction other than where that damn storm is heading." Amy dropped two cold cans of beer into the drink holders between the front seats. After lighting a joint she said, "Last thing the cops are gonna do is stop us for drinking beer and smoking weed." She ignored Bartholomew.

Bartholomew offered a beer to Earl who just shook his head. Bartholomew lifted his opened beer towards Amy and then emptied the can in three long swallows. Earl exited left out of the parking lot and headed south. The radio DJs were all delivering severe storm and tornado alerts for all affected counties, cities, and towns. Traffic was starting to slow as more cars appeared on the streets. It was as if a dead nightfall arrived—still--no wind gusts, no rain. As traffic slowed to a crawl, Earl tilted up his side view mirror to see what was happening behind them. Now half dollar sized rain drops slammed the windshield and pinged the car roof. While Bartholomew's left hand switched from FM to AM stations listening for any weather updates, he looked out at the sky. Amy offered Bartholomew a toke.

"Pass," he said. She lowered her window halfway and blew the smoke outside.

"Wouldn't want to get you fly boys high with second hand smoke." Earl pulled out of the traffic jam, swinging a right turn into a 1950's era neighborhood.

"This street could use a little tornado remodeling," said Amy. She moistened her finger with her tongue and smoothed out a wrinkle in the remainder of her joint. Bartholomew spotted the spout of a twister—maybe two miles away, at most, he guessed. The end of the distorted funnel soon disappeared behind the house rooftops.

"There she is, and she's about to wreck up the place," said Bartholomew, pointing out his window.

"Whoa, that's cool," said Amy, sliding over to the opposite side of the car and pressing the window button. She pressed her face against the lowering window. Earl slammed the brakes, jerking the car to a hard stop.

"No stupid stoner babbling from you, hear me?" barked Earl. Amy raised her hands and her mouth opened as if to object. Her squinted eyes lowered from Earl's and she slumped back into the seat, popping open a can of beer.

"We should move on," said Bartholomew in a lowered voice.

"Got it," replied Earl, punching the accelerator and pinning them back in their seats.

"I smell rain," Amy said, blowing smoke out the window. She flicked the joint out onto the street.

"The tornado is touching down," said Bartholomew. Earl exited the residential street, turning right onto a major road, keeping the tornado at their three o'clock position. Glancing right, he saw the ash colored funnel, four semi-trucks end-to-end wide, grinding up and spitting away bricks and shattered sheets of wood, dry wall, and fatal bent long pieces of metal. The mortar, wood and metal mixture of the remnants of homes orbited like satellites around the slow churning funnel. The funnel stuttered and shifted direction as if running into an invisible wall and changed to a smoky white color, appearing to alter its physical characteristics and then careened off north in a tight jagged angle, flinging debris out of the tornado's orbit and turning them into deadly projectiles.

The tornado moved aft toward their six o'clock as he motored north. The first torrent of rain smacked the windshield.

He slapped the windshield wiper handle full up to get the wiper blades going full speed.

"Earl, why are we heading into the dark part?" screamed Amy, shaking and shrinking into the backseat. "Shit is flying everywhere. My God, Earl. Get us outta here, now, Goddammit!"

He swerved into an empty parking lot of a supermarket, turned left and drove along the side of the building where the delivery trucks unload produce. He slowed the car to a crawl and edged to within three feet of the building stopping the car at the corner. Sheets of rain and trash can rubbish were falling at a thirty degree angle. Plastic bottles of all colors and sizes were spinning and sliding over the asphalt. Newspaper sheets stayed airborne, swirling about trying to find a resting place. He parked with the supermarket upwind to the storm. Earl was able to lean forward and peer around the corner of the building.

"Storm's blowing through," he said. Turning right he tried to locate the tornado.

"Lost the twister."

"People are hurt." Store signs and stoplights now went dark.

"It's gonna get chaotic around here with the power being knocked out," said Bartholomew. Six red plastic handled shopping carts whirled about the parking lot on swivel wheels, splashing through wind rippled rain puddles swelling into the size of farm ponds. The carts appeared to be confused while rattling about in a dizzy circle before four of them crashed into a navy blue station wagon and the other two into an old white sedan parked in front of the supermarket. The radio was filled with bitter static. Earl could not find an operating radio station.

Then the rain stopped falling in angled sheets. The straight downpour was deafening. Then, sheets of rain as the gusts resumed.

"The front's moving pretty fast," yelled Earl. "Look, the clouds are not nearly as dark over there," pointing north where they had first spotted the tornado. The engine turned over and Earl pulled away from the wall protecting them. The hard rain blasted the BMW's hood as soon as it was exposed.

"Where now?" asked Bartholomew. Earl turned wide, away from the shopping carts but splashing into large shallow rain pools, and pulled onto the empty street.

"Going to where the tornado just passed over," said Earl.

"To do exactly what?" shouted Amy, lifting herself up higher in the backseat.

"To render aid and comfort," said Earl in a monotone voice, as if reciting from a Government Pamphlet on Natural Disaster Response. Bartholomew looked at Earl, realizing that would have been the farthest thing in his mind—and his expression admitting as much left him feeling small. He loathed feeling small. He also knew to keep the loathing centered on himself and not Earl, but his anger arrived anyway.

"Tell me exactly please, exactly what the connection is between being poor and being unable to clean up all the junk in the front yard," said Amy, full stoned and staring out the window and pointing at two old pickup truck hulks, a dented and scraped gas stove, and small piles of pipes, wood scraps, strips of bent corrugated steel sheets and a severely faded blue tarp covering God knows what, anchored at the corners by broken masonry bricks.

"Miss Amy, please note the sense of organization of the stuff in the front yard. The proprietors clearly don't view curb appeal as a priority over the consolidation and separation of potentially reusable resources," lectured Bartholomew, looking straight ahead, never once looking at the source of Amy's scorn. He did not need to. Where he lived, many yards had their stuff organized in the same way, although the heights of the surrounding grass and weeds did vary. He failed to recognize he was imitating Earl's cool demeanor, but Earl noticed.

As Earl drove north, the rain stopped and normal afternoon daylight was fast returning. Bartholomew saw no further signs of any tornado. Earl slowed and turned right into another neighborhood of Sixties style single story homes. From what he could see, at least six of them were homes no more. One hundred yards ahead the street was impassable. The tornado ripped the houses to rubble, three on the north side and three on the south side, before it continued on south. Two four-door sedans of early 80s vintage were resting upside down in the ruins of two of the homes on the south side. What caught Earl's eye was the long six wheeled vehicle overturned on its side with its exposed drive shaft drooped in the lawn, no longer connected to the rear drive train. It was occupying the front yards of the two demolished houses on the north side. Earl pulled over near the south side curb, turned off the ignition. His creeping sense of who might be inside the overturned vehicles turned him nauseous for an instant, and then calm enveloped him. They saw no one.

"What the hell are we doing here?" whispered Amy, now squeezed down on the floorboard peering eye level through her window, as if to protect herself from the panic papering over her stoned mind. She wished her brother would have kept driving north, kept driving on highways with no other cars and trucks. Just driving away, with nothing but miles of cotton fields on both sides of any two-lane, and cloud dotted blue skies along all horizons.

"What do you think?" said Bartholomew as he got out of the car and shut the door. Up until Amy asked the question, he also did not know what they were doing. He was not thinking ahead, not even about the next sixty seconds. He was just riding shotgun in Earls' car. Earl was driving and I'm along for the ride, he thought to himself. Bartholomew knew he let himself go passive and let events happen before him. It irritated him when anyone else would just go along for the ride. It was the quickest way to earn his disdain. But he had a gut trust in Earl for reasons he was not sure. The whole day--from being ordered by the Commander to get a ride in order to leave base to following Earl--he did not feel right. He was out of sorts, out of his carefully cultivated orbit around himself, out of his sphere of assuredness. Uncertainty was clawing at him rather than exciting him and he could not figure out why, adding to his anger. Earl got out of the car without saying a word. It was the first time Bartholomew could ever remember hesitating to do anything. But no way was Earl going to look for survivors alone. He jogged to catch up with Earl as he approached what now appeared to be a school bus.

"Listen," said Earl, as Bartholomew caught up with him. Earl slow turned a complete 360 degrees looking and listening for something, anything.

"Not a sound, no yelling, nothing," said Earl.

"Not true," said Bartholomew, one eye closed and head cocked sideways, his ear tilted towards the faint whine of a siren. Earl and Bartholomew looked into the front windshield of the bus as it lay on its side. The seat belt was around the bus driver but his head and shoulders were not visible because they were outside the driver's window, between the front lawn and the side of the bus. The passenger door was ajar but they had to climb on top of the right front fender and drop down the door in order to get inside. Multiple sirens could now be heard. Standing on the upturned front right fender was the only way to look inside the bus door. Earl climbed on top of the wheel first, placing his right foot on the fender, and bending over to look inside. His mind was severely charged and his chest heaved, inhaling full lungs of anxiousness in a preparatory reaction to what he expected to find. Right away he knew who the young boy was. Bartholomew began to climb up on the wheel when Earl raised his right arm and waved Bartholomew away.

"Check out the rest of the area, I'll search the bus," said Earl. Without a word and grateful, Bartholomew ran around the end of the bus and began searching for persons in the house rubble.

Earl stepped onto the edge of the bus driver's seat and carefully stepped over the boy. He was standing on the smashed window of the second seat behind the driver. The first seat was occupied by the body of the driver's son. Earl found no pulse on the boy's neck. He did not have to check the driver's pulse to know he was dead. "God, there's so much blood", Earl said to himself. The blood had lost its rich red color. The boy's father's head was crushed between the side of the bus and the ground. Earl searched the rest of the bus by walking on the sides of the seats until he reached the rear door. There were no other kids on the bus, which reinforced his initial instinct, which was that the driver had dropped off all the other kids and Dad and Son were returning to the bus depot or more likely, going home. They both had Dallas Cowboys lunch boxes. Both boxes clutched to the boy's chest.

Earl popped his head out of the topside window and saw Bartholomew picking up a section of wall siding and searching underneath. He stepped back onto the edge of the driver's seat and propped his butt up onto the doorframe, pivoting his legs around to the side of the fender and jumped down from the bus. Taking another deep breath, bowing his head and steadying himself against the upturned bus wheel, he prayed,

"Lord, may these two creatures of your love find you in willing embrace and eagerness to accept them into your eternal fold, Amen." Out loud, he added, "And give me strength to face what I find next." The blistering sounds of sirens and strewn rubbish and wreckage surrounded them. Yet no ambulances or fire trucks were seen on the street. Bartholomew was talking with a middle-aged man amidst what was left of a home across the street. A mid-thirtyish couple scurried up the sidewalk and stopped to look inside Earl's BMW. Bartholomew figured they were checking to see if Earls' sister was all right. Joining Bartholomew, they listened to the man's story about the collapsing of his roof, and neighbor's as well.

"Supposed to be tornado resistant they said," turning around and pointing to nothing specific, just moving his arm up and around as if tracing where the house stood.

"They sold me and Donny a tornado resistant home renovation kit that was supposed to prevent the roof from blowing off by diverting the air flow in some kind of different way throughout the house. What saved us was the cellar, not the Panhandle Home Protection Company. Damn cheats. Lucky we survived. That congressman is a double crook."

"Cellar saved us," Bob repeated to himself, whose wife and young daughter were just emerging up from the cellar, sickly pale and clinging to each other very tight. They did not scream or go hysterical. Mother and daughter were in shock, numbed by seeing the ripped remains of what was left of their home.

"The bus driver and a young boy are in the bus," said Earl. He shook his head. "Must have finished his route, with one school kid left to go, going back home with his Dad."

"Who's a double crook?" asked Bartholomew, distancing his consciousness from Earl's discovery.

"Congressman Steen. He's a politician, which means he's a crook, and his family owns the Panhandle Home Protection Company, the company that sold us the tornado home protection stuff. Look around. Look like it worked to you? He's a double crook."

Bob then walked away and joined the couple shuffling up the sidewalk. It was as if they aged forty years in an instant. The other man put his arm around Bob and he was able to quicken their pace across the street to check on Bob's neighbor Donny. In this part of the city the tornado cut across the parallel streets. As a result, Earl and Bartholomew could see a path of leveled homes that stretched at least three streets north and south. Residents began to wander outside to inspect for damage and check on their neighbors. A fire truck and ambulance finally arrived and stopped in the middle of the street, just in front of

Earl's car. Two police sedans arrived shortly after. The cops were unraveling and wrapping yellow police cordon strips around fallen power line poles and directing people to stay away from the wires until utility repairs could be made. Bartholomew pointed the ambulance attendants to the school bus and together they lifted the bodies of the driver and boy onto gurneys through the windshield frame that had been kicked out from the inside by the first attendant inside.

Earl was not sure who arrived first, the TV van or the Congressman's Cadillac. Earl overheard a resident who recognized the Congressman. The street was now choked with emergency vehicles, gas company trucks, and the TV van was blocking his BMW. Sunlight was returning in streaks through slits in the thinning light grey clouds. Soon the sky would be clear. The humidity seemed to be dissipating. His mouth was cotton dry.

The Congressman's assistant was attending to him, straightening his red tie and applying some face powder. The thin pale cameraman wedged his cigarette to the corner of his mouth with his tongue while positioning lights to afford the best possible view of the destruction. Residents and neighbors began congregating around the overturned bus. Earl became perplexed watching Mom's, Dad's and children build into a crowd around the bus. Mom's clutched their children who clutched whatever comforted them to hold—blankets, dolls, toy animals, and live ferrets and tiny cages containing horned toads. They were coming from what was left of their own homes—they were survivors who no longer had a living room sofa to sit and watch TV, a refrigerator to grab a piece of cheese and a soda, and a toilet in which to pee.

The fireball arrived in an instant, just before the loud boom—collapsing everyone to the ground either by force of the explosion or by instinct. With his eyes closed tight as he lifted off the street, his mind's eye captured the explosion as a silhouette resembling a brilliant orange traffic cone. Earl did not immediately fall, he bounced off the side of the TV van and landed back on his feet, directly in the path of the panicked Congressman who was picking himself off the ground and scrambling towards his car. Earl pivoted around the Congressman brushing past him, grabbing the back of the congressman's shirt and suit collar and yanking him to a stop.

"Where you going, sir?" said Earl, his mind racing but focused.

"Who the hell are you, mister?" screamed the Congressman. His silver dollar sized eyes were evidence enough. He was enraged and frightened, and if Earl did not release him he would have to add hysterical to his description of demeanor. Letting go of his collar, Earl replied, "I'm offering my services to personally assist you in tending to your constituents."

"Get away from me, you ass," screamed the Congressman, squinting his eyes at the sudden white light in his face. The skinny cameraman backed away from the Congressman to avoid his weak attempt at a roundhouse punch.

"Tell us Congressman Steen, don't you believe in assisting your constituents in need?" asked the big-haired brunette reporter, shoving her microphone towards his face. He straightened and stiffened, and his face transformed in a flash to one absent of any expression. He swatted the microphone away and dashed past the reporter and into a small crowd forming behind them who were caring for the three or four injured lying amidst the fresh rubble.

Facing her, Earl froze. She lowered the microphone and extended a forefinger to click off the miniature recorder she held in her other hand. Behind her, slightly to the left, Earl's eyes caught Bartholomew waving his arm above his head and he took off to meet up with him, shaking off an increasing dizziness in his head, and leaving his mother standing alone amidst uniformed men dashing around trying to do something about the chaos and destruction and death.

Chapter 10

"Stay outside with that," demanded Bartholomew, as he tossed a match onto the charcoal bricks. Amy took one last toke and tossed the end of the joint into his BBQ grill before going back inside the house.

"And no cigarettes in the house either," he added, as she slammed the sliding glass door shut.

"Real nice," said Bartholomew, flicking the last ashes of the joint to the side of the grill.

Earl's apartment roof lost sheets of shingles during the storm and water quickly waterlogged the cheap ceiling causing it to collapse in his bedroom and kitchen. So he and Amy moved the sofa, chair, dining room kit, and his bed away from the wet mess of the fallen ceiling, packed some clothes and toiletries and went to stay at Bartholomew's rental house.

Bartholomew guessed correctly that small homes were available for rent around the university and besides, the idea of living in an apartment complex never appealed to him. A couple of years of dorm living was a couple years too many in his mind. His neighborhood was older but the homes were well kept. If the druggies ever robbed his house he figured he had nothing of real value except his .357 handgun for comfort and shotgun for quail hunting. They were both loaded and accessible. His vintage TV weighed a ton. Let them haul that big thing out of the house, he thought. It will take two druggies twenty seconds to realize it is not worth it to lug it out of the house.

"Exactly what was ya'lls plan today?" said Amy, sitting cross-legged on the well worn wall-to-wall carpet, facing an equally worn puffy gray leather couch. Dark green was such a downer of a rug color, thought Amy. Earl did not answer, waiting instead for Bartholomew to close the glass sliding door as he entered from the patio.

"Yeah, what was the plan?" echoed Bartholomew, as he strolled into the kitchen to scrub the charcoal and lighter fluid smell from his hands.

"Simple—avoid being flung across the Panhandle by the tornado and help some people," he said, adding, "And we did both."

"We were stuck there for damn near four hours!" said Amy. It was nine thirty in the evening and they had not been in the house for more than a half hour.

"We'll have a thick steak and potatoes and a tossed salad and we'll all feel better," said Bartholomew, removing the last steak from the microwave after defrosting. He plopped the last steak on the plate, grabbed three big aluminum wrapped potatoes and headed for the patio.

"You like your steaks-- how?" he asked.

"Medium rare," said Earl.

"Well done," said Amy.

"I don't do *well done*," said Bartholomew, closing the sliding door behind him.

"Why'd he ask me then?" shot back Amy.

"He's kind of an ass," she said.

"So are you," said Earl.

"I'm not talking about me," she said. Earl did not want to talk. Exhaustion from the afternoon's tornado caused his mind to slow down and ignore any talk requiring a moment of thought. The father and son in the bus. The young family of four, eventually all found dead, after being ejected from their unsuccessful hiding place. Being amongst the firemen, emergency medical technicians and local residents-local survivors-shouting and rushing about accounting for neighbors, tending to cuts, broken limbs, and severe head trauma, searching for potential fires, all the while waiting for the fire trucks, ambulances and public utility vehicles to leave so he could drive away. Amy finally had enough and screamed at him to jump the curb and drive on the sidewalk to get around all the first response trucks. That was soon after they finally tracked down Bartholomew.

His street did not lose power in the storm. Must be in part of the electrical grid that gets reset first, thought Bartholomew, fork and spooning a lettuce and tomato salad.

"Get something to drink and let's eat," he said, grabbing another beer and sitting down. Amy flicked on the TV before going to the fridge.

"Good steak," said Earl out the side of his mouth, savoring the first piece as if days had passed since his last meal. He dropped a thick slice of butter into to his potato, watching the steam rise and butter melt. A collage of film clips showing the death and damage from the tornado glued their eyes to the television. They ate quickly and in silence, letting the excited talk of the TV reporters mingle with the sounds of their knives clinking against the plain white plates as they cut into their steaks. No word from Amy how the steak was cooked, thought Bartholomew. Must have been good enough. Nothing left but the gristle.

"Look, that school bus," said Amy, pointing with her fork at the television. The film clip showed two white-sheeted bodies lying next to the front of the bus.

"Look," cried Amy. Bartholomew was in view during the last few seconds of the clip; seen walking away from the dead. The next footage scanned across the rubble and wreckage left by the tornado. The final clip showed Earl grasping the collar of the Congressman and his angry reaction to being yanked around and confronted. The editors elected to include the segment of Earl asking the Congressman where he was going--but his angry reply was muted and replaced by the reporter's voice over. However, the clenched lips and pumping fist of the angry Congressman was included for all to witness. The film flash of him losing control of his composure was as memorable as the tornado's aftermath.

"Shit…that's Mother!" shouted Amy, slamming down her beer. She turned quickly to Earl and gave him an inflamed stare. Her stare seemed to burn as her eyes began to water.

"It's been a long day, and I gotta lie down and shut my eyes for a while," said Earl.

"Air mattresses are in the first room on the right. Pillows and sheets are in the top of the hall closet," replied Bartholomew.

"Thanks for the steak. I'll be up at five tomorrow. Sorry to wimp out on cleaning up."

"Go to bed," said Bartholomew, gathering up Earl's empty plate and half empty beer bottle and placing them near the sink. "I got the rest."

"Night," said Earl to Amy, with a slight nod and tight smile. Amy kept her stare squared on Earl as he turned and went into the bathroom. Changing his mind, he returned to the couch to watch the rest of the news.

As Bartholomew took away her plate she said, "What are you, a clean freak?"

"Maybe. I don't get living in a mess of my own making. Rather live in a place that's, you know, free of roaches and rodents."

"Yeah, what about it?" demanded Amy.

"Your brother accommodates your desire, Miss Piggy?" said Bartholomew.

"Up yours—he's a clean freak too. What is it with you two?" She had worked herself into a lather. Bartholomew had no clue as to why and wanted no part of this act.

"Listen, I'll leave a couple of empties on the table for you—if it makes you feel better. I'm going to bed. We gotta go to the base early tomorrow."

He went outside and turned off the gas grill and locked the sliding door on his way back in. A local car dealer commercial came on the TV. Pointing at the television, he said, "That woman reporter stopped me and asked me a lot of questions about your brother, most of which I couldn't answer. She was fascinated by him it seemed--you know--grabbing the Congressman and calling him out for basically being a jackass."

"*You're* the jackass," said Amy.

"Jackass?" replied Bartholomew. Bartholomew went to bed, leaving her alone at the dining room table. Amy got up and bent over close to Earl slouching on the couch and hissed, "Why didn't you tell me Mom was here? Do you hate her that much not to tell me?"

"Now I'm really going to bed," said Earl, attempting to get up before Amy shoved him back down.

"You will sit—and we will talk—now. About Mom. About why she left and about why you and I have not talked about it. About why she and I talk now and you and her don't talk."

"Not tonight."

"Yes, tonight," screamed Amy, anger flushing her cheeks and hardening her stare. Earl got up and led her outside through the sliding glass doors, knowing cigarettes will be littering the small concrete patio after all is said. Her resistance to his arm about hers was nil.

*****

The next day flying was cancelled at the air base, though the skies were clear by the previous midnight. Earl received permission to go back and take care of business at his damaged apartment complex. A seemingly logical decision that only propelled gossip and speculation because on base it appeared everyone watched Earl grabbing the Congressman on TV the night before, and for those few who did not watch, that night Earl made an international debut when the tornado coverage was picked up by one of America's most popular national broadcast networks and transmitted around the world.

Comparisons to the tornado of 1970 filled the local newspaper for a week. Experts claimed and the anemometers positioned around the city verified that both were F5 strength but the 1970 tornado wreaked three times more damage and killed twice as many people. Therefore, last week's tornado was officially classified as an F3 on the Fujito scale. The funnel appeared to return to the blackened storm clouds, according to witnesses, like a film of the event was played backwards. If that had not occurred, it would have had at least three miles of residential area in all directions to rip apart and speculation was the damage and loss of life would have doubled that of 1970.

Certain Air Force leaders believed they had found an ideal representative to interact with the local residents and fanned Earl's increasing popularity, which found him initially cautious yet excited to be invited to the Lubbock tornado victims fund raising rallies, which turned into community protest rallies, which were soon commandeered by political organizations and turned into candidate platform rallies.

"How did you get my phone number?" said Bartholomew.

"You have to believe one thing about reporters, we're tenacious. We're doing a follow up on your friend Earl," she said.

"Why not talk to him?" he said.

"He's not very talkative. And you don't seem to be the shy type."

"I don't know him that well."

"Well, enough I think to get a fellow pilot's perspective," she said.

"We're not pilots yet."

"Sure you are—the Air Force just hasn't recognized you all yet," she said.

"You've attended the last three events he was invited to, right? "

"So."

"So, is Earl coming up with those words up on the stage or is someone helping him?'

"Ask him."

"The crowd adores him. They want to touch him. They want him to hold their babies. He's so quiet. He doesn't say anything. He just stands there and listens to their ramblings about how unfair it all is."

"What about you? How many times did you go back to that neighborhood and help those people? You two go together and help them, or does Earl just go by himself? I know he goes back on weekends to help those poor people."

"Maybe he doesn't trust reporters," he said, ignoring her questions, adding, "Or, maybe he doesn't trust you." Bartholomew certainly did not trust her. She was pushy and cocky. She was his mother's age and she acted like she ran the TV network. For Bartholomew, he could not imagine being with a woman like the reporter. Sure, he knew some like her at college, but they weren't women yet. They weren't his mother's age. By far. He wanted to tell her off and hang up. He just hung up instead and went to the fridge and grabbed a beer, leaving the phone off the carriage so she wouldn't call back.

*****

Chapter 11

Plotting the path and gauging the ferocity of a hurricane is a titillating exercise, especially if its destructive nature causes no harm to body or property. Ocean temperatures stimulate and steer the ocean beast. At Category 5, hurricanes rule. The awesome view from a satellite image speaks for itself, but left her speechless as she pondered the immensity of concentrated force bearing down in a destructive rage only a sociopath could fully appreciate. But she was not a sociopath. Destruction was not what fascinated her about hurricanes. That up until recently they were only named after women did fascinate her, however. Abby identified with the nature of hurricanes up to and short of the wake of their destructive effects. In her mind it was a sad day when women demanded hurricanes also be named after men.

Abby Westmoreland was also not the first woman in her family to attend college. She came from a long line of college women. Educated women, who by rare exception, married wealthy and were never inclined to pursue a career other than ensuring they stayed married to a very well off provider. This was the way of the Westmoreland's. Between Mr. Westmoreland and his two brothers, only one had a son, and he was killed in a jeep accident during the Korean War.

In Abby's day, women whose family could afford it went to teachers colleges or nursing schools. Nurturing, while never explicitly discussed, was a women's destiny. It was taken for granted. Look around town and even to the larger towns and cities in west Texas. Women filled the hospitals and primary and secondary schools. The only businesses women ran were ones started by their husbands and named after them.

In Texas, Abby's family was in the oil field supply business. They owned ten trucks that delivered whatever the riggers and roustabouts needed out in the field. Anything they needed, the Westmoreland's made sure to have it on hand. Their warehouse was a leftover aluminum aircraft hangar hastily built in the late '30s and taken apart, sheet by corrugated sheet, and reassembled on the Westmoreland property outside of Hobbs, New Mexico, located far enough east of Hobbs to be in Texas. This was also the northern boundary of the Permian Basin. Not too far south, the Santa Rita # 1 blew on May 25, 1923. Some New York City investors, a small Catholic women's group, suggested the rig be named Santa Rita, the patron Saint of the Impossible, since the apparent likelihood of striking oil there seemed remote. Maybe the strike was due to the effects of blessed rose petals offered by the women to scatter about the area from the top of the derrick--another request from the New York investors.

The Westmoreland women married doctors and lawyers, and shunned oilmen. They were too loose. She thought she was afraid of them, but her fear was merely the shroud that concealed her excitement being around such men--and their dreams. She was afraid of the excitement they generated inside her. They were Texas loud and arrogant, and bursting with sudden confidence of sudden wealth, or at least the prospect. But they were also the most alluring as far as Abby was concerned. Oilmen were dreamers. They talked big, acted big, and possessed big appetites. At least that is how Abby viewed them. Lincoln fit their mold. He was a six-foot two-plus tall man with spanning shoulders and a genetic disposition that prevented him from looking like every other man his age. He remained lean and sinewy. He never cared to eat much. Eating was not a pleasure but a necessary function. High-end whiskey and cigars were a pleasure. And he was disciplined in moderating his pleasures. He wore his dense wiry hair short with thin flaring sideburns a quarter inch short of his ear lobes. At one time the color of his hair could be described as bright gray, or maybe the color of a rain puddle in a county road composed of caliche. His long chin complimented his authoritative nose. He had steel blue eyes through which he would squint to size up a person or check out what's out yonder. He was always looking beyond someone, scanning just short of the horizon.

"Never know when I'll spot a stretch of ground that's begging for an oil bath."

Westmoreland, originally from New York City and an attorney himself, is thought to have made his big money wildcatting throughout Kansas, Texas, and New Mexico with close associates of Tom Slick, known as the King of the Wildcatters. His relationship with the New York Catholic women who were talked into investing in Santa Rita # 1 is assumed to have been more of a courteous church-social nature. It was in the City, where a widow named Claire Deforest approached Westmoreland after ten o'clock Mass, seeking his advice on a wildly speculative investment opportunity. According to most, this is how Westmoreland arrived in Texas the first time.

Abby was born in Midland and was seven years old when her mother died. She was the youngest and her mother was 32 at the time, considered well past due by most back in those days to be mothering children. Abbey's memories of her mother are now limited to two incidents that occurred just before her mother was quarantined. To this day, these two memories influence her actions and attitudes towards how she approaches living her life, including her views on her marriage and her relationships with her children. Those memories are her life touchstones and she considers them sacred and therefore must be protected. Abby never mentioned these memories to anyone. She has no plans ever to reveal them. His wife's sudden death of influenza emboldened Westmoreland's decision to remain in the West. He always referred to the 'West' with a capital W to ensure the recipient of his writings or utterances recognized that he recognized the West not only as a special place but also as a unique state of being. As for remarrying, the thought of having to be retrained by another woman--under the bonds of matrimony--to her ideals as to the proper habits for men was extremely unappealing. Westmoreland loved his wife but he felt he'd been trained long enough. His desire was to remain as is until his time was up.

Little was known of Mrs. Westmoreland. Lincoln Westmoreland never spoke of his wife after her death and the sisters found little motivation to inquire about her background. But she was a looker of the extraordinary kind. In their wedding photo album, her beauty transfixed the photographer. All the photos in the album placed Julia Westmoreland in the best possible light and framed in the most flattering manner. Not because it was necessarily good for business, but because he had never photographed a woman of such beauty. When the girls finally noticed this fact pouring through one of the old

66

footlockers filled with odds and ends from their parents' life in
New York, Westmoreland just uttered, "Ladies, that was the
man's job, to capture your mother's beauty on her wedding day.
And fine job he did, too." But even Westmoreland knew what
the children had discovered. Julia's beauty was alarming. In
truth, her beauty was not truly captured by a photo, no matter
how skilled the photographer. Only in her presence could one
attempt to measure the effect. It took Westmoreland a better
part of two years living as husband and wife to finally be able to
take his eyes off her.

"Now, that's beauty," he'd say to himself and himself
only; every night when he gazed at their wedding portrait
hanging above his nightstand. Funny, he thought, the girls never
recognized that earlier, especially seeing how obsessively
important facial beauty was to women. But then again, they
were all blessed with their mother's beauty. Too bad my genes
got jumbled in the mix otherwise they'd have to be locked away
for fear of inciting riots, he thought, chuckling with satisfaction
that he contributed something positive to humanity.

The girls divided their time between San Antonio and
their ranch house near Midland. They attended boarding school
at Incarnate Word, spending summers helping their father in the
Permian Basin area, between Hobbs, Odessa and Midland.

Winnie Porter was their nanny and housekeeper. The
girls loved her as a mother. With no family, Winnie was
grateful for their love, but stayed with the Westmoreland's only
until the youngest, Abby, left to find her own way. There are
few Winnie Porter's around today. She was what the times
produced, a black woman widowed young in West Texas, with
no chance of starting over in marriage. There were just no other

black men available. She made the best of what came her way, and in her mind caring for the Westmoreland family was a Godsend.

Lincoln Westmoreland laid down his firm view of the way-it-is to his girls prior to shipping them off to school back East.

"You want steady and secure? Find a doctor finished with schooling and learning his craft. If you want soft comforts with a little excitement in the form of uncertainty then latch on to a lawyer...but the same rules apply to him as well. And unless you have children, expect to be bored with both because you girls are too damn smart to be counting bedrooms and spending weeks on end thinking about kitchen appliances while dedicating thoughts to designing your next dream house. Young ladies, you may just have to venture out there into the great unknown. Know one thing--because I'm telling you--that for better or worse, it's a man's world. And at times it's scary, even for a man."

He made the same speech to each daughter prior to leaving home. Abby was the only one who did not cry. In fact, she smiled and ran to hug Westmoreland, who was much more than taken aback by her reaction. Behind her back and unbeknownst to Abby, tears formed in his eyes as they clutched each other. Winnie Porter also offered them advice.

"Listen to your father. He's the only man I ever met who makes any lick'a sense. Now, if he told y'all to run for Governor of Texas, then I'd be a'might worried. But he don't say things he don't mean. And children; he ain't mean neither, and that's the key to life the way I see it. Seems there ain't many men like him, which also don't seem to make a lick of damned sense when you put two thoughts together. Wonder what God was thinkin' when Adam fell…"

Abby always wondered if the reason Winnie stayed so trim was because of her father. No other woman around stayed as trim as Winnie Porter. She was not a beautiful woman. Way back when, some smart aleck started describing certain women as handsome, and in Winnie's case it was an appropriate description. Ms. Porter and her father were never seen together, except after dinner in the kitchen, and she refused to eat at the dinner table with the family despite Westmoreland's insistence she join them. He began to press her to join them one year after she hired on to care for the girls. Maybe she was hurt because he hadn't asked earlier, but Abby didn't think that was likely. She was not that naïve. No, she thought, Winnie had another reason for eating dinner in the kitchen. Choice. Winnie Porter had a choice, and she chose to eat alone, twelve feet away and behind a swinging door to the dining room, where the separation was always obvious to everyone in the household. Now why Winnie Porter chose to eat alone Abby was hesitant to speculate. What this arrangement did do however was to get everyone, including Lincoln Westmoreland, to clear the table and help with the dishes. It was in the kitchen where they were all together, and despite Winnie's protestations she could not prevent them from helping clean the kitchen. It was then and only then when Lincoln and Winnie would converse with each other, almost as if in code. Only Abby noticed how they'd look at one another and detected the softened tones of speech they applied only towards one another. They learned to convey the key essence of their daily thoughts to each other from the simplest of routine questions about the weather or some trivial daily happening. On rare occasions Lincoln would allow himself to be dragged into gossip. He hated gossip and Winnie Porter knew he hated gossip, but she loved gossip. Winnie had excellent sources the FBI would steal for. And on even rarer occasions, she'd engage in mean gossip about some of the families nearby and include a few of the prominent folks in Midland. Westmoreland would then give her the eyeball and she'd switch subjects immediately. Westmoreland commanded the girls to their rooms to study or elsewhere as the kitchen duties neared completion. And it was then and only then that Lincoln and Winnie were alone together. Abby also avoided thinking about why Winnie left as soon as she went to college.

Abby had no interest in staying in West Texas and sharing the oil dream, and welcomed her father's direction to attend school back east. She met Theodore Neuhaus just after graduation. He was a CPA with the New York firm Barnard, Fink, and Kelly. She was hired as an executive secretary not only for her looks but also for her obvious self-confidence. Abby carried herself as if she were her father's stature, despite only being five foot and a half. She had slim but athletic legs, compact hips, really not much of a waist to speak of, and freckles, which for years kept everyone guessing her age. Regular comparisons to the actress Doris Day were common—if only she were a brunette then the comparisons would linger. It was once a source of irritation, and eventually her irritation gave way to a gracious acceptance of the comparison as an ego lift. Abby's eyes, nose, mouth, and ears were small and her face was remarkably symmetrical, which she was reminded of over and over by her husband, whose passion was portrait paintings. Abby was never sure he appreciated her for her actual looks or the confirmation of what he learned as a student of the great European masters.

"I'm married to a classic face--and if guys ever laid eyes on a female athletic body like Abby's, they'd understand." She'd heard a version of this line too many times at parties. Abby married for what she thought was the whole package, not just the wrappings. She married because she understood that vows were a permanent commitment to one another. But her understanding of how marriage was supposed to play out sprung from a cultured naïveté, and sixteen years later, with a daughter and son, she felt her life was being strangled playing the role of a spouse and mother with narrow dimensions, and the routine that demanded cultivating--selected societal intricacies that formed--in her mind, the foundation of something actually hollow, further antagonized her as she felt strangled by what she came to believe; an inextricable demand for subservient role-playing in order to sustain some faux sense of order within society's stilted bounds. Her husband was never around to be committed *with*. Commitment in absentia was not in Abby's vows, and therefore, Abby reasoned she was relieved of her spousal role. Escape from motherhood was obviously another matter. She had dreamed of being a mother.

Yet also, Abby possessed the escape gene and the dream gene. Inherited from what others thought was her father. But, it was perhaps from her mother, who died not to escape, although Abby could certainly see death as an escape from a life. Abby's mother's dreams died when she died. All except for one. She explained to Abby that she must inhabit a future that offered a chance to dream, a chance to place the dream upon a wheel, like a potter's wheel, but in her mind's dream wheel, and with a mind's finesse and power, shape and build her dream. Then carefully, extracting the dream from her mind, from the mind's kiln...

Her mother said, "Dreams are the yeast of life and escape delivers them. They are your creation, a real living thing, something of your making."

According to her mother, Abby's dream should be like a cylindrical hologram upon which both the inside and outside walls were of the nature of kaleidoscopes--manipulated by her mind's eye. Her mother said, "Your mind's eye observes and through observation forces the kaleidoscope to show you a world you want to be a part of, but more than just be a part of, to design and mold and apply treatments that will be extraordinarily rich in visual beauty, inducing a helpless wonderment, and always leaving pathways away from that particular world, pathways that in full radiation extended away and outward. Brilliant hologram rays are the pathways, the escape routes to the next world."

This is what Abby's mother whispered to her one bright, cloudless, hot dry day, as she lay drenched in perspiration, soaking the pillow case with matted long brown hair, a pool of sweat forming on her beautiful pursed upper lip. Luscious red lips from the fatal fever, spilling sweat down from the pool around her full mouth, and trickling down around her sculpted chin, causing her pulsing neck artery to glisten in a hurried heartbeat rhythm, catching sunrays from the window Abby's mother demanded no curtains ever close, even at night.

Abby melted into her mother's fevered reverie, fell entranced, believing every word her mother spoke and nodded her head over and over again as her mother, over and over again, made Abby promise to build her own dreams and have the courage to escape when the time demands.

"I have one last dream. Escape Abby. For me. Never be afraid to escape Abby, never be afraid to escape. No, don't do this for me. Do this for yourself."

It was not, contrary to what everyone who knew Abby and her family, her father's instilling of independence that might be the source of her decision to leave her family. Rather, it was her mother's delirious delivery on how to build a dream in order to prepare an escape to live that dream. And that is what Abby did; she felt the need to build upon an earlier dream of hers, finally galvanizing her courage to escape. Abby escaped because she could no longer see her future. She felt she simply was not present in *any* future. Not just invisible to others-- not present. Absent. That was more frightening than anything she could imagine and the flush of panic caused her to run to the bathroom and vomit.

She thought of Earl and Amy, wondering if they wondered why she was not preparing pork chops and peas, along with French fries. Abby loved making that dinner because it was the only combination both Amy and Earl loved. Abby thought, they *love* pork chops and fries. Plus it was the only way for them to eat vegetables, including broccoli and asparagus. Abby became nauseous and vomited as tears streamed into the toilet bowl. She sat on the cheap linoleum floor, putrid green tiles with red and yellow specks, not from her vomit; the tiles were actually designed with red and yellow specks sprinkled about. She broke into laughter upon her realization the tiles were designed with vomit specks. Abby slept easier that night, waking at 330am without the aid of the alarm to drive to Florida for her first interview with a local TV station. Her husband, soon to be ex, arranged it, with no knowledge he had actually done so. A business partner owned the Miami affiliate station. Abby followed up on her own, through deft, disguised conversations with the business partner's wife. All part of her dream plan--from the kaleidoscope. But she never forgot for a day, her children. She knew she would return to them. In her own time, in her own way. First, Abby calculated, she would reclaim her daughter. And she knew she would succeed. But her fear kept her from thinking too much about her son, even more so after seeing him in Lubbock.

Abby recalled all this driving to Midland to visit Winnie Porter, whom she called frequently but had not seen since her wedding day. She left Lubbock, the tornado, and her daughter and son to talk to Winnie and to tell Winnie what her mother told her. Winnie was waiting for her. Winnie would always be there for Abby.

Chapter 12

Lt. Bergsten received an official atta-boy for not pranging the T-37 onto the runway, or worse, stalling and crashing on final. The first gusts of the big storm that generated the fateful tornado created havoc for pilots attempting to land. The wind shear and gusting crosswinds up to 30 mph scared instructor and student pilots alike. Most instructors with any amount of aviation humility took over controls from their students and landed the jets themselves. At least that is what the flying squadron commanders hoped as they accounted for their aircraft. Being solo, Bergsten did not have that luxury.

"I was too scared to think about being scared," he told Earl and Bartholomew a week later at the bar. Bergsten rarely made it to the bar on Friday because his fiancé did not care for the military, much less pilots. She was in Florida getting her master's degree in nursing but that did not seem to stop her from persuading Bergsten to avoid the O'Club bar on Fridays. Bergsten drank beers all night for free and Bartholomew promised him that Earl would get him to his VOQ room safe. Bergsten lived on base to save money. He was already planning on starting a family and started socking away money for that eventuality.

"Well, if that is what it takes to get you to the bar on Fridays Karl, then we may have to convince the flying schedulers to make sure you fly on bad weather days," said Bartholomew, handing him another beer, knowing he would not deliver a wise-ass comeback. Which was a shame, thought Bartholomew, walking to the men's room. My god, he thought,

Karl won't even give me a hard time for giving him a hard time. Bergsten doesn't seem like a weak type.

"Somehow that's gotta change," Bartholomew said aloud as he relieved himself of the last three beers. Bartholomew liked Karl Bergsten, knew he was a strong pilot, and began to admit only to himself that Karl was probably the best student in the class. Different guy, thought Bartholomew. Why the hell would you live on base in the cramped VOQs going through pilot training? The base was ten miles away from anything in Lubbock.

Bartholomew arrived back at the bar to find Earl's sister had arrived. She was wearing tight jeans and a low-neck white frilly top. Her hair was tossed around in some kind of purposeful disorganized look. As she bent down to grab cigarettes from her purse resting on the top of the brass foot railing her blouse billowed revealing her black half-cup bra showcasing firm round breasts. Rising back up she noticed Bartholomew and said, "Perfect timing. Got a light?" Perfect timing is right he thought, knowing she knew that he knew what she meant. He unzipped his arm sleeve pocket and removed his lighter, flicking on the flame and lit her cigarette in one continuous motion. She nodded as she drew her first drag, turning her head to blow the smoke towards the bartender who had just arrived with her Chardonnay.

"Sorry bud," she said to the bartender, standing on the foot railing and leaning over the bar to touch his arm. The bartender's view of her breasts quickly dissipated any frustration from the smoke. Earl and Karl were oblivious to the scene. Bartholomew was convinced Amy orchestrated the little episode.

"Where we goin' tonight boys?" asked Amy, interrupting Earl's conversation with Karl. "My name's Amy," she said, and pointing at Earl, added, "I'm with him." Definitely the too-cool-for-school type of chick, thought Bartholomew, with a mild irritation starting to build up inside. The cure for these types is to ignore them just enough to keep them off-guard, and out of their comfort zone of manipulation.

"Karl, this is my sister Amy," said Earl, shifting his eyes to Bartholomew and sneaking him a flash of a smirk.

"Oh, you're the one who landed in the tornado all by yourself, right?" she said.

"Not really, I mean, not really in the tornado," said Karl.

"Still, you saved the airplane, right?' said Amy, taking a sip of wine and extinguishing her lipstick smeared cigarette butt in the metal ashtray on the bar.

"I just landed it and taxied back to parking."

"Well, I wanna guy like you to be flying when the weather turns real nasty," she said, accentuating the 'real nasty.' Her flirting was over the top, thought Bartholomew, and she was quickly becoming a bore. No way I'm going out tonight with her in tow.

"You're coming with us tonight right" she asked.

"Uh, well, probably not," said Karl.

"Come on Karl, go change and we'll pick you up in front of your room. What's your building number?" said Earl, surprising himself by inviting Karl out.

"C'mon Bartholomew, you're comin' too. We're going to a kicker bar and teach you some two-step," she said. The way she drew out the syllables of his name was beginning to wear thin. It was going to be a long night he said to himself. May have to get drunk just to put up with her.

The Rusty Moonbeam Dance Hall was a new joint, and a college age crowd favorite. The tornado did not pass near the place. Regardless of their musical preference, the guys showed up because the place was filled with girls on Thursday and Friday nights. From the guys' perspective, the downside was they had to learn to dance if they stood a chance with the good-looking set. The upside was many of the girls were more than willing to teach a decent looking guy that wanted to learn to two-step. The downside was the girls danced for an hour straight. The upside was that most girls were beer drinkers and the place ran nightly beer specials. The gals could hold their own drinking beer with most anyone. Thursday nights The Wood Brothers played marathon length sets starting at 830pm and going near non-stop until midnight. On Friday nights Lanky Frank manned the turntable and he too was relentless. Before it became the Rusty Moonbeam the converted warehouse was a roller skating rink. It was perfect for a dance hall and soon after arriving in town had become Amy's main hangout. There was not much to the Rusty Moonbeam; two giant beach ball sized mirror balls suspended over the parquet dance floor, giant half moons made out of rusted rebar hanging over the two bars at either end, and fifteen or twenty patron tables on both sides of the dance floor. Overworked swamp coolers did a lousy job cooling the place. It deserved its nickname—'Sweat Palace.' None besides Amy had been there before. She led them to her favorite table near the far end bar, waving and yelling out to fellow regulars along the way. Girls mostly. Amy smacked her hand down on an empty table, evidently a command to sit down, and shouted for four beers to one of the bartenders.

"I got the first round, flyboys," she declared. Returning from the bar with a tray of four beers, she plopped each one down in front of her companions. She stood leaning in towards the middle of the table with her beer bottle raised and breasts heaving from her brassiere.

"A toast. Here's to a good night with the boys," she said, clinking each of their raised beer bottle necks. After taking a swig and lighting up a cigarette, she arched her head straight back and exhaled.

"Now, who here likes to dance?" she said, shouting over the music.

Without waiting for a reply she knew would not come, she said to Karl, "How 'bout it Tornado boy?"

"No country bars in Minnesota," he said.

"None that you'd admit to knowing about, you mean," she said.

"C'mon, I'll teach ya," she said, grabbing his hand, yanking a bewildered Karl out of his chair, and dropping and stomping out on her fresh lit cigarette.

"Ahh…no," he said.

"Ahh…yes," she said, "Unass your chair and let's dance. You owe me for the beer."

Bartholomew raised his beer in approval.

"Don't think about leaving. You're next," she said to Bartholomew, taking Karl by the wrist and leading him to the dance floor.

"That's how she got her first husband," said Earl.

"She's married?" said Bartholomew.

"Was. Lasted maybe a half a year."

"Karl has a serious girlfriend-a fiancé I believe," said Bartholomew.

"He's safe," said Earl, adding, "It's you she's after."

"Oh sweet joy," deadpanned Bartholomew, swallowing the rest of his beer. He got up, grabbed the tray Amy left on the table and went to get another round. Bartholomew handed Earl a fresh beer and returned to his chair.

"How'd you end up a Religious Studies Major?' asked Bartholomew.

"How did you?" asked Earl.

"On paper, I'm a Philosophy Major," said Bartholomew.

"So am I. Kind of odd…"

"My Dad's a truck driver and got me interested in philosophy," said Bartholomew.

Earl put down his beer and stared at Bartholomew.

"I'm serious as a coronary thrombosis. He listens to tapes of college professors' lectures on the road. Didn't have much of a choice listening when I rode with him on trips. By the time we got back home I was kind of hooked."

"Hooked on philosophy?"

"Maybe not philosophy right away, but thinking about Big Questions, like, 'what's it all about?' Then I got interested in theology as a result. You know, Augustine and Aquinas. In particular, Augustine. Gutsy."

"And you were a football player? I'm sure you confused the professors."

"Yep, especially when I turned on my West Virginia dialect and let them know my uncle's a big-shot Baptist preacher."

Imitating a professor, he said, *"What's a yokel like you doing in a place like this---Oh, you're a football player."*

"Damn if that snot-ass attitude didn't change after the first exams. God, I loved getting under their skin. Told a philosophy professor I was thinking about converting to Catholicism--you could see knots form in his neck."

Earl grinned along with Bartholomew. Earl pointed at Karl and Amy on the dance floor. It appeared Karl was a quick learner. Amy danced like a dance hall pro.

"My Dad called me The Ruminator."

"I think I was just called 'quiet,' said Earl.

"Well, you gonna tell me why you became a philosophy major?" asked Bartholomew.

"Because my Dad wanted me to become something else entirely," said Earl.

"Like what?"

"Lawyer."

"Your Dad a lawyer?" asked Bartholomew.

Earl shook his head. "CPA."

"That also why you joined the Air Force?" said Bartholomew.

"Partly," said Earl as he got up to fetch another round. Earl was a different breed of cat, quick on the take, and not the least bit showy, thought Bartholomew. He seemed to be very aware of his surroundings but at the same time he was not too concerned about what was going on around him. Unlike himself, he thought. He admitted he seemed to be always aware of who was around him and how he was affecting others. He was charged by his affect on people because he was very aware of his affect on people. This seemed to feed upon itself, he thought.

Earl returned a few minutes before Amy and Karl. Bartholomew noted he brought back four beers. The dancers worked up a sweat. Bartholomew stole a glance at Amy, thinking she actually glistened rather than sweat. Her heaving glistening breasts were very difficult to ignore.

"What've you two been up to?" asked Amy, blowing smoke up in the air and cooling her forehead with the condensation from her chilled beer bottle. Earl displayed a short smile and lifted his beer. Nobody answered.

"You as lively as my brother?" she asked Bartholomew.

"You gonna teach me two-step or smoke cigarettes?" said Bartholomew.

"Both-C'mon."

"Not with that butt sticking out of your lips I'm not," said Bartholomew.

"Baby," she said, this time extinguishing her cigarette in the cheap metal ashtray on the table and throwing back a half bottle of beer.

Bartholomew let her lead him around the dance floor and explain the elements of the two-step. After one trip around the dance floor he took command. He was graceful for a big man, displaying subtle footwork. Amy yielded, although it was against her first and second inclinations.

Catching her on the return after spinning her out, he asked, "Why'd you really come to Lubbock? "

"The weather," she said, swirling away from him. He caught her around her waist and led her around and around with him, side-by-side.

"Maybe, and then again, maybe you're bored and like attention. Or maybe you do like the weather—rough, nasty weather, like tornadoes," he said.

She reclaimed the lead by grabbing his hand that was wrapped around her waist and spun out and away from his grasp. He let her lead.

"Doesn't seem to be botherin' you much, does it?" she said.

"Not unless the weather tries to kill me," he said.

"Hey, I wasn't the one driving around with a tornado raging about," she said.

DJ Lanky Frank transitioned to a slow song of yearning for an ex-lover who just won't leave a wistful man's mind alone.

"I'm takin' a break," said Amy, "besides I'm dripping sweat."

"Thanks for the dance and the beer," said Bartholomew.

"Anytime," she said, letting go a quick smile, and walking off the dance floor towards the ladies room. Bartholomew caught it and thought it sure seemed to take a lot of effort for her to smile. It may actually have been genuine. He returned to their table.

"She can dance," he declared.

"That, she can do," said Earl. Karl chortled in agreement then realized his response might be taken the wrong way and shrunk back in his chair and resumed sipping his beer. For the next hour Amy took turns dancing with Karl and Bartholomew. Earl nursed his beers, never leaving the table until he informed them all it was time to go home. He and Karl did not say much when Bartholomew was on the dance floor. They were both comfortable in their respective silence. Bartholomew on the other hand loved to converse. He's a thinker; I'll give him that. Not many would even be bothered to think about what Bartholomew liked to talk about, thought Earl. A mix of western philosophy, religion, politics and American music—all jumbled into a stew of conversation. Can't imagine too many military types share his wide range of interests, he thought.

Earl was not going to put up with any games between his sister, Bartholomew and Karl. He instructed Karl would drive them all back on base because he had the fewest beers to drink, and Earl would drive from base back to Bartholomew's house and drop him off. They learned tonight that if Earl went out, he always decided who would drive and when. Earl thought about those things.

For all of them, it was the first time since they joined the Air Force they did not think about learning to fly jets, about putting up with stupid military rules and restrictions, and about what a crapshoot pilot training is actually turning out to be. And they found others to commiserate with when the bullshit of Air Force life, or life in general, became intolerable. Bartholomew had forgotten all about his need to get drunk just to put up with Amy. It was also the first time Amy wished she met these kind of guys five years ago. Which was one reason why, after her brother turned out his bedroom light, she showered, changed into a soft summer dress, put on some eyeliner and lipstick, and tip toed out of the apartment.

Chapter 13

The body does not function well at two thirty in the morning. Not well at all. Yet that is the time Bartholomew's father woke him to start the day. It was the end of May and the air was clean and cool; school had just let out for the year and the buzzing excitement of anticipating summer began to clear his groggy morning head. Football practice did not start until the first week of August and he had until then to earn some money for books and a new pair of jeans, shoes, and shirt—plus a little fool around money. But before he went to work during the summer, he worked for his father. His father did not call it work; he called it personal improvement time, or PIT for short. But Bartholomew knew it was a time for his father to show him why escape is so important and how it can shape a man.

More to the point his father said, "You have to recognize opportunities to escape. But, acting on that opportunity is entirely another thing altogether."

Every year he would proclaim, "I'm fortunate to find long haul as my method of escape and the measure of a man is determined by not what you do but what you accomplish while on the loose. You don't have to pick my method, in fact, don't, because that ain't escapin', that's mimickin'. As I say, there's a time and a place to mimic, and then you gotta let that go too. So, let's be off." And with a wave of his rumpled brown, stingy brimmed fedora, he climbed up into the cab, turned over the gigantic diesel engine and let it warm up for ten minutes, climbed back down and went over the trip checklist in his mind that he memorized long ago. He hated wearing baseball hats and had a special loathing for the plastic mesh kind, the kind you size adjust by snapping the little plastic nub into the hole.

His father stood just under six feet with a full head of brown hair, square shoulders, a slight pouch that he would actually lose on the road, and hands you would never guess were those of a trucker. He was not handsome, his face and nose too fat, but he was not ugly. The square jaw helped and his green eyes were his secret weapon, according to his wife and dozens of waitresses throughout the Midwest, plus a few in California.

"Take care of your hands, and always have a few good pair of gloves—heavy duty leather gloves and cold weather gloves. Take care of your gloves too." His father had no qualms about dispensing advice to Bartholomew but at least as far as he could tell, his father kept his mouth shut around neighbors and strangers alike. Bartholomew never was present if he gave unsolicited advice to his only sister. She was eight years older and they never interacted much once she reached junior high school. It was like she was in a different family and only stopping by to eat, change clothes, and do her laundry. She started doing her own laundry in seventh grade. Kept her room clean and did her own laundry. Kept her out of mother's hair and her mother kept mostly out of her life and that was exactly the motivation for cleaning her own clothes and room. While still living at home, Bartholomew never considered if it was their father that advised his sister to do these things. He figured his mother mothered his sister and his father fathered him.

On Bartholomew's final trip before leaving for Officer Candidate School, he joined his father delivering wrought iron backyard lawn furniture to a giant all purpose store in Ohio, just a hundred miles from home and then they were to continue west

86

to California to pick up a load needing delivery somewhere back east. His father didn't say what he was picking up or where it was being delivered. He scheduled his trip on purpose so he could visit some favorite stops. As usual on these trips, he brought along two Honda motorcycles. They would ride their cycles together on particular stops to check out places the big rig was not suited for, which, save for a couple of scenic views, were most places. As an independent, he scheduled his own trips or sometimes accepted referrals from longstanding companies he hauled for. He treated his road trip with Bartholomew as one of his two vacations a year. Sometimes it was his only vacation, depending on his wife's disposition approaching vacation time. His wife's parents were long buried and she and her sister were not close. Bartholomew met his aunt on his mother's side only once—at grandmother's funeral.

Bartholomew never knew the route his father intended to travel, or the places he intended to stop, or the particular spots he intended to visit. This trip was no different from the others, except this time his father had a surprise visit arranged.

They said goodbye to Bartholomew's mother last night as well as packed the truck with their personal things. The release of the air brakes announced their departure and a short horn blast pulling out onto the road in front of their house was his mother's signal she could rollover and go back to sleep. The drive to the highway was unhurried and silent. Father and son slow- sipped from their aluminum coffee mugs. Past the four-way stop entering town they lowered their windows, letting in the cool air from the dark morning and the low raw rumbling sound of the big diesel engine. His father had accumulated many habits that transformed into rituals over the years--leaving home in unhurried silence, lowering the windows past the four-way stop, and ejecting the last few drips of coffee from his mug out the window and nestling the mug in its place holder in between the seats. The next stop was for breakfast and the morning constitutional. His father knew the best places for both. Some are co-located, some are not. The objective he said on Bartholomew's first trip was to find the right place to satisfy the needs of the body at dawn's light. Bartholomew learned about 'food and flush' from overhearing another trucker as he climbed down from his rig, stretching and rubbing his lower back and shaking his legs into motion as he joined a couple of other truckers entering the restaurant. Maybe it was just that one trucker who used the term, Bartholomew did not know, but when he mentioned the phrase to his father, the pouting scowl on his face after hearing it was all Bartholomew needed to see what his father thought about that saying.

Two lane highways, the meandering paths through the land of small towns that appeared as oasis' amidst the open spaces--that is what his father loved. He said every small town is an oasis, some are alive and growing, most are just getting by, and some are dying. Or sometimes he would drive the Interstates—odd numbers go North and South, even go East and West—because it excited him to enter the big cities of America.

"Big cities generate big dreams," he said, "And if you're gonna dream, it might as well be American big." He seemed to never tire of telling Bartholomew to dream.

"Always dream son, and always dream big. Huge dreams. Out of your mind huge. No harm in dreaming, so why limit yourself?"

Bartholomew often wondered if his father spouted the many snippets of advice and aphorisms to himself when he drove alone. Or if he talked back to the recordings he would listen to on the road. His father possessed a large collection of lectures from a company that sold copies of recorded academic courses by various professors. History, religion, science, literature, philosophy—his father's collection included them all. He told Bartholomew many of the professors were distinguished in their respective fields.

"Most times I have to play the lectures over a few times until I get the gist of what they're lecturing about. I think I get most of it by the time I'm finished with the series. But who knows for sure."

It did not appear to matter to his father one way or the other.

"It's funny," he said, "I wander the highways with a purpose you know, to get the job done and get paid. But I wander in my mind and don't seem to have a purpose. But I have a need. There's a purpose hiding somewhere I guess."

This last trip, he told himself, Bartholomew was going to ask him about the librarian.

Chapter 14

"Is your friend a Christian?" asked the righteous Reverend Delroy James.

"Uncle Delroy, who are you talking about?" said Bartholomew, looking at his puzzled face reflecting off the microwave oven door. He was bent over watching the rotating popcorn bag expand by exploding kernels. He was not about to let another bag of popcorn get ruined by his inattention. The phone cord was stretched to its limit.

"That young man I saw on TV a short while ago—helping out during that terrible tornado y'all had over there in Lubbock," he said. "I saw you too, in the background."

"That's Earl Neuhaus," said Bartholomew, punching off the microwave and removing the steaming hot bag of popcorn.

"Neuhaus, eh?" repeated Uncle James, "Good name, too." This was the first time Uncle Delroy ever called. He had never even met the man until the last road trip with his father. He retrieved a beer from the fridge and sat down on the stool at the kitchen counter. His head had that hangover hurt and beer and buttered popcorn seemed to the best remedy at the moment.

"Is he Christian?" his uncle repeated.

"I don't know, probably," said Bartholomew, confused and in no mood to talk.

"What's all this about anyway?" asked Bartholomew.

"You mind askin' him if he's Christian?" said his uncle.

"Where's he from?" he asked.

"Northeast somewhere," said Bartholomew.

"Hmm, might be Catholic—well, maybe he's lapsed," said Reverend James, mostly to himself.

"Anyway, how you doin' in pilot school—gonna be one of those fighter jocks?" he asked.

"Doin' alright so far," he said.

"Great, great," said Uncle Delroy. Bartholomew knew he could care less. He had something cooking in his mind about using Earl. Seems Earl's become a magnet to those in search of something. And yet, Bartholomew could not figure out what it was about him. Those two Colonels from the Officers Club last Friday seemed to be on the same mission as his uncle. They had flown in an F-4 from some Air National Guard base near Houston and were already hanging out in the bar when Earl and Bartholomew stopped by. The F-4 got everyone's attention that afternoon. Any airplane other than the white trainers on the base always caught their attention. The F-4 shot into the airfield traffic pattern and performed some practice touch and gos. On their last low approach to a full stop landing, they sucked up the landing gear and leveled off fifty feet above the runway, accelerating. Just past the end of the runway the afterburners lit off and the pilot pulled up sharp and crisp, and then cranked in a tight turn to inside downwind. The engines quieted to idle as the gear, slats and flaps extended. Just as the gear locked into place, they banked and descended in the final turn, touching one hundred feet down the runaway. The drag shoot deployed to further slow the jet. Earl and Bartholomew did not require anyone to explain to them why flying fighters was their only choice. God bless the saps flying heavies. Someone has to, thought Bartholomew.

"Who were you talking to?" said Amy, finally coming out of the bathroom. She had showered and dressed and Bartholomew thought she looked no worse for wear, considering there was a lot of drinking and not much sleeping the night before.

"My Uncle, the esteemed TV Reverend, Delroy James. Seems he has taken a shine to your brother after watching him rip into that Congressman on television. Wants to know if he's a Christian. Wants to recruit him."

"Well, that wasn't who I expected to be calling," said Amy.

"Beer and popcorn?" she asked, grabbing a few hot pieces from the just opened bag.

"Heavy buttered popcorn--cures what ails," he said, plopping down on the sofa and in rapid fire fashion, tossing butter soaked popcorn, one-by-one, into his mouth.

"Not sure how to take that," said Amy, unlocking the sliding glass door and going outside for a smoke on the back patio. Bartholomew watched her as she perched on the edge of the patio chair, profile to him, smoking with casual yet deliberate intent. Slow movement to place the cigarette to her lips, a deep inhale, exhaling the smoke as if she were the femme fatale of Lubbock, knowing she was being watched. She cupped the ashes with her other hand and when finished extinguished the butt by squeezing the lit end. Amy slid open and closed the door and dumped the butt and ashes in the trashcan under the kitchen sink. She used the liquid soap dispenser on the sink to wash her hands.

"Recruit Earl? For what—a TV preacher?"

"That's what I suspect. First time he's ever called me. He's a real operator my dad says," he said.

"So it runs in the family," she said, grabbing her purse and keys from the counter.

"See you around," said Amy, blowing him a smoky kiss and walking out the front door.

"Jesus." She stopped suddenly in the blinding sun bright doorway and fished in her shoulder bag. She pulled out a pair of sunglasses, slipped them on and shut the door.

Chapter 15

Before Bartholomew's father became an independent long haul trucker he and his mother were in the Air Force. Both were retired; his father as a Senior Master Sergeant, his mother, one rank higher, as a Chief Master Sergeant. His mother's small inheritance was used to buy the cab. Nothing too fancy, but it was new. His father rarely mentioned what he hauled around the country and he never seemed to be looking for new customers. At home, the only job talk was about the weather and road conditions. Bartholomew remembered when he was a high school freshman his father talked about coming upon car wrecks. Three or four car pileups with multiple fatalities. His mother made him stop talking about car wrecks at dinner. This suited Bartholomew just fine. He did not like to think about the dead, or worse, someone crushed and dying in what used to be the front seat of a car.

"Truckers don't die driving," he said to Bartholomew on their first trip together. Pointing down at the cars passing by he said, "We're way up above everybody else on the roads, we can see further up the highway, and our rigs are big and built like tanks, not soda cans." His father could never understand why people bought small cars.

"Son, when it comes time to get a car, get a heavy duty pickup truck," he said.

There was plenty of silence on the trips and Bartholomew easily adapted to the silence and stared out the window during sunny cloudless days. He would cat nap off and on as he pleased. He could think of nothing at all if he pleased. Around 1000 am his father played the radio or listened to his tapes until they stopped for lunch. He never asked his father if he could drive because he knew he would never let him. Bartholomew was just fine being a passenger. This trip started with blue skies absent of clouds and absence of chatter in the cab. He opened his lazy eyes to view the Fort Steuben Bridge spanning across the Ohio River. They were arriving into Steubenville Ohio on the Highway 22 Bridge, with the old railroad bridge off to their left. He had been asleep for over an hour. His father drove north up the east side of the Ohio River on Highway 2 and joined Highway 22 west to get to Steubenville, the first break stop.

He stopped at a strip mall, parking on a utility road behind the complex. Bartholomew stepped down and stretched his arms over his head and bent over to get blood circulating from his legs to his head. Shaking off drowsiness, he followed his father around the complex and into a delicatessen. It was 1030 in the morning and they were the only customers. Greeting them was the upfront aroma of Italian bread as well as a short stout man tending the counter, wearing a crisp new Cincinnati Reds baseball hat and a starched white apron. His father ordered two Italian Specials—giant hoagies filled with thin sliced Genoa salami and pepperoni--in between the salami and pepperoni the deli man built a two-inch thick layer of paper-thin slices of prosciutto, capicola, and pastrami. He only used mortadella and mozzarella. Two slices of both. Thin sliced tomatoes below slices of purple onion were slapped on top of the meat mound-- and no lettuce. Plenty of black pepper but only pinches of red pepper and garlic powder. The black and green olive slices were alternated and placed with deliberate intent. Before combining the hoagie halves, with reverence and vigor, the deli man sprinkled extra virgin oil on both sandwiches like a priest applied holy water on newly baptized twins. On his hip rested a knife holster, on his right a black handled bread knife, and on his left a white handled salami slicer. That's what the deli man called it in an accent Bartholomew could not recognize. Whipping out the bread knife the deli man sliced both sandwiches in fourths. With similar flair he wiped the knife free of hoagie particles with a damp white towel lying on his counter and exaggerated his movements holstering the knife. Accepting the bagged hoagies from the deli man Bartholomew thought they must have weighed at least two pounds a piece. His Dad grabbed three 16-ounce bottles of water from the cooler and paid in cash.

"Your son?" asked the deli man. His father nodded and smiled.

"Strong," said the deli man.
Walking out his father said to Bartholomew, "Best Ukrainian deli man around. These will last us all day." Approaching the truck, he gave Bartholomew the bag containing the water bottles.
Bartholomew opened the bag and looked inside, recalling his dad bought three bottles of water.

"Let's go meet the librarian," he said, walking to the end of the strip mall, in the opposite direction of the truck. He stopped in front of the computer store and looked around the parking lot.

"She'll be by soon," he said.

"We are having lunch with her. I'm buying, she's driving."

He smiled, knowing Bartholomew was perplexed. Moments later his father waved at a white sedan that stopped behind the cars parked in front of the computer store.

Approaching the car the driver's window motored down and they were greeted by a brown haired, sun glassed woman whose age and looks Bartholomew could not discern. He gave her a hesitant wave and quickly went behind her car and entered the passenger side back seat.

"How was the trip?" she asked.

"Fine. Beautiful day to drive,' he said.

"Well, you look the same, which is not bad," she said.

"Same to you Julie," he said.

Pointing behind him, he said,"Bartholomew, I'd like you to meet Julia Davenport, the big shot librarian at the University." Julia punched his father's arm.

"I take that back, she is the tough, big shot, pretty librarian at the University,' he said, rubbing the top of his arm. Her return glance gleamed.

"He's awfully proud of you Bartholomew," she said, extending her hand. Bartholomew shook her hand with a firm grip, knowing his father would be grading the handshake.

"Very nice to meet you Ma'am," he said.

"No ma'am's please," she replied with an engaging smile.

"Congratulations on your scholarship Bartholomew. I'm sure you realize how difficult it is to be accepted there. It's quite an accomplishment."

"You mean, for a son of a trucker from West Virginia," said his father.

"No, Harold, I don't mean that," said Julie, "And you're not from West Virginia, either. "

They lived in western Virginia but his dad always said they were from West Virginia. Only when his mother got angry did Bartholomew ever hear his father called Harold. His father smiled and motioned them to sit down and eat. Bartholomew ate in silence, watching people settling in the grassy spaces to study and talk, while others strolled through the campus. With the exception of Julie asking about his mother and where they were heading on this trip, Harold and Julie ate in silence. Bartholomew was unsure if his presence halted conversation between them. Then again, his father never said much to his mother when Bartholomew was around.

"Your father and I were in the Air Force together," said Julie, wiping crumbs from the table and placing her sandwich wrappings and empty water bottle in the white paper takeout bag.

"And your mother, too," she added.

"I like your father because he likes to read and is not afraid to admit it," she said, again smiling at Bartholomew.

"Time to hit the road."

"Again, very nice meet you," said Bartholomew. Julie kissed his cheek.

"You'll be just fine at that university. Don't let the uppity types get under your skin, because they'll try hard, they surely will. They want you to feel smaller than them, forever."

"I won't, Ma'am--I mean Miss Davenport. I'll take your trash and get rid of it."

His father handed over his lunch wrappings. Julie pointed to the nearest trashcan, a short distance opposite the direction where she parked. He felt strange that he was relieved to let them be alone. She did not correct him, so he thought she was not married. He was uncomfortable eating lunch with them. He was an intruder, invited yes, but intruding all the same.

And a day later, after visiting his uncle the Reverend Delroy James, Bartholomew affirmed what he had been feeling since last Christmas. He felt like he was an invited guest in his father's life. More so with his librarian friend than his brother Delroy, whom he had only met once before when he came to visit them at Langley AFB, but never the less. They had to visit the Reverend because he insisted once he found out they were traveling together. Thank God they just stopped for lunch. His church was a former office building that seemed perfect for the future of Reverend Delroy's vision. The first floor was never configured for offices after the investors defaulted on their loan. Delroy's ministry grabbed the property cheap. He was more attracted to the four story parking garage that for some reason had been completed first. Delroy wanted plenty of parking spaces because he fully intended to fill his new church. After the tour they ate lunch at his Uncle's favorite diner.

"Kentucky suits me fine," said the Reverend, cutting a large slice of Salisbury steak, swirling it about in the brown gravy soaked mashed potatoes before shoving it in his mouth. He whipped open his cloth napkin still lying near his plate and quickly wiped his mouth while still chewing his steak. He chewed in violent bites, taking two sips of black coffee to help swallow the gigantic forkful of food. He was trying to talk through his food. He was a man on a mission for sure, observed Bartholomew, and in a rush to get there. His father was just the opposite. He was a very deliberate eater. Cut his meat, put down his knife before placing the portion to his mouth, and grounded his fork as he chewed. His father was a deliberate man. Bartholomew never gave any thought to eating. He ate to satisfy his hunger and quit eating when there was no more to eat. He could not remember the actual act of cutting meat, or putting the fork to his mouth. What he did recall was noticing the serving plates were empty. Then he was done.

His uncle the Reverend interrupted his own knife and fork attack and said, "Now Bartholomew, you've got a glimpse of what I'm proceeding to build here in Kentucky. It's gonna be a huge church with a multitudinous congregation, yes sir. What do think?" He tipped up his coffee mug and drained the last drop before reaching over the condiments islanded in the table center and grabbed the coffee thermos.

"About what, uncle?"

"About what? Why, about this enterprise of the Lord! What do you make of it? All of it! Or some of it! Like for instance, that your uncle's spreadin' the Good News over the TV!"

"I don't know what to say. But congratulations to you and—I don't know, um, best of luck?"

Reverend Delroy looked at him, making Bartholomew very uneasy. Then his uncle burst out, "Luck? You know, you're right son, I could use some luck. I could use a lot of things. But I could use some luck too." His softened voice was more of a surprise than his outburst. Bartholomew's father finished his lunch as if neither of them were sitting there. Delroy resumed his attack on his steak and listed off all the tasks yet to be accomplished before his new church was open for business. Bartholomew felt like he was among complete strangers.

Delroy asked if his father's rig had been blessed. Bartholomew didn't think it mattered how his father replied, the Reverend was going to bless the truck anyway.

Bartholomew felt complete relief as he settled back into the cab. The diesel roared to life. That was blessing enough, thought Bartholomew. His father eased into second gear and they left his uncle waving in front of his church to be.

******

During Bartholomew's parents last duty location they lived on base at Langley AFB, where there were plenty of kids to run around with and a few that joined Bartholomew to race their bikes to the closest spot near the flight line where they would not be shooed away by the security police. The home of the F-15 Demonstration Team was at Langley and Bartholomew and his buddies rarely missed an opportunity to watch the Demo Pilot practice his routine. The plumes from the afterburners shot out from the back of the jet two station wagon lengths and the deafening roar vibrated their chest cavities and left their ears ringing for what seemed like hours. Bartholomew never forgot the *feel* of the raging afterburners and the up close sight of the fighter jet bending its turns, flipping over on its back and then powering out of a low, slow speed loop. Everybody on the air force base wanted to be that Demo Pilot, thought Bartholomew, kids and big people alike. He badly wanted to be that Demo Pilot.

But he forgot all about fighter jets when he fell in love with football in high school, which led him to receiving a full ride football scholarship to college. Bartholomew threw a football far and accurate and he had the kind of quick release coaches can't teach but only hope they can find. He was big and tall, with respectable speed for his size. His feet were quick in the pocket and he could scan over the defense and predict whether his pass would connect just after his receivers had taken their first few steps into their routes. His only interceptions occurred when the ball deflected from his receivers' hands, hanging in the air long enough for the defensive back to grab. The college football recruiters noticed that statistic as well.

Chapter 16

Earl's father did not attend Undergraduate Pilot Training graduation. He could have, he was available finally. After 39 months in prison his father had begun a new life on the West Coast. He started in Seattle but hated the wet gray, low hanging gloom. It did not help that he rented a small apartment the week after New Year's Day. He knew he was not attracted to the city enough to wait until a cloudless day arrived, no matter how beautiful the city appeared when sunlight was permitted free reign. Graduation day caught his father enroute to a promising job interview in Portland and he was as excited to leave Seattle as he was about the realistic prospect of employment. No matter how wet and cold Portland could be. He promised himself he would not gripe about the weather if he landed the job. Demand for a highly experienced CPA in growing investment firms remained. All he had to do was come clean with why he was sent to prison.

Theodore "Chance" Neuhaus earned his nickname late in life, in prison, in fact. Once the inmates learned about him from a TV news broadcast someone took to calling him "Chance" during evening chow and the nickname spread like a salacious celebrity rumor. Theo never referred to himself as Chance, but eventually responded to it when it became clear no one was calling him "New House" anymore. Even the guards were calling him Chance. Inmates finally stopped asking him whether he actually had to shell out the $13 million fine that was affixed to his sentence. The others who were in for fraud knew better. The small thinking white collar scam artists and embezzlers did not. None had come close to accumulating the mass of wealth

Theo had in five years. Theo never said a word to them about money. Theo never said a word to his lawyers and the prosecution about *all* his investments, just the investments that were known. It made no difference whether or not he was going to prison, no effect on his sentencing, and had no further impact on his business associates and partners. Theo's investments were strictly a solo endeavor; every aspect of protecting a portion of his assets was overseen by him alone. He spread them all over the world, one dozen different 'enterprises', as he referred to them. Account numbers and passwords were kept in his mind only. Three drives that stored other information were hidden away. No one would find them unless Theo revealed their location. He regularly drilled himself by writing the phone numbers, account numbers, and pass codes down on a three scraps of paper. After writing the numbers down, he shred the notes and deposited the scraps in three different places. Theo used time tested memory association techniques he learned as a boy. Back then he wanted to be a magician. He memorized 248 numbers for all twelve enterprises. The number twelve represented the Twelve Tribes. But Theo made up his own names of the tribes. Two names were pioneer rap artists popular in the late 1980s.

To hear Theo tell it (one which he crafted and honed by facing himself in the mirror and assuming the role of a prosecutor attempting to find any traces of inconsistency in his own story) Theo woke up one day and realized he was neck deep in fraud. He was the chief accountant, not the Chief Finance Officer. The only time Theo told that story was on the witness stand and his attorney begged him not to. Theo maintained he only presented the facts on spreadsheets and provided assessments based only on facts. No material evidence ever was produced that countered his claim. Problem was that everyone indicted in the fraud charge was singularly focused on saving their own skin. Theo fully recognized this as well as fully anticipated he was going to be found guilty of some of the charges. The prosecution asked Theo if, at any time, did he think he was doing wrong.

Theo said, "Yes, ten days prior to the indictments, on a Sunday, drinking coffee alone in the kitchen. It occurred to me something was not right about a meeting I was in earlier that week. I started thinking about things. I then began to doubt we were above board."

His lawyer turned pale but continued to jot down notes, consciously slow, hoping no one noticed his pallor. His lawyer was convinced Theo was going to get trapped into a confession, but he was wrong. The questioning went on for two hours as the prosecutor used every technique possible to extract more information from Theo. But Theo knew nothing could be proven one way or the other. He knew there were no recordings of meetings or any other notes that the prosecutor could use against him. Even when the prosecutor demanded to know why no memos or meeting notes were ever recorded, accusing Theo and the company of being business imbeciles, Theo told the prosecutor that was their business practice and it suited his work style. He was paid well for an extraordinary capacity to memorize large amounts of data. That bit of information he kept to himself.

However, there was no way Theo would escape a heavy fine and prison. No one in America was offering a scintilla of sympathy to rich accountants and lawyers on trial for fraud.

Especially when it was portrayed as wiping out pensions and savings, regardless if that was actually taking place. The obvious question in his mind was—how much time was he going spend in prison?

He received a five-year term and was released after 39 months when a review of his case resulted in the finding that Theo was not nearly as involved with the mechanics of the fraud as was claimed by the prosecution the first time around. Good news was Theo was confined in a minimum-security facility. Bad news was he was in prison.

Earl wrote his father every month. Theo replied to every letter with an equal detail, although much of Theo's letters involved describing fellow inmates he liked and loathed. They both forwarded their correspondence to Theo's lawyer who then sent the letters on to Theo and Earl. Earl did not care if his father's letters would come from prison, but Theo did. Just one small measure to insulate his son from his incarceration. They never wrote of Earl's sister or his mother. They shared dreams and fears and hopes and realizations. Just between them.

"You never left me and I'll never leave you," wrote Earl in his first letter to his father. Theo called Earl after his release and prior to checking into a hotel in Alexandria, Virginia.

"Earl, I'm switching service providers and picking up my new cell phone tomorrow, but I wanted to let you know I'm out."

"Let me know what you need from me, Dad."

"Will keep you posted on how well my plan's working," said Theo. His optimism was leaking through the phone and to Earl that was the best feeling in the world--hearing his father's excited talk about the future.

Theo had a plan. He spent the first few months concentrating on nothing but his plan. Earl knew no details. Theo's lawyer knew few details. Theo destroyed his notes as soon as he knew that part of the plan by rote. He believed the sequence of his initial actions were critical because they would determine the timing of setting into motion subsequent actions. Theo knew he could not predict the timing of events, but he felt confident he could predict the outcome of events. His objective was straight forward; return to society as seamlessly as possible given his circumstances and set about to do something entirely different than what he'd done before he was convicted. He was more than just free; he was to start over-- not completely over, because he had more money than he'd ever need to live out his life. It was as if he was one those, those of inherited wealth. He craved for something much more than monetary wealth. Much, much more. Theo had 39 months to contemplate. He wasted no time with regret beyond coming to terms with his willful blindness to the realization his firm was duping their investors and everyone else. He resolved to fight to his last days any temptation to dupe himself. It was this resolve that led him to another realization; that he had to choose. Theo had to choose between absurdities. Like his son, he further reduced the absurdities to two choices. Any other absurdities were just outgrowths of the two. The first absurdity was to believe, or more theologically, was to have faith in the absurdity that something can indeed come from nothing. To have faith that eventually some scientists will discover the mysteries of the first cause. To be convinced that civilization will be able to completely bypass the question of 'why' life exists by a determinant resignation that pursuing the "Big Why" question will become irrevocably irrelevant. That by resigned faith, life on Earth just happened. Yes, with full certitude of the human mind. For no reason other than the physics of the cosmos, particle action and reaction. Particle mass, predictability, probability? Particle behavior? Why? Why-- is irrelevant. The facts will turn up to prove there is no "why" when it came to the beginning of the cosmos. If there is no "why" then there is no need for the second absurdity. It makes no difference and therefore should be removed from the question list. Forever.

God exists –that was the second absurdity and Theo still chuckled to himself when Rabbi Benny told him, "Theo, believe this, God does not give a sliver of shit about your stratification of absurdities."

Rabbi Benny was dying in prison and Theo volunteered to be a caregiver. Rabbi Benny was convicted of killing his wife. She thought he was embezzling money and she was wrong. Running over her in the driveway of his synagogue never made national news. He said he did not mean to kill her, he did not mean to harm her. But he was blazingly angry when she accused him, yelling at him in the parking lot while approaching their car, screaming at him that he was a scheister. Rabbi Benny did admit to the jury he stomped on the accelerator in anger to her shouting while backing out of his parking spot. For this, he received five years. He was found to have third stage pancreatic cancer while awaiting sentence. He became bunkmates with Theo. Such events change lives. Rabbi Benny was well known and his influence matched his notoriety. For six months no one but Theo knew he had incurable cancer. The Rabbi forbade his physician to say a word to anyone. Rabbi Benny told his lawyer that if anyone found out about the cancer he'd make sure his days of comfort, wealth, and lawyer privilege were over. Rabbi Benny may have had a cozy and friendly sounding nickname—Benny—but he was as much of a hard ass as any hardened soldier, or con for that matter.

And it was from Rabbi Benny that Theo was informed about the choice between two absurdities. Rabbi Benny said, "Jesus Christ was Divine? Well, good luck with that Theo. You know my peoples' position…Another absurdity--that is an outgrowth of the number two absurdity. But I'll say this; I'm not counting it out, because once you've committed to the second absurdity the concept of a son of God is not all that farfetched. Jesus was a Jew after all. But, I'm only a dying Rabbi guilty of killing his wife. Take that for what it may be worth."

Rabbi Benny went on to say, "To my doubters in my congregation--who had enough guts to express their doubt, I'd say to them, 'To be less human is to believe that something can come from nothing for no reason other than you are feeling putting upon. Your desires are being impeded by what Kierkegaard said— impeded by a trembling and fear to know that God knows every thought and motivation towards what you desire. So I dare them to assert aloud that God does not exist and to live their lives in accordance with their accumulated whims. Because, I'd say to them, 'Your whims were created from nothing, so they mean nothing. Therefore, make the best of nothing, because it matters not whether you are more or less human, other than what others say. Go then and continue to become the best mimic you are capable of. Find what you desire in others and mimic them until the end of your days.'

Benny laughed. "That certainly seemed to clear my office of the doubters. They all understood sacred sarcasm, for that's what I told them I was dispensing. I claim no credit for their change of heart or mind."

They released the Rabbi to die in a hospice. He had one daughter and Helen was as near and dear to him as Earl was to Theo. She wrote as often as Earl. Helen called every Sunday. Theo met her a few times during her visits, and wished his daughter Amy would think to visit him. Theo was able to spend the day with Benny on his second to last day in prison. He gave Theo an enveloped letter. Rabbi Benny's letter made sure Theo would never forget him. Theo never had a better friend. They spent their days together. They shared their thoughts on sleepless nights. Benny was the only person Theo ever talked to about his son and daughter. Together they followed the news about Earl and the tornado. Theo did not know how to approach his own daughter. He felt he'd lost her for all eternity. To help him, he would have to call upon Earl. Benny thought it was the best chance for Theo to re-connect. It deep-bruised his heart not knowing whether he would ever succeed.

Chapter 17

Undergraduate Pilot Training graduation was far and above more satisfying than anything they had accomplished prior. That is what Earl, Bartholomew, and Karl admitted to each other after their third beer. Bartholomew claimed perfect thinking of any phenomenon after finishing the third beer—thus his announcement after every beer triad, "I have achieved three beer clarity." After six beers Karl told him his clarity turned to stupidity. Earl couldn't agree more.

It was Karl that initiated the question what was the most satisfying day of their lives. He pressed Earl and Bartholomew for their answers.

"Getting my wings. Yep, that's it Karl," answered Bartholomew, banging his long neck beer bottle against Karl's. Earl nodded in agreement and clinked his bottle with theirs. Their friendship had grown tight over the last eight weeks, hanging out together during the day whenever they were not flying. Karl's short, plump and very cute girlfriend was a patient kind, noted Earl. She knew it was their night and she gave them enough distance to let them celebrate together. She would press Karl later that night whether earning his wings was really the most important day of *his* life. She had already met Karl's parents in Minnesota. His parents were able to attend the graduation and stopped by the graduation party, just to make an appearance. Dinner was buffet style, catered by the best B-B-Q restaurant in town. Earl sat with Bartholomew's parents and his uncle, opposite Karl's parents and fiancé.

The Righteous Reverend Delroy James was animated and eager when talking with Earl.
He asked about Earl's parents figuring no one else would.

"My father had the job interview of a lifetime and could not reschedule. He didn't want to take the chance of being passed up."

"Your mother couldn't make it either?" pressed the Reverend, leaning in towards Earl so as not to be heard by his brother or nephew. The dining room was packed full and loud with chatter. There was little worry of someone overhearing a conversation.

"I don't keep in regular contact with my mother," said Earl, savoring the Texas brisket, but not the conversation. The Reverend employed nothing but the most soothing of tones as he rubbed Earl's back to congratulate him on his accomplishment.

"Well, son, you can call me anytime you'd like to and talk about anything on your mind—and I mean anything," said Delroy, slipping Earl two of his cards.

"You are an impressive young man and if I could I'd make you one of my top preachers!" laughed the Righteous Reverend, beaming a wide toothy smile.

"I saw that interview of yours during that tragic tornado, yessir, and you crushed that Congressman with ease! You're a natural! Yessir!" patting Earl's back. He leaned close towards Earl and whispered,

"I'm serious son, you *have* it. And I know what the people want, what they need. That's my calling son. I'm called to tend the flock. And young man, you could lead them anywhere you choose." The Reverend's brown eyes blazed. He later could not recall a more inspired performance. Earl had

created a loud and constant buzz in his mind. He fantasized Earl
expanding his ministry all through the southeast, down through
Louisiana, Mississippi and Texas and into California.
Nationwide in fact, is what Reverend Delroy James dreamed of.
He had visions of capturing the world through his ministry.
Delroy only thought big. The Word needed to be delivered in
large ways, not small ways, he thought. And he knew he did not
have the full gifts required to grow his ministry to the heights of
his dreams. That's alright, he thought, because now that he
actually met Earl and talked with him he was absolutely
convinced he found the man who could. He could not explain it,
and he was not in want of an explanation. Delroy just felt it and
felt he had been given a gift to give back to the Lord. Now he
just had to pray that Earl might call him one day. Hopefully,
sooner than later.

"Amen, Amen," he said. "Amen."

"Sir, what is it do you think I have?" asked Earl, not ever
having believed he possessed any trait that would attract him to
the preacher. Earl thought of himself as a good student, could
focus on the task at hand, and complete a task well. He was
willing to listen and learn and then move on to something else;
skills he did not think all that unusual. Yet he knew what the
Reverend was referring to. But Earl had no intention of
discussing it with Reverend Delroy.

"Aw, c'mon now son, you *know* what you have," said
Reverend Delroy laughing loud at Earl's feigned ignorance.

"You're not afraid to die, are you son? The crux is, why
not?" Delroy's smile reached across the room as he excused
himself from the table and stepped outside the O'club to seek
some quiet and think. Earl did not want to think too much, but

couldn't help pondering exactly why Reverend Delroy asked him that question. Earl froze in contemplation.

Outside in the calm dry air a quick thought pierced Delroy's mind. Was it feigned ignorance? Or did this young man have no idea what affect he had on people? Did he not know he presented himself as a blank slate upon which others fill transfer their fears, their desires, their hopes? Certainly he had to know, thought Delroy. He most certainly had to know. Then again, maybe it was because Earl did *not* know or realize this. Which now made Delroy think further; what made Earl become like he had become? What did Earl have inside him? What swirled in his mind? His heart? Where was Earl's mother in his life?

Inside the Officers Club was buzzing with testosterone, beer, and tequila. The band was playing classic rock songs that anyone with two functioning legs could dance to. Loud and raucous, with occasional screams and laughs piercing the air by excited young women. Bartholomew was fixated on those women; every one of them, looking to see who was attached and watching their eyes to notice who appeared to be not too excited being with whom they were with. He had wings on his chest, an assignment to F-15C training along with Earl, three beers and a shot of the best tequila in his belly, and a building tension in his loins. Karl graduated number one in the class and was coming back to base as a first assignment instructor pilot. Earl and Bartholomew knew he wanted a fighter and he accepted the assignment with classic restraint, impressing Earl. Karl had his full respect. He was going to marry his girlfriend and she was very happy he was returning to the base. To her, training seemed a much safer pilot job. They had immediate family plans, just as their parents did before. Maybe, thought Bartholomew, she told Karl she wanted him to stay and be a training instructor pilot.

Later, at the bar Bartholomew found Earl on a seat at the corner. He was talking to his sister Amy and another woman; plus the same two Colonels from the Texas Air National Guard who were here a few months back. He noticed the Colonels right after the graduation ceremony, standing off to the side observing Earl being interviewed by two local TV stations. Lubbock was not going to forget an Air Force pilot who stopped and cared for them. A few families from the neighborhood attended the formal graduation ceremony. Earl returned to the neighborhood a number of times to check up on the families, and always asking about the woman who was wife and mother of the bus driver and young boy. This is what Earl confided in Bartholomew about—his thoughts about that woman. He wanted to meet her. No one seemed to know where she lived. Or if she still lived in Lubbock.

Earl captivated the TV interviewers. Humility cloaked him and no one escaped notice. Nor was the TV audience immune to his penetrating, immediate presence. Reverend Delroy was right; Earl absorbed the feelings of others, yet yielded no response other than conveying a countenance of what others may have been searching for, conscious or not. And Bartholomew was convinced it was a willful countenance. From where it came he could not begin to offer a theory. Earl had become a regional phenomenon. Bartholomew watched the colonels watching—trading comments but nonetheless measuring the response of everyone's reaction to Earl. Bartholomew knew they were exploiters sizing up a prospect.

He knew the very same about the large bellied, black suited man now joining them --the Righteous Reverend Delroy James, Bartholomew's uncle on his father's side. He had not seen Bartholomew but one other time as a young boy, he thought, and yet he was not going to miss his graduation from pilot training? Bartholomew was convinced he could see everything, and now could see what was in it for them. It was clear in his mind. It was as transparent as the human condition can reveal itself, he thought, tossing back one more tequila shot.

"We're going back to the hotel Bartholomew," said his mother, sneaking up on him as he slammed the empty shot glass down on the bar. She kissed him on the cheek. His father winced, but Bartholomew ignored his expression and kissed her cheek.

"Go on and celebrate with your friends. Your Dad and I know about you pilot types," she said, beaming a wide warm smile. His father shook his hand and slapped his back and then left to corral Delroy, who had interjected himself in a conversation with the colonels. They all drove together and Bartholomew's father knew all too well that unless he relieved the graduation attendees of his brother's overreaching benevolence, the blame may rest on Bartholomew's shoulders for inviting him—which was not true. Reverend Delroy James invited himself.

As Bartholomew said goodbye to his parents, he again noticed the woman standing next to Amy. Now he recognized her as the weather reporter who appeared after the tornado. Remarkable the resemblance, he thought. She was having a grand time with the two old colonels. Earl caught Bartholomew's eye and gave a slight head nod towards the side exit, where everyone filed in and out to smoke. Earl joined Bartholomew to go outside. The patio was almost as crowded as the dance floor. Only a few were smokers, the rest were just catching some fresh air and tired of yelling over the band. They felt the warm air begin to cool, coaxed by the lazy breeze. Conversations were filled with anticipation of the near future, the next event in their lives. Earl and Bartholomew were no exception.

"Who's that other chick with you and Amy?" Earl laughed and punched his arm.

"Chick?"

"Ok, who's that woman?"

"Why, you interested?"

Earl could read Bartholomew's mind, which in this case was not difficult. Earl was enjoying the moment.

"C'mon, Earl."

"You're whining, big fella," smiled Earl. Two other guys in their graduation class came up and they congratulated each other.

"I'm going back inside," said Earl.

"I can only take her in limited doses," he said.

"Take *who*, goddammit?" yelled Bartholomew as they stepped back inside the bar.

"My mother," said Earl, not looking back at Bartholomew but at the two old fart colonels on the dance floor with his sister and mother. It was a slow song.

"Your mother," said Bartholomew, burying his amazed disbelief, as they watched the two couples dancing and his mother and sister laughing at whatever the colonels were saying. A few times the couples would converge and the colonels exchanged some banter while his mother Abby and sister Amy traded smirks. Bartholomew was not sure who was playing whom out on the dance floor.

"Did you visit with her after the tornado?"

"No, and I don't plan to visit with her now."

"She tell you she was coming to your graduation?"

"No. She invited herself—or probably Amy invited her. They get along pretty well considering." The slow song ended and both couples started to leave the dance floor as Amy waved to Earl and Bartholomew. The band's lead guitarist began the infectious riff of the Rolling Stones song, "Satisfaction." The two colonels transformed into fervent rock and roll stooges, yelling at each other and raising their arms in the air. They then grabbed Abby and Amy, begging them to stay and dance. Bartholomew grew angry with envy, poorly disguised as disgust. Amy looked back at her brother and Earl, and signaled to them just one more dance. Earl's mother was oblivious to his whereabouts and seemed perfectly happy to dance all night.

"What do you want to do?" asked Earl, motioning to Amy that he was leaving the club. She shrugged her shoulders, tossed her head back and laughed and began a slow grind dance in front of her partner, lowering herself slowly to the floor.

"Considering what, Earl? Amy gets along with your mother considering…"

"Considering she left without saying anything." Earl remained fixated on his mother and sister.

"Left?"

"My mother left us and no one, not Amy and me, not my father—none of us knew she was leaving. Only afterwards, a few weeks or so, did Amy and I find out why." Turning to face

118

Bartholomew, Earl said with dead eyes, "And her reason for leaving? Her reason? She felt trapped and had to escape. That's how my father initially explained it."

"What do you want to do?" asked Earl. Bartholomew wanted to get laid in the worst way and at first did not care if he bedded Amy or Abby.

"Let's get out of here and out of these damn dress blues," said Bartholomew.

Chapter 18

The doorbell rang as if being punched by a slow motion jackhammer. Bartholomew awoke in his bed with no idea where he was. Accompanying the urgent doorbell ringing was the front door being pounded by something hard, giving off a sharp sound. It was everything Bartholomew could do to focus on the red LED to read 323am on his alarm clock. He was naked and could not find any clothes to put on. The ringing and pounding was in his head now and he grew nauseous. He and Earl had finished the evening solving the world's problems at the Rusty Moonbeam. Bartholomew swallowed beers all night while Earl sipped and mostly listened.

A woman screaming epithets of all persuasions pierced through the pounding and ringing. Bartholomew's name was in the mix of verbal vulgarity. He found his boxer shorts lying in the entryway of his bedroom and stumbled and bounced off the hallway wall putting them on.

Amy was furiously drunk; Bartholomew's head was in the furious middle stages of a hangover. Bartholomew tip toed to the front door and put his ringing ear to the door. She was sobbing and sniffling, still screaming and cursing. Bartholomew's head ached and he was dying for a gallon of cold water. He kept all the lights off and crept into the kitchen. The light of the refrigerator door was enough for him to see the numbers on the telephone. He dialed up Earl. He was not letting her in the house. Then the rapid ringing sounds were replaced by slow pulses of ringing. She was getting tired. The pounding on the door stopped. He could now barely hear her raspy sobbing voice.

"Hello."

"Sorry Earl, but Amy is at my door screaming and crying and drunk out of her mind. Or she is something out of her mind. I'm not letting her in and I'd be grateful if you come and get her."

"On my way," he said, with no hesitation. There was now silence. Neighbor dogs were barking. The high-pitched yip yips of tiny dogs startled and agitated. Bartholomew returned to the entryway gulping water from a plastic jug he retrieved from the fridge. Again he pressed his ear to the door and heard nothing, but smelled cigarette smoke. He sat down in the foyer and gulped from his jug. Water leaked from his mouth down his chin and dribbled onto his belly. The waiting made his head pound harder, but the cold water streaming into his undershorts seemed to bring a soothing salve. He grew angry--a mean kind of angry that lead him towards mean thoughts about Amy. And about himself. About why he was getting so angry over her. She was playing him like she played every man she met. She played them because she could, because the men she played were weak. Bartholomew was played too, he thought, and now the game is over. He knew she was still playing and he was self-eliminating from her game.

The single, prolonged doorbell ring startled him. He'd been droning in his mind and wasn't sure how long he had been sitting on the foyer tiles. He grabbed the door handle to help lift himself up and peered through the peephole and saw Earl looking at him.

"Well, at least she had the courtesy not to spell out the entire phrase," said Earl, pointing down with his head at the knife scrawled carving in the door as it opened.

"FYA," said Earl.

"Fuck You Asshole?" figured Bartholomew, bending over to pick up two cigarette butts extinguished on his welcome mat.

"Correct."

"Her truck's gone," said Earl. Bartholomew left the door ajar and walked back to the kitchen, flipping on the light.

"Thanks again for taking me home tonight," said Bartholomew.

"Amy and my Mom were both out to get riled up and weren't thinking too much about anything else, it seems," said Earl. Bartholomew detected his sad disappointment.

"I think you did right not to let her in. I'm just worried about where she is now."

"Your mother is quite the act, Earl, my God."

"First time I've ever seen her that way. But then, I have not seen much of her over the past years."

"And, while we're at it, you're becoming quite the act as well. You get loud and obnoxious when your belly's full of beer—talking like you're already a fighter pilot. You're a big guy Bartholomew, and getting bigger," he said, smacking Bartholomew's bloated belly with the back of his hand and then smacking his forehead—like a Three Stooges slap around. If Earl was hurt by his mother's performance last night it never showed. But Bartholomew was not going to forget the sadness soaking in his voice. He accepted Earl's words with a shoulder shrug.

"Seemed like peas in a pod to me—watching them tag team the two colonels."

"Yeah. They wanted to convince themselves they *were* sisters and I went along with the charade. Kind of pitiful, actually, but I figured it best to go along rather than tell the colonels one of the chicks they were hitting on was my mother."

"I should have let her in," said Bartholomew, filling up the empty water jug with tap water.

"I'm not so sure," said Earl, turning to leave, "I'll call you when she pops up. And, she *will* pop back up."

"Pretty weird last night Earl, your mom pretending to be your older sister—and Amy...she's too damn much. Did she learn her whole act from your mom, or what?" Bartholomew winced at his stupidity for blurting out about his mom.

Earl stepped off the porch to walk to his car. Over his shoulder he replied, "I think *'or what'* is probably the right question."

"Sorry Earl, I didn't mean that," shot back Bartholomew, his stupidity igniting self-loathing. Maybe, he thought, he was getting back at Earl for calling him out for trending towards the habits of an obnoxious sloth. Without looking back Earl waved off the apology. It was a wave of forgiveness.

"You really had no idea she was coming to graduation?" Earl shook his head.

"She wants to see me more often. Wants me to call her, keep her in the loop on my life."

Quickly changing the subject, Bartholomew asked, "Those colonels, why were they here again? Did they talk to you?"

Opening his car door, he said, "Amy swears they're trying to get me to join the Texas Air National Guard. They claim I have big potential in Texas. She said the Governor is also a Guard pilot and he wants to meet me. Says he saw me on TV handle that stupid Congressman in Lubbock after the tornado and he wants me on his team. Whatever that means. More drunk talk, that's all." He laughed, waved again, and drove away into the early morning darkness. Earl did not want to think about things, but he could not help but think about Amy's whereabouts. And Earl's mother? He did not want to think about her. The dogs had stopped barking.

PART II

Chapter 19

The dogs stirred just like the other animals reacting to the change in humidity and stillness of the sticky air. They did not bark in unison, more like a call and response, like an expression of uncertainty that permeated the backyards, beaches and pine and shrub parcels just north of the Panhandle, this time the Panhandle of Florida. Looking south over the gulf the sky appeared bruised—a gigantic swath of blotched grey and deep blue and purple was visible for miles. The northern face of the largest hurricane in thirty-three years was creeping towards landfall—somewhere between Mexico Beach and Pensacola Florida.

Almost six months prior Earl would never have believed hurricanes roar through this part of the country. Then again, after leaving Mississippi he never saw much beyond the swath carved through three story pines bounding Interstate 10, just hazy laced blue sky. Arriving at Tyndall AFB, the foul acrid stench released from a nearby paper mill seeped into his BMW and choked him, distracting Earl from noticing the orange tinted sunset on display beyond the undulating inter-coastal waterways. His air conditioner was fixed but that didn't prevent the stink from filling his car. A lone boat motored away from him at high speed, evidenced by the three foot symmetric white topped wake that diverged and eventually bumped up against the shorelines.

Earl suggested living in Mexico Beach, a slow motion beach community eight miles west of the air base. However,

Bartholomew got to Florida first and leased their shared apartment 25 miles east, in Panama City Beach, within safe drunk driving distance of the biggest and rowdiest beach nightclubs along the Emerald Coast.

Earl and Bartholomew were almost finished training, well ahead of their classmates. Quickly adapting to the F-15, Earl received quiet praise from the instructor pilots, many from operational squadrons that had flown in the Gulf War. Earl's confidence in his evolving flying skills fueled his aggressiveness. As a wingman, he always targeted, identified, and 'killed' the training adversary, frequently killing both his adversary and the adversary the instructor pilot was paired against. Earl's hand-eye coordination combined with aggression made him lethal and even the hard-dick, cantankerous instructor pilots gave him his due—although reluctantly. Part of the reason was that Earl was not the type to suck down beers all night while arguing fighter maneuvering techniques, yapping about squadron politics, and openly lusting after the brand new pilot wives.

On the other hand, Bartholomew also received attention, the kind of attention that came with dealing with a personality that overwhelmed any room as well as a clear ability to fly the F-15C as if he had 1000 hours in the jet. His basic fighter maneuver skills were becoming well known. He was waxing every instructor he flew against, and thrived on their frustrations with him both as a pilot and as a bloating, big talking second lieutenant student pilot draining beer from the taps in the squadron bar and Officers Club bar. He loved to lust over his fellow students' wives. He'd been slapped more than once for whispering his oral sex fantasy into their newly wed ears. Earl was the only student pilot that could stand to be around him. Fellow student pilots grew so frustrated they finally stopped pulling Earl aside and asking him why he stood by him. Barely eight weeks into their six month F-15 training and Earl had become ostracized because of his unwillingness to disassociate himself with the obnoxiousness on display known as Bartholomew.

"Keep your sleazy pickups out of the apartment," said Earl, when he agreed to room with Bartholomew. Bartholomew violated that rule 48 hours after moving in their furniture.

"I wasn't going to roll around with them on the carpet Earl," he said. "Besides, our place is a helluva lot more convenient for me than some chick's hotel room. They all flock down to the coast together and cram into one room. That doesn't make for a relaxing environment to get it on, y'know?"

He paused, and then added, "I'm not so sure you do know Earl, do you?"

Chapter 20

Hurricane Amy threatened and the F-15 instructors were hustling to get as many students through training before she hit landfall. Until it formed into a Cat 5 storm and threatened most of the Panhandle Earl and Bartholomew enjoyed the best inside joke two friends could have, at least according to Bartholomew. Earl's laugh was acceptance enough for Bartholomew yet he overstepped the line by offering up the crudest types of hurricane metaphors to describe the real Amy. Earl called him on it and he backed down.

"Your Mom's back in town," whispered Bartholomew, in between stuffing his mouth with jalapeno popcorn, the only food Bartholomew ate in the squadron bar. He leaned over the counter and topped off his beer mug. Earl said nothing. The bar was filling up because the commander was going to give a quick overview of the evacuation plan. The F-15s were too vulnerable to remain on the airfield and every flyable jet was to be hurrivac'ed to Virginia. They were departing at dawn the next day. Earl's mother was on TV reporting about Hurricane Amy's advance. Now Abby Westmoreland was the current weather darling of cable TV news. She was reporting from Gray's Beach, east of the Panama City Beach. The shore break was reaching overhead size. Local surfers were catching the biggest waves of their lives. Abby's yellow rain coat was open, revealing her low cut V-neck purple t-shirt. Bartholomew noticed. He looked back at Earl, but knew better than to expect a response. The on-shore winds wrapped her hair around her cheeks. She moved her head side to side while consciously using her first finger to pull back hair strands off her face as she reported on the nearness of the hurricane.

"I'm going to the woodshop before it closes for the hurricane," said Earl.

"Laying in the frets."

"What kind of guitar is it again?" asked Bartholomew.

"Acoustic-electric cutaway."

"I thought you told me you only play piano."

"I play piano and I'm building a guitar."

"Can I again ask, why?"

"Sure. Making a guitar is sensual." Earl enjoyed watching Bartholomew grow flustered.

"Like erotic sensual?"

"No. I don't get sexually aroused building a guitar."

"What gets you aroused?"

"Why the interest?"

"Trying to figure you out Earl, just trying to figure you out."

"I'm not wired like you Bartholomew."

"No shit, dude."

At the wood shop Earl was known as the guy making a guitar. He loved the wood shop. He checked in, retrieved the guitar neck from the rental locker, and went into the far right corner of the shop where the smaller projects were worked on. He wore his big blue-cupped ear protectors he was issued in pilot training. Nearly all the machines were occupied—the table saws and miter saws—all were screaming away as men concentrated with due diligence on their respective projects. To a man, all were absorbed in their tasks, behind protective masks and goggles, and under ear protection. Absorbed in their own micro worlds, oblivious to others around them. Cocooned by the sound of high pitch saw blades tearing wood, higher pitch meant soft pine, lower pitch meant harder wood, like cherry and oak. The air was saturated and scented by fresh cuts and machine oil, as oil also clung to their blue jeans and t-shirts-- mixing with the sweat on their foreheads and forearms. Today the shop was also permeated with a sense of urgency. They knew they might not get a chance to work on their beloved wood after the hurricane hit landfall. Their place of refuge was vulnerable, leaving their creations vulnerable. So they cut and lathed and joined pieces together as if to complete themselves. This is how Earl felt. He was amongst like-minded men, and rarely a word was spoken between them. There was no need. Earl thought about what he needed to complete himself, or whether he was already complete.

Earl laid out the stainless steel frets and set about implanting them into the maple neck he finished during pilot training. Looking out the window, he observed the sky was free of rain and beautiful blue. Tomorrow night was going to be a different story. After installing the frets, he drove home, arriving at his apartment close to nine pm., bringing with him all the pieces of his guitar, uncertain if he'd have an opportunity to work on it over the next few weeks, or worse, have it become damaged or destroyed by the hurricane. He retrieved a hard plastic storage box from the general purpose closet under the stairs. After triple wrapping up the neck in a bit of old blanket, now velvet soft from years of use and washing, he laid the neck on top of the guitar body already wrapped in the remainder of the faded blue blanket. The rest of the hardware--tuning pegs, extra frets, and small set screws were kept separate in zip-lock bags and tucked in the corners of the box. The box, along with an Air Force issued A-3 bag full of clothes, and his backpack crammed with pilot training books and notes, were coming with him when the time came to find adequate shelter.

"Pack your clothes and gather your stuff so we can leave quick." The note was posted on the Fridge and Earl slipped a copy of the note under Bartholomew's bedroom door. They were both on call to be ready as backups to fly out the F-15s if any of the instructors fell out of the lineup. Being on call prevented them from evacuating, like most of the residents had already done, or were finally getting around to. The sheriffs were all over the local TV stations warning residents about remaining in place and chest poking the locals from TV land to leave the coastline immediately. They were simply not manned to enforce mandatory evacuations. They knew they would never hear the end of the harassment complaints if the hurricane caused little damage. Yet law enforcement had to prepare for the worst case, including rescuing the stubborn, the stupid, and the resistant during and after a direct hit.

Earl calculated he would have to find shelter nearby the apartment. No way I'm staying in our place, he thought. If the apartment complex survives at all, it will take weeks for the debris and wreckage to be cleared, much less the chance of electrical power. So no air conditioner and no hot water—no thanks.

Three phone calls came through and two were for Bartholomew. One was from his uncle the preacher—the second from his father. Both asked that Bartholomew call them back. It was 1130pm before Bartholomew returned to the apartment. Earl was on the couch watching a special report on the hurricane, wondering whether to tell Bartholomew about the third phone call.

"Clouding up and the air is getting dank," mumbled Bartholomew, going straight to the Fridge and grabbing a jug of water.

"Thanks for the reminder," Bartholomew said, waving the note from the Fridge door reminding him to pack. He tossed the note on the counter and settled on the opposite end of the couch, chugging cold water, some leaking from his mouth and dripping onto his shirt.

"How much water does it take to sober you up?" asked Earl, still watching the TV.

"Damn near three jugs. I starting pissing after chugging the second. By the time I finish the third I'm pissing every ten minutes." Earl turned and grinned, shaking his head like a disapproving parent. Bartholomew shrugged and kept chugging, emptying the jug and going to the kitchen sink to fill it for round two.

"When'd you quit drinking beer?" asked Earl.

"Half hour ago—been drinkin' on a no-fly forecast. No way we were gonna be called to fly those jets out tomorrow."

"Your dad called three hours ago, right after your uncle. Both want you to call them tonight."

"What's up?"

"Neither said and I didn't ask," said Earl.

"Call them back tonight? Hell--for shit's sake…" Bartholomew chugged the rest of the water in a continuous series of gulps, spilling water all over his chest. He wiped his face with his forearm and stuck the jug under the kitchen sink faucet and watched the water fill the jug as he listened to the phone ring through the headset.

"Is Dad there? What's up?" asked Bartholomew.

"Yeah, I was out. Earl said to call you tonight. What's going on, Mom?" Earl clicked off the TV and remained on the couch. Bartholomew grabbed the filled jug and took quick sips while listening to his mother. He paced back and forth across the kitchen in big steps, squeaking his tennis shoes while pivoting around.

"In six hours? Damn, Mom!" He finished the call while tromping up the stairs to use the toilet. He returned downstairs five minutes later.

"Everything alright?"

"Fuck no."

"My dad's arriving in town in six hours—with my damn uncle. Somehow he holy talked my dad into transporting a load of relief supplies down here. My uncle's leading a damn caravan of church volunteers to help out. Unbelievable!"

"Your truck full of gas? You packed?"

"Lay off, Earl." Earl rose from the couch and stepped in front of Bartholomew.

"Go fill your truck now and then come back and pack up. Get five gallons of water and beef jerky and cans of chicken. Let's get ready for tomorrow." Earl's confident and quiet tone calmed Bartholomew. He said nothing as he left the apartment. The wind had picked up and the air was sticky with swelling moisture. Now, thought Earl, if the real Amy can just get here before her namesake hits landfall. The third phone call was from his sister. She'd never been to Florida and felt a calling to visit. Earl did not protest. It was a wasted effort and would yield no satisfaction.

"Hope I'm still here when you arrive," he said.

"My apartment is the last place to sit out this hurricane. We're on the Grand Lagoon and that is not a good thing."

"We'll just have to make the best of it, won't we Early boy?" chirped Amy.

"It is beyond foolishness to drive into a hurricane," he said.

"But—I have to!" He sensed the titillation she was feeling. She wanted to be part of the glamour of hurricanes. Earl believed Amy glamorized destruction, regardless of origin. Amy had to place destruction center stage, in full light and for all to see. Destruction gave her a purpose.

"Mom's down there somewhere too, showing off those store-bought titties she just got installed! The TV loves her titties!"

"Call me when you're fifty miles out," said Earl, disgusted.

"I'm in Montgomery."

"Like, I said," and reminding her, "Watch your speed through those small towns."

"Thought they like white girls in Alabama?" she giggled. Sure sign she was high, thought Earl.

His BMW was packed—three coolers, two filled with ice, one with jerky, cans of chicken, and vegetable soup. He had a nine-roll pack of toilet paper, a six-pack of soap, and five gallons of water and five gallons of gas. He declined to take one of Bartholomew's handguns and ammo. Bartholomew was ready for an armed gang, complete with a pump shotgun and two Glock 9mm. He had more than enough ammunition to put ten rounds each into two hundred men.

Earl was in bed when Bartholomew returned. Both lay awake, with Bartholomew whisper-cursing having to urinate every twenty minutes. Separately, they listened to the wind swoosh and tear and bend the trees and rattle the loose doors. Rain now fell in swirling sheets. The bedroom windows flexed in and out. Earl fell asleep just before the phone rang at 600am. He wasn't sure if it was the phone, hearing only one ring. He rolled back over and cinched up the sheet under his chin. He thought about the fan still blowing. The white noise and airflow across his face had always been relaxing. It stilled his thoughts as he lay down for the night. Fan on meant electrical power was still on. But for how long? He heard the rain slam against the sliding glass door. The cheap plastic vertical blinds bounced against themselves, tinkling like plastic blinds do, revealing a hint of dawn light—as if a weak flashlight was attempting to shine through stacked layers of grey tinting. The wind was flinging branches or something hard against the apartment complex. Earl flipped on his other side and noticed the hallway light from under his door. He tore off the sheet and shot out of bed.

Bartholomew was not in the apartment. Earl clicked on the TV and went back upstairs to shower and get dressed. He thought of his sister. She should be calling soon. The phone must have ringed and Bartholomew answered, he thought. His father must have arrived. No place to park his semi near the apartment, so Bartholomew went to him, Earl concluded. The hurricane expert showed the path of Amy. She was hitting landfall between the air base and Panama City Beach. She had been upgraded to Cat 5 and just miles from landfall. Now the phone rang again.

"Bartholomew?"

"No, this is Earl."

"Is he there? Can I speak with him please?"

"He's not here. I think he left 20 or 30 minutes ago."

"Well, we're here—God only knows how and I'm parked with the others in a big church parking lot—Saint Basil's I think, just off Highway 98. We're not going anywhere soon. The highway is jammed, the hurricane's close. I'm listening to the chatter on the CB. Tell Bartholomew I called--will you please? "

"I will."

Bartholomew's father said, "Not sure I'll see him anytime soon—damn this is going to get real, real bad." Earl could barely hear him now, the wind conjuring up a screeching and persistent whistle—a panic whistling, not caring about the notes, just about panic. This is stupid staying out here; I have to go, thought Earl. He pulled on a sweatshirt and grabbed his slicker. Lacing up his flight boots the TV went silent and the lights went out. He ran back upstairs and pocketed his wallet and put on his watch. He grabbed his keys off the kitchen counter and struggled to insert the key to lock the front door against the buffeting wind and stinging rain. As he left the parking lot branches and pinecones behaved as projectiles, slamming into his BMW. Dawn was not coming this morning. The sky above was black, only looking towards the North could he glimpse some dull light. Two young men were flailing about trying to tie down a blue tarp across whatever was in the back of their old red pickup. Then one of them let go of a rope and the

136

tarp. Only secured on one side, it began to flap above them. A sudden reversal of the tarp swiped the man with no shirt and the attached rope whipped him to the ground. Earl kept his car running and got out to help.

"Get outta here man, we got it, we got it. Go man, thanks!" said the other man, now lifting his friend and clinging to the loose tarp by the rope end that was for an instant a whip.

He was not alone on the debris cover road; cars were moving in both directions, slow and steady, crunching over tree branches and swerving to miss remnants of boxes, and outdoor plastic trash cans forgotten on the roadside now amongst the traffic, puking their rubbish onto the asphalt as cars smacked them and the roaring wind flailed the weak hinged trash can lids as easy as an open cardboard box. Sheets of soaked newspaper clung to windshields in a last desperate act to avoid being blown away forever.

Chapter 21

Bartholomew spotted the black pickup next to the pay phone outside the 7-11 store, which was closed and the corners of the plywood sheets were slapping against the store front windows they were nailed in to protect. Getting there was lucky. Now the traffic stopped all movement. He saw no chance of driving away. He banged on the driver's side window of the black pickup and pressed his face against the glass to see if she was inside. He could see a figure scrunched down on the passenger side floor.

"Open the door. Open the fuckin' door, now!" Amy's arm crept along the bench seats, first snatching her purse, then lifting herself up to see who was banging on the window. She unlocked the door and Bartholomew clutched her wrist and pulled her from the pickup.

"You're an idiot," he yelled, dragging her outside and into her raging namesake. He began to trot away from their trucks, sloshing through ankle deep water and buffeting against the overwhelming wind and stinging bullets of rain.

"Where are you taking me?" she screamed. He ignored her and began to jog. Around the stand-alone building he found the three parked small sedans and a Black Cadillac Escalade. He banged on the private entrance door to The Shelter, the most popular strip bar in Panama City Beach.

"What are you doing? You full-scale asshole!" screamed Amy. Bartholomew banged with both fists until the door popped open. Billy D's lit Cuban was extinguished immediately by a sheet of rain. Newly unwrapped Cuban, just lit up. He tore it out of his mouth and gave it a moment's disgusting stare, tossing it high over Bartholomew's head as he pulled Bartholomew inside, dragging Amy with him. She tripped on the single step and Bartholomew had no intention of picking her up. Billy D was no less furious than Amy, and dragged her by her arm into safety.

"Bartholomew, are you a complete insane motherfucker?"

"Thanks Billy D. Thanks for letting us in."

"Hope no other dumbass customers are looking for shelter in my club," shot back Billy D.

"There's no one behind us," said Bartholomew.

"Well, I should hope not. I guess you're one of the lucky stupid people," said Billy D.

"But I'm sure there's a story to be told and by God I love a good story—especially if it's true." Billy D chortled and led them out of his office and into the girls' dressing room, finding towels for them to dry off. Not much bothered Billy D for too long. Even hurricanes.

"There's clothes for you, sweetie, if you want to shower and get out of those soaking things. No clothes for you big fella," said the grinning Billy D. Bartholomew finished drying his head and arms while following Billy D to the long bar. He could barely hear the screaming hurricane.

"Do you realize the 100 mile an hour wind is about to hit us? My God, man, you would have been blown to Atlanta!" He poured another cup of coffee and handed it to Bartholomew. Four girls were smoking and playing pool at the far table. None bothered to pay much attention to them.

"Now you know why I built this place the way I did," said Billy D.

"You spend a bunch of typhoon seasons on Okinawa and you gain full appreciation why those tiny Okinawan boys built all their damn buildings out of concrete, with thick-thick walls choked full of rebar. They got sick and tired rebuilding after every typhoon. No shit. No damn hurricane is gonna wreck my club."

The exact reason Bartholomew remembered The Shelter. He'd been in more than one conversation with Billy D carrying on about how the place was built to withstand a bomb attack. He bragged about his two backup generators and on and on about all the extra supplies he had stored away. Small wonder other frequent patrons didn't think to flee to The Shelter.

Mrs. Billy D appeared from the storage room behind the main bar. He had met her only once, the last time he stopped in—just last night.

"Young man, I figure Billy D has already told you what a lucky stupid shit you are—what's your name again?" she asked. Billy D and the Mrs. were the same height, about 5' 8", both stocky around the middle. Mrs. Billy D was old school, big hair, plenty of makeup and finger long eyelashes. Her tits were so big she appeared to lean slightly aft to keep from tipping forward. She used to be pretty; almost beautiful, thought Bartholomew, but the cigarettes pruned all the corners of her face. Her red hair may have been real at some time, but whatever perm she had in place made her hair look shiny and brittle. Billy D was a full black haired man of middle fifties, the Mrs., maybe a few years younger. He wore crisp white shirts tucked into black jeans with tight-ironed creases. His gold baht

chain looked to weigh a half-pound around his neck. His Rolex
was the old kind, with the red and blue bezel faded from the
action of past years. He was a retired Marine and he made you
remember that fact. His jaw was soft and round and he seemed
sensitive to that—he wore a close cropped mustache and goatee.
It was the only visible silver hair on his person.

"Well hello there, sweetie. You with the big, lucky,
stupid guy?" Mrs. Billy D gave Amy the once over, the is-she-
stripper-material kind of once over. Bartholomew was unsure of
her assessment, as was Billy D. Amy wore a borrowed white
sequined halter-top and loose black short shorts that were meant
to be ass tight. Her hair was bundled atop her head, wrapped in
a towel.

"My cigarettes are soaked."

"Angie Lee!" yelled Mrs. Billy D. The short brunette
looked up from her pool stick.

"Give this wet waif a smoke, por favor." Amy met Angie
Lee halfway.

"Amy."

"Hope you like menthols," said Angie Lee.

"I'd smoke anything right now," said Amy, leaning over
to light her cigarette from Angie Lee's plastic lighter.

"You from here—or Alabama?" asked Angie Lee,
tiptoeing up to sit on a barstool. She was a tiny thing, with
expensive tits that paid the bills and then some. She was still
cute, a perky look with hard brown eyes and straight brown hair
parted down the middle that draped down to her waist.

"Recently? From nowhere's in particular," said Amy,
smiling weakly and flicking moisture from her right eye. She
was sober and sorry she drove into the hurricane. She knew her

foolishness had finally permeated her denial. She was never so aware of her habit of magnetizing herself to the loser class. The stupid men, the shallow men. She was shallow and allowed herself to act stupid. The trap was real—she knew she did not have what it takes to escape. Amy had a barrel full of tears straining to be emptied. Her eyes yearned for their full release.

"Why didn't you get Earl to pick you up?" Bartholomew was thinking about his father; he must be here by now.

"Power's out, buddy, phones too. You two are here with us for the duration. Make yourself at home," said Billy D.

"We got regular smokes if you want 'em," said Mrs. Billy D, taking Amy by the hand. "Let me introduce you to the other girls. They're gonna like you, especially when they see your tattoo." Amy had black angel wings a foot long spread across her back and bordered by her sharp shoulder blades.

Mrs. Billy D laughed at her realization. "You're not the cause of what's goin' outside?

She whispered in Amy's ear to relieve her of her confusion. A weak laugh escaped her, and Amy prayed it wasn't her fault.

Chapter 22

Earl thought he was now an official member of the stupid people. His BMW was getting slammed in the near full fury of Hurricane Amy. She was just offshore and angling towards him. The wiper blades were just shy of useless as he navigated north on Allison Ave. Two cars filled with other stupid people were in front of him. Earl was now concerned about low spots and flooding and stalling his car. He pressed up to 40 mph before he felt the volume of water spewing out in from of him as his car slowed, propelling him forward against the restraint of the seat belt. He was gambling on the big sky theory applying to stupid people driving on suburban roads barely in front of a Cat 5 hurricane. The big sky theory holding that the likelihood of hitting another airplane, in particular at night or in clouds, was very low simply because there's a lot of sky for airplanes to fly in.

"Lord, let there be no other dumbasses on this road but me," prayed Earl, wiping condensation off the inside of his windshield, nose close to touching the windshield as he scanned for any other cars approaching the cross sections. Red lights were the same as green lights to Earl. To him they all signaled go go go.

Turning left into the open parking lot is when he noticed the semi, with its trailer end backed up against the first steps to the entryway of St. Basil's. A large white passenger van was parked next to the truck. A few other cars were nestled close to the main entrance. No one was outside in the fury. Earl parked on the north side of the semi, attempting to shield himself from flying debris as he sloshed through a rising torrent of water flowing under the trailer. The door opened for him and he leaped inside. Soaked boxes were being slid across the entry foyer and lined up against the front inside wall of the church.

"Lieutenant Earl!" cried a big man bouncing down the middle aisle. Reverend Delroy James bear-hugged Earl, who was drenched to the skin from the run from his car.

"I'm Bartholomew's uncle. Met you at your graduation from pilot training. You recall?"

"I do."

"Bartholomew's dad is here too. It's his truck parked outside."

"Need your help son," said Reverend James. The black raincoat did not hide his girth. Reverend James was still a fat man. His second and third chin wobbled as his head turned around to describe what was going on.

"We passed by stranded cars out there on Highway 98—women and kids stuck in their cars. It's too disorienting out there to drive in all this damned rain. We need to get them here to this church. We got a lot of women here and not many men." Earl counted off the women moving about, seeming to organize boxes, large stuffed plastic bags, open boxes of cereal and crackers and boxed food. They all looked like church women. Organizing supplies that did not need to be organized, waiting for the hurricane to do its worst and leave.

"Hey Earl." Bartholomew's father entered the church from the same door Earl used. His red rain jacket hood was cinched tight around his face. This man was dressed for a hurricane.

"Grab a pair of rain boots over there," said Harold James. "We'll need to get out on 98 and bring in some stranded families. Bartholomew's with you, right?" Sitting in a pew, Earl untied his flight boots, wet laces stubborn to loosen. He unpeeled his socks and wrung the water from them.

"He is not with me."

"Where is he then?"

"Don't know. I figured he was with you. He left early right after I heard the phone ring. I figured it was you calling."

"Now just where the hell could he be?" pressed his father.

"I think he's with my sister, somewhere nearby," said Earl standing up inside a worn pair of farmer rain boots. They were tight.

"My sister announced she was arriving in to visit and I think he may have gone out to get her, but I don't know." Harold James stood equal height to Earl and leaner than his son. Much leaner, observed Earl.

"Don't ask Mr. James—it won't make much sense to no matter how long I try to explain."

"She crazy?" asked Mr. James.

"She's lost."

"Well, she better not lose my son." Earl knew Bartholomew did not need Amy's help losing himself. He wondered if his father agreed. Earl was in a familiar mental place,

"We taking that white van out?" he asked. Mr. James motioned with his head to follow. The van's engine roared as Harold James stomped the accelerator. His truck radio was sitting in between them in the front seat with a cable trailing over the back of the seats to the back of the van. Only static. He pulled out onto the highway and turned left. Hurricane Amy banged the van in pulses of wind and rain and in front of them tree branches snapped free from their trunks. The wiper blades were worthless. They approached the first car parked off on the side—warning flashers distorted by the rain pouring off the windshield. Harold plowed to a stop. Earl pressed his face against the window. Seeing no movement, he forced open his door and was blown to the ground before slamming the door shut. He crawled to the stranded compact and rose to look inside. He banged on the window. The wind hissed and scowled as Earl open the door. Empty.

He flipped around and leaped to the van door. Harold accelerated slowly as Earl dove inside. The next vehicle was dark. Right away Earl was sitting in a pool of water from his drenched clothes. His socks were already soaked. He could not tell if the quiver of his lips was due to being cold or something else. They approached a maroon mini-van tipped on its side. Harold pulled up close to the wheel up side of the mini-van. Earl exited and ran around to look inside the windshield. Small arms were flailing about inside. Their muffled yells were mixed with blunt screams. He ran around and tried to open the back door. The wind heaved Earl against the door, and his distorted face pressing against the window only served to extract and expose the desperation from the now high-pitched screams coming from inside the vehicle. It appeared locked as he hit the window with his fist, yelling at those trapped inside to open the door. Now the door opened and Earl stuck his head inside. There were small children, maybe three or four years old, all crying and screaming in waves of panicked ferocity.

A young woman, gigantic, pale and still, was slouched over in shock. Mouth agape, she stared at Earl in silence. Earl opened the door and grabbed her arm and she tensed and withdrew like a moccasin had bitten her.

"We are leaving now, miss. Now." Earl's low lid eyes, attempting to connect to her with his gaze as he placed both his arms on top of her shoulder, matched the hollowness of her stare. She was twisted in the turned over seats and her face was a window to her suffering. The children stopped crying and became still. The wind howled outside.

"Grab my arm. Now," he said, in a commanding low and slow voice. Two girls reached for him. He pulled the first over the seats and tucked her into his abdomen as he guided the second girl over the seats.

"Stay right there," he told the second girl and swooped up the first girl into his left arm and transferred her into the waiting arms of Harold James, who had the sliding door opened to receive them. Harold held her tight, waiting for the next child. The last of the four children were now safe in the van driven by Harold. The woman screamed in pain as Earl attempted to lift her up from the seat.

"Earl!"

"Earl!" He heard Harold the second time and climbed over the back seat and opened the rear door.

"They are tellin' me there's another kid in that van! They swear there's another kid in that van! Name's Jonah!" Earl turned around and looked back at the woman. She weighed well over 400 pounds.

"Where's Jonah?" The woman shrieked as she flung her head side to side—strands of her sweat stained stringy hair sticking to her bloated cheeks. Spittle gathered on the corners of her mouth. Her face was blotted red. The windshield cracked as a leg-sized tree branch bounced off the front of the van. Earl knew where Jonah was.

On two subsequent forays out to the highway they found two couples in separate pick-up trucks, each with a disabled spouse, each huddled together, each trembling for their loved one. They found no others on their fourth trip out, and they returned to St. Basil's for the night. The priest quietly celebrated Mass in the only area not filled with survivors and supplies, in a small space between the altar and sacristy. Earl sat on the tile floor left of the altar with his arms clutching his propped up knees, too exhausted to get up and receive communion. Earl stared into the closest candle light, emptying his thoughts to be burned away by the swollen flame, swelling yet larger by his offering. The altar candles shimmered in violent unison as the gusts from the shattered windows invaded the celebration yet remained lit until extinguished afterwards by some woman rescued from the highway. With slow and painful effort, Earl straightened his legs and lay down on his side, falling asleep in an instant. Another woman slipped a pillow under Earl's head and covered him with a thin scarlet blanket.

Chapter 23

A second white van cut through the flooded church parking lot; a brilliant white light beamed out from the side window. The driver parked next to Earl's BMW. The church doors were now open and two figures were carrying a large cardboard box inside. The driver of the second van got out and ran to follow them. The main door slammed shut just after the driver slipped through. A thin bent figure shouldering a TV camera with a brilliant white light attached emerged from the side of the van while a rain-coated figure burst out of the passenger side—both now running towards the church door. The woman peeled off her hood and yelled at no one in particular, "Where is Earl? Earl Neuhaus! Where is Earl Neuhaus?" The righteous Reverend Delroy James trotted to her. "Who are you, please?" Mutual recognition occurred.

"Reverend James, right?" James was very pleased. Fortune, within the trials and tribulations of humanity. He felt a sensuous surge flow inside him. A warm validation of his destiny.

"He will be here soon, I hope," he said, now closing his eyes and beginning a forceful prayer inside him, further hoping the cameraman would begin to film. The Reverend struggled to recognize her. Familiar, definitely now, yes, she looked familiar. I feel I know her. I feel I'm connected to her.

"What's going here?" the woman demanded.

"We are preparing for them to arrive here."

"Who?" the woman asked.

"Those stranded out there." The Reverend ignored her insistence and placed his hand on the free shoulder of the cameraman and asked if he was well. He nodded and switched on the spotlight. Reverend James watched as the red 'record' light came on. He quickly stood back and watched the woman set up a microphone and check connectivity.

"May I say something?" asked Reverend James.

"Go." Earl's mother placed the microphone below the Reverend's chin. The cameraman took his eye out from the camera and made a fuss over her tousled and matted hair. Impatient and irritated at his insistence, Abby fluffed her hair up and in front of her face. She lowered her raincoat zipper. The low cut V-neck T-shirt was wet and her chest glistened. The Reverend was exultant in his restraint in not casting an eye towards her twin globes of temptation. He drew a deep, deep breath from his nostrils—subtle now, very slow, so as not to appear obvious. He began to talk slowly, loud enough to be heard over the menacing wind threatening the high roof structure of Saint Basil's. He was very familiar with the life of Saint Basil. Catholic teachings were a particular interest of his at the seminary—especially the fathers of the church. Reverend James knew to be here because he was chosen to be here. Right here, in this place, at this time, during this hurricane. Yes, yes, he thought, I am where I need to be, doing what needs to be done.

"Don't speak about Earl, Reverend, not yet," she instructed. Reverend James understood. He too is doing the Lord's work. Reverend James was now convinced. He must recruit Earl and the world must be a witness. This woman reporter was to be the window for America to see. Oh blessed be, he thought, blessed, blessed be the Lord. I am so thankful you have chosen me. His blood felt hot, pumping through him.

His mind buzzed. Don't get dizzy, he commanded himself. Breath. Slow. Breath deep. Slow. Hold onto the pew rail. Steady. Be ready. This is my day.

Chapter 24

"Sweetie—that your boyfriend?" Amy picked the stray strand of tobacco from the tip of her tongue and examined it. She drew the menthol deep, so deep as to tickle the bottom of her lungs. She exhaled out the left corner of her mouth; her head cocked up and to the left to prevent Mrs. Billy D from being exhaled upon.

"Friend of my brother. "

"So you drove from--where now? You drove into a hurricane to see your brother?

"Amy, my Lord child--like the name of this damned hurricane?"

"Like the very name of this goddamned hurricane—the very name." Amy's smile was official notification she was in possession of a secret. And she wanted to let Mrs. Billy D know she was in possession of a secret. This secret was the sum total of her possessions, for within the secret held the sum total of her worth, her importance for being, and therefore her very reason for being. With the exception of that impossible man, she thought, glancing over to look at Bartholomew, who was listening to Billy D explain exactly how the Okinawans build typhoon proof structures.

Mrs. Billy D knew Amy, or she knew her kind. Let her keep her secret, she said to herself. Inside every secret is where they think they safeguard whatever it is worth protecting. Mrs. Billy D could see through Amy as if her skin was that of a skinned lychee. She was as naked as they came. And Mrs. Billy D was there to care for them. She ran the strip bar precisely for these women and she would never tell them…ever.

152

But it was too early to know for sure about Amy—she may be lost permanent-like. Too soon to tell. Too soon.

Chapter 25

Harold James flung open the door with one child in arms and the other clinging on his back with a death grip around Harold's neck.

"Two more outside," he said, handing off the girl to one of the Reverend's female volunteers and leaning down to deposit the boy on his back into a pew. The girl burst into tears, not believing she had more tears to relinquish. The boy said nothing. Reverend James dashed outside for the other two, nodding to the cameraman to follow.

"I'm going back for Earl," announced Harold, to no one in particular.

"And we're going with you," commanded Abby Westmoreland, mother of Earl. Harold registered no expression and said nothing as he returned to the van, brushing by the Reverend. The cameraman saw Abby point to the van and he jumped inside and maneuvered to the back seat, placing his camera and gear next to him. Abby slid in the passenger seat as Harold gunned the vehicle and spun around back onto the highway. Now the van rocked as the wind pummeled them with gigantic globules of rain. Abby flinched at the loud bang as hard debris bounced off the opposite side of the van.

"Get ready now." The cameraman focused on the rearview mirror between Abby and Harold and handed Abby the long microphone. She held the tip just above the seat.

"Ready—go!" said the cameraman pointing towards her as she started her report.

"We are heading east on Highway 98, in search of stranded motorists."

*****

"You have got to move and you will move." The tone in Earl's command was low and monotonous. Inches from her, he held her face between his hands. He looked through her anguish, which was surrendering to shock. Her pallor was beginning to look permanent as she continued to hyperventilate. He held her to slow her breathing, hoping to gain her trust.

"We are all leaving this van. You are going to grab the top of the seat—here—grab right here and squeeze tight and pull towards me." She did as he instructed and began to pull her weight forward towards Earl. He leaned back and lifted the lever to the seat back. As the back seat collapsed forward and his arms now under her armpits, the gigantic woman poured onto Earl and pinned him against the front windshield. With the back of his boot heel, he slammed against the windshield. She began a crying moan as his nostrils filled with her stench. He could now see the legs of the boy that had been trapped under her. He released the yell of an Olympic weight lifter as he pounded the windshield with the heel of his boot. Her weight prevented him from getting full breaths and Earl became dizzy. He focused on shattering the windshield as her crying moans filled his head—her mouth was pressed against his left ear. His vision narrowed. Earl could not see the lifeless body. The windshield would not give way. The branch cracked the windshield corner on his first swing. Harold's second swing shattered the windshield and Earl and the gigantic woman writhed out of the van and into the torrent of rain. Water rushed in.

"Inside," cried Earl. Harold crawled in amongst the shattered windshield fragments and pulled Jonah's limp body out and carried him to the van. Abby and the cameraman captured the entire scene. She reported in shouting, punctuated, rhythmic phrases during brief lulls in the pulsing wind and rain. Saving the woman, carrying and laying the boy in the van, the volley of rain and debris bouncing against them. The cameraman filmed the gigantic woman being shoved into the front passenger seat, laying Jonah out on the second bench seat and then switched off his light and camera and crammed in the far back seat. Earl slam closed the back van door from the inside and crouched in the space between the back door and the far aft bench seat. The van lurched forward and they all slid left during the violent turn back to St. Basil's.

*****

Billy D. mixed two special Bloody Marys, sliding one over to Bartholomew. He preferred the short, wide-mouthed glass. Two supreme sized pitted green olives pierced by a long red plastic toothpick that had first skewered a fresh thick wedge of lime. He stirred in quick short motions with the miniature red plastic naked figure of a big breasted woman on top, squeezing lime juice first onto the olives before it settled into the drink. Bartholomew thought the drink stirrer woman was the same figure on the big trucker's mudflats. Billy D. made them stiff, otherwise what's the point of drinking a Bloody Mary? The Shelter had been on back-up generator power for six hours now and no problems yet.

"Your girlfriend ever danced before?"

"Not my girlfriend."

"Even better," said Billy D.

"Always, repeat, always results in trouble when there's a man hanging around them. The best dancers are in between boyfriends or husbands. Motivates them to frustrate you guys, if you know what I mean." Billy D. had a Marine laugh. You had no doubt he thought something was funny, especially when he said it.

"Truth be told, learned everything about them from her," pointing over to the misses.

"She picks them and she's the one that sends them back out into the world. Sometimes they don't know if they wanna go back out into the world but Mrs. Billy D does. Sure does. She sends them back when the time comes."

"She fills their troubled minds with advice all along the way, too."

"Wanna know what her number one piece of advice is, bar none?" Bartholomew finished his Bloody Mary, the vodka just hitting his brain. He felt like the world was created just for him. He loved the first three drinks. That one counted for two, he thought.

"Huh?"

"The number one piece of advice…Know what it is?"

"I think so," said Bartholomew, with vodka clarity.

"Stay away from men that love strip bars," said Bartholomew.

"Right on the money," said Billy D, adding, "Stay away from dudes like you." It was impossible to tell what was going on outside. The only window was in the office and that had been shuttered since yesterday afternoon.

"Why do you own and operate a strip club then?" asked Bartholomew.

"Help the ladies get back on their feet. I'm just the owner and make sure the place runs smooth. Mrs. Billy D is the brains behind the operation. She's the one who told me to build this place. Me? I wanted to own a charter fishing boat and hire a crew to catch all the tourist dollars I could. I'm tired of workin'. She promptly informed me that boats are worse than women and far more work, so I took her advice and opened this club." Stabbing the bar counter with his stub of an index finger he said, "And I'm here to tell you that this here place is a pain in the ass to run right and make some money. "

Bartholomew cackled.

"Listen, you're the most free when you're well away from any reach of power, the power of our Government, the power of the police, the power of the law. Stay way, way back in the periphery. That's when you're most free. Plus, don't be an idiot and don't associate with idiots. Idiots hate freedom—scares the living shit out of 'em. You always can spot the ones that are scared of freedom---Jesus they are so easy see."

"I could run amuck in this place—gamble, prostitution, take every flavor of drugs, fuck everyone and everything—total freedom. But you cannot, I tell you, you cannot be an idiot. Idiots are scared to death of freedom."

"Not that I'd do any of that stuff," said Billy D, draining the last of his drink.

"Leads to idiocy, always, always does."

"Excuse me while I check on the dames." Bartholomew turned and watched Billy D. He walked erect and with purpose. Nothing casual about his walk—all business. He kissed his wife on a willing cheek. She smacked his rear end. A love tap.

158

Bartholomew wondered where Earl was now. He wondered where his Dad was now. The Shelter shielded his thoughts from Hurricane Amy—that was easy. But Amy in the flesh he was unable to forget. She stood hip cocked to the right talking with the strippers and Mr. and Mrs. Billy D. Their faces beamed like being at the first hour of a family reunion. Bartholomew watched as if he was watching a life sized movie screen. He suspended disbelief and he wanted so much to believe. But he didn't know what to believe. He believed the hurricane was destroying homes and buildings and cars and bridges. He believed humans and animals were in a paralyzing panic that they were going to be crushed or drowned or carried out to sea. He believed he was paralyzed and he could not stand up from the barstool. The pang of hurt spread inside his chest and forced an exhale so violent he wobbled off the stool. His knees would not lock to support him as he grabbed the edge of the bar. Bartholomew held onto the edge of the bar waiting for his legs to respond. Once able to walk, he opened Billy D's office door. The ringing in his ears prevented him from hearing Billy D. Bartholomew's hand was pulled off the door handle leading to the parking lot.

"Where in hell are you going?"

"To find my Dad."

"Not now, not just yet, L T."

"It's raging outside and you're staying inside—right here."

"I gotta find my Dad."

"Back to the bar L T—now. Go lie down on one of the sofas." Flat black painted ceiling tiles—the porous kind to absorb sound—appeared to be lowering. The ceiling was lowering, thought Bartholomew, staring up from the black leather sofa in the lap dance room. Bossa Nova--faint but the airy dreamy chords flowed through the Brazilian rhythms. The ringing stopped. His chest hurt left him. The second Bloody Mary locked his mind from family ruminations and Bartholomew closed his eyes.

Chapter 26

The cameraman was a pro, being the first out of the van and filming Harold and Earl transferring the body of the boy inside and returning back again to lift the gigantic woman from the vehicle and drag her into the church. Abby reported into a recorder shadowing her cameraman. Reverend James was the first to rush up and help place the boy onto a blanketed section of the pew. Another woman pulled the Reverend away to tend to the boy's body. The Reverend replaced Earl and together with Harold they steered the giant woman away from the boy towards the front of the church. She was still in shock. The woman tending to the dead boy rushed over to the giant woman and barked commands to Harold and Reverend James, who then motioned two other volunteer women to follow the woman barking out the commands. Harold turned around towards the back of the church and counted heads. He could swear there were more people here now than when he left. Some were frozen in place, heads down in disbelief or worse, three or four moved about not desiring any purpose other than to not sit in any pew, still others plucked supplies from the card board boxes and dispensed them to those lying and sitting in pews. Harold finally noticed the stained glass fragments all about his feet. The rain was coming in from the south facing upper windows. Through the windows he could now hear the howling, the raucous swirling sound of Hurricane Amy. The cameraman filmed Harold gazing upward and wiping rain off his face and panned down to the shards of stained glass around his boots. He turned again and filmed Earl sitting and sipping something hot. Abby watched a woman placed a blanket over him. She talked into her recorder. Now the cameraman and Abby joined up again and Abby wiped her face, adjusted her hair and lowered her raincoat. She reported into his camera and he followed her slow rotations in order to capture the sanctuary and tending to the rescued and those welcoming shelter. The camera light extinguished and the cameraman un-shouldered his equipment and stored it in a black canvas case. Then, without notice, Abby and the cameraman left the church and returned to their van.

Chapter 27

The miles thick dark storm was moving off to the east. Daylight through thinner cloud cover caught Billy D's eye. He was just outside his personal entry door, assessing the surrounding area. He knew the hurricane changed course and was becoming weaker. He sensed the worst for them was over. Everywhere appeared the aftermath of what a disaster of this magnitude was expected to look like. No area without debris and rubbish about, traffic lights lying in standing water in the streets. No birds, no sign of life. Peeled sections of metal roofs turned to cartoon sized blades pierced building walls. Floating gunk, plastic soda bottles and black bags of household garbage ejected from their trash bins lay still in brackish water wanting for a current. Billy D felt no rain and knew soon the stench of rot would infect the air. Bartholomew pushed open the door.

"It's moved on east. Still dangerous to drive. Where do you live?" Bartholomew's legs were fully functional and his head was fuzzy but not aching. Billy D could see he was leaving and he had no intention of stopping him.

"An apartment off North Lagoon Drive."

"Forget going back there. It'll be all wrecked to hell."

"Not going there."

"Can Amy stay here?"

"Sure sure."

"Thanks." Bartholomew's truck had been thrashed with flying debris, but the building protected the windows and it started up. He backed up and headed west, away from the darkness. The semi-truck came easy into view as his eyes were guided by the half dozen police vehicles with their blue and red rooftop lights fully blazing leaving the parking lot of St. Basil's. His father's semi was still parked backed up to the front entryway. Cars and trucks completely ignored the white lined parking spaces and formed a semi circle, with his father's truck in the middle. He drove around the vehicles and parked up on the sidewalk, high enough to avoid wading through the flooded lot. Both main doors were open and the inside of the church was loud, hot and tense. He saw Earl's BMW parked next to his father's truck. In the center of the middle aisle was the righteous Reverend James engaged in an intimate conversation with a priest. Bartholomew was welcomed by a tired thin woman with stringy brown hair offering him a Styrofoam cup of warm tap water. She smiled, wishing there was ice in his cup and left him standing alone. Now he saw Earl over on the north side aisle. He was standing and staring at Bartholomew.

"Bartholomew!" His father grabbed his arm and spun him around. The hug was quick as he pressed his heart against Bartholomew.

"I had to get Amy," and pointing over to Earl, now approaching them, "his sister, to a safe place. Couldn't leave to look for you until just now. Saw all the cop cars leaving and spotted your truck outside."

"She's fine, Earl," shaking his hand and smacking his shoulder. Earl nodded.

"Mom?" asked Bartholomew.

"She's at home, watching on TV and worried sick like everyone else. Pissed off too, I imagine."

Chapter 28

Earl's father never loved driving cars, any car. Theo 'Chance' Neuhaus never thought about cars. He thought about how to make money from nothing. That's what he told the inmates. He made money from nothing. He was not going to teach them about financial packages that are constructed from nothing of material value. But he did lecture to those who cared about how he developed his well-honed hunches about people and whether a loan can be paid off. However, after the third conversation with Rabbi Benny those thoughts vanished, allowing new thoughts. Rabbi Benny only thought of making money. It was his crime against God, he told Theo.

"What a perfect excuse! I'm Jewish for Christ's sake!" Prison gave him the realization of his true sin, he said, "Not running over his wife." Now that he no longer thought about making money he felt he was free. Prison gave Theo Neuhaus the same realization. And as well it should, thought Earl's father.

Theo now discovered he loved driving a car. His first long trip by himself. Barely a week in San Francisco and his new firm pleaded with him to accept a position in Houston. Bumped his salary by $25,000 dollars and gave him a $25,000 bonus, bought him a new, loaded BMW 5 Series and agreed to pay for the first year's rent in a city apartment in the high end district. Fully furnished. Theo knew Earl owned a BMW and it made him smile every time he shifted into drive. He thought of his son as often as he did in prison. Theodore Neuhaus was driving to Houston and he now loved to drive.

The only reason he switched on the TV was to get an update on the hurricane. Theo bounced his suitcase on the double bed in his hotel room in Las Vegas. Numb from the road, he knew he pushed it too far. Nine hours of driving in California highway traffic left him too tired to grab a bite to eat. He lay out on the cloud white bed spread next to his suitcase, too exhausted to remove his new black shoes. A mistake to drive in these things, he thought. Not the best way to break them in, leaving only heel blisters on both feet. He stared at the ceiling when he heard her reporting on Hurricane Amy. Exhaustion vanished in an instant as he sprang up like a sprung trap. He watched her eyes and her mouth the words, his eyes looking within hers for signs of recognition. Scooting to the edge of the bed, he leaned forward and closely watched her reporting from inside of St. Basil's. Now he saw his son, and his ex-wife Abby walk behind Earl seated in a pew tending to a small boy. He looked for her face to register any recognition of Earl. None—as if her son was not there in front of her. Something now about a rescue on a highway, something about a stranded van of children, one of them died. Now a segment on the highway showing what appeared to be Earl transferring a small boy from a turned over van into another van. A quick shot of a morbidly obese woman being almost dragged through the driving wind and rain and into the van by Earl and another man. Then back to the church as Abby concluded her reporting. And the segment was over.

Theo had driven nine hours with no radio on. He wanted to see without any distractions other than the sounds from the road and the thoughts in his mind. He thought of Earl in the path of the hurricane and thought of Earl in the path of the tornado. And that Earl's mother was there both times with him, reporting on him as if he were just someone else. He thought of his family as a family and knew that was an illusion. His family was like a round of buckshot in a shotgun, and when the triggered pulled they spread in a pattern that was extremely difficult to find, much less put back into the shell. But he was going to find them and put them all back in the family casing. Never would he give into temptation—the temptation to lay blame to anyone other than himself. The Rabbi taught him as much, for he was his confessor. The prison priest was a certified asshole. What the asshole could learn from Rabbi Benny, thought Theo.

"You can live with doubt, but grief and guilt will kill you," said Rabbi Benny, laughing at himself. Theo remembered Benny laughed at himself with confident ease. He swore he was turning into a Catholic, and that made him laugh out loud.

"Wait, wait! Next I'll be babbling about grace!" Theo swore he'd never forget that moment they shared, sitting by themselves on a hot sticky day next to the barb wired adorned cyclone fence. Theo referred to himself as the slow awakening idiot, not quite what his attorney called him when Theo made sure he'd never get a penny of his sequestered savings. He instructed his attorney to be the guardian of his savings and further instructed him to make Earl the only other person with full access to his accumulations. Theo revealed to his attorney that he had others monitoring his actions regarding his savings.

"If you steal, I'll know in an instant, and you are ruined." Theo had only to tell his attorney this once and he savored the seconds on the phone warning his attorney. Mutual distrust was a very good lesson to abide by when dealing with lawyers, he

167

affirmed time and again. His attorney told him he was an idiot by taking away his financial safety net.

"Think so? Then why do I find myself smiling?" said Theo, to his attorney, a man completely absorbed in his own anger. Theo wanted to always remember the brief phone conversation. He opened the nightstand drawer to confirm the presence of a bible. His smile persisted, thinking about what Rabbi Benny said to him in prison about the bible.

"It is nothing if not a contradictory compendium of questions and only one paradoxical answer. For those of faith, the bible remains a mystery and undergirds the soul as mystery—that is, mystery revealed as an unknowable mystery. So much for a firm basis of support—'Hey, look, here's a path out of the dark and towards the light!' Not much firmness of ground, with that promise, eh?"

"Mystery impels the agitated to attempt to conduct a rational inquiry to reveal. But mystery is a source of yearning and wonder, a yearning for truth and wonder as to the existence and source of truth. Why mystery is considered a human agitation or a difficulty, much less something that must be overcome? I'm such a sucker for my wonder of mystery." The Rabbi, thought Theo, was one of God's best messengers. The complete confessor of and practitioner of human contradiction and euphoric in his practices.

In the morning, Theo called again but phone service in the Florida Panhandle remained unavailable. He slept in interrupted spurts; grateful that he could fall back asleep each time he awoke. That night he left the bible in the drawer and the next day he kept the car radio on.

Chapter 29

Abby could always tell the moment she passed her limit.
She felt her speech slow, in an effort not to slur. She lost the
ability to focus on someone's face in conversation –staying
fixated too long on any object made her aware of her dizziness
followed by a wave of nausea. Her eyes skittered around in
what seemed random patterns of distraction; a routine to get
herself somewhere, anywhere to get some fresh outside air—
alone.

They'd driven to Dothan Alabama and performed a
quick edit in the TV station affiliate. Her Hurricane Amy report
went international. Her boss loved it—a tight, tense life and
death drama reported under extremely dangerous conditions and
with matter-of-fact reporting—by a woman. Abby was now the
hot item on television. Her boss had every intention of getting
her back into studio headquarters and back in front of a camera,
looking sensuous. With Abby, he fantasized. God, she was
worth it, he thought.

Abby made her way out the side entrance of the bar and
walked along the hotel perimeter sidewalk. Fresh air was not
helping and she was losing confidence she could keep from
throwing up. She paced back and forth, five steps out and back
along the sidewalk. Thank God no one was around, she thought.

"Abby!" Her cameraman had poked his head out the side
bar door. She ignored him and continued to pace back and
forth.

"Get away," she warned.

"Gonna…" she slurred and dove between two parked
cars and emptied her stomach onto the asphalt, her vomit

splashing on the driver's side door of a red Ford pickup. She waved off her cameraman. She didn't want him or anyone else near her. She had to get back to her room but she couldn't stop puking. Anger welled inside her now empty stomach. She was going to walk back to her room, she told herself. Now she attempted to command herself. Her cameraman ignored her resistance and grabbed around her waist and led her to her room. Abby's resistance tapered off as they neared her room, letting herself be led.

"Boss wants us on a plane now. Wants you back at headquarters."

"That means we gotta start drivin' real soon, Abby."

"Will you please stop chuggin' Manhattans as if they were light beers?" The cameraman led her to her bathroom and shut the door. "You got ten minutes to clean up and get dressed. I'm packin' up your stuff and I'll be downstairs in the van. "

"Hear me, Abby? Got me?" he barked into the closed bathroom door, hearing her yell that her Daddy drank Manhattans and to piss off and go to hell--in that order.

Ten minutes later the cameraman let himself back in her room, lifted her from her bed where she had fallen asleep, and fireman carried her to the van, laying her on the back seat, and roared off into the crystal clear night.

Chapter 30

Bartholomew returned to The Shelter to bring Amy to St. Basil's. Except for most of the stained glass windows, the church fared well and was now the temporary accommodation for nearly seventy-five survivors. He banged hard three times on Billy D's private entrance door and again three more times until Billy D opened up.

"How is it out there?"

"Hurricane's gone north and east. Shit floating everywhere, but the water's starting to back off on the bigger roads." Billy D lifted his flared nostrils up and sniffed a couple of times. Bartholomew wasn't sure what he smelled for.

"Amy's fine here, L T."

"Her brother wants to see her—over at that Catholic Church off 98." He let Bartholomew inside and shut and locked the door. The girls were all sitting at the bar, giddy, topless and drunk.

"Our favorite customer is back!" yelled the platinum blonde, by far the prettiest—which more than made up for her small and natural tits. They were sculpted cup-size tits, with beautiful brown quarter-size areolas. At least Bartholomew believed them to be so—until Amy turned around. He couldn't remember much from the one night stand in Lubbock. The room remained dark that night. He barely remembered squeezing her breasts—but he remembered her half inch erect nipples. And now he saw them and Amy threw a crumpled up empty cigarette carton, hitting him on the forehead.

"Will cost you this time, big fella!" Amy laughed hard and loud.

"Earl'd like to have you come with me. He's helping out at the church down the road. "

Tight lips replaced Amy's cocky grin and she cupped herself in her hands and ran to the dressing room. Bartholomew turned and walked past Billy D saying to him, "Please tell her I'm waiting in the truck." Bartholomew sat waiting with the windows rolled down. The humidity seeped in, along with the stank of contaminated floodwaters. He thought of Amy's breasts.

Leaning into the passenger side window, Amy said, "Mrs. Billy D takes care of her girls. You know that? She takes care of them, like a momma." Amy got in the truck and then pointed out the front window and all Bartholomew could see was trash and debris everywhere.

"Then she makes them leave and go back out there, out there to the real world again. She won't let them stay but three years and then she makes them--she make *us* go back out there, and there, and there," said Amy, pointing out in different directions, in and beyond the destruction of the Hurricane.

"Earl will be happy to see you," said Bartholomew.

"You really don't know him that well, do you?" said Amy.

"That church is a crazy refuge now —everyone helping everyone out," said Bartholomew, dying for the conversation to end. No way, thought Amy. She was going to prolong whatever trumped up thoughts of agony floating about in his pussy-dreaming mind. Amy was embarrassed at his return to The Shelter. At The Shelter, she'd forgotten him and most everyone

and everything else she screwed and screwed up in her life.
Under Mrs. Billy D, Amy immediately felt safe, and her bimbo
talents, her primary survival tools, didn't need to unconsciously
kick in as a means of survival. They slogged through streets of
floating shiny brown-gray sludge of unknown origin, kicking up
its spray at opposing vehicles, pick-up trucks mostly, trying to
reach what was now lost. The sun shone as if completely
unaware of the passing of Hurricane Amy. The sun was
bringing what the sun always brings—and the heat turned the
dead to a gagging rot.

Chapter 31

"How do you know so much about him?" said
Bartholomew. He felt as if he received a stabbing wound, just
below his heart. He was so engrossed in his own story even he
couldn't tell if he was acting. Reverend James thought, "*It feels
right. I am right. I am right!*" His heart and mind pounded in the
same sacred rhythm he felt when he went outside himself
delivering his best sermons. Reverend James could see himself,
looking down on himself, when he spoke in a way that
righteously delivered the message.

Delivered!
With Righteousness! Lord, have Mercy!
My sweet and gracious Lord, have Mercy!

Bartholomew's father grabbed his arm when he and
Amy strolled in through the front door and pulled him into the
far aft pew on the left side of the center aisle. Amy had
wandered up the right aisle. Earl and Amy huddled and
whispered in the nearest pew to the sacristy on the north side of
St. Basil's.

There seemed to be no escape from his father—whom he
realized he missed—and his ass pain of an uncle—the Reverend.
It was his father he wanted to be with—just he and him. And
this surprised Bartholomew.

"Do you hear me?" Reverend James said. Bartholomew
was clearly distracted and had forgotten what he asked his Uncle
in the first place.

"I do know him! I've done some checking on your
friend," said the Reverend.

"Why are you so interested in him?"

"Because no one comes upon two natural disasters like a killer tornado and devastating hurricane and begins to save—not in this day and age—No Sir!"

"I was there too."

"That you were, that you *indeed* were." Looking at Bartholomew's father, he said with a gleam, "Sure you weren't intending to name your son Peter?" Reverend James's burst of laughter silenced the church for a moment. His father popped him on the shoulder when Bartholomew said, "Get off it," to his Uncle, the Reverend.

"Do you know who Earl's father is?" Uncle Delroy asked. Bartholomew's fatigue was furrowed deep yet did not prevent him from seeing the continuous flurry of the frightened and panicked failing to be comforted by the volunteers. Shrieks and moans erupted throughout the church. It wasn't chaos, wasn't panic, observed Bartholomew, it was something he couldn't describe. It was a foreign sight to witness. Bartholomew could not visit with his father. They had to try to get back to the base. In fact, it was Bartholomew's father who insisted.

"You have a duty, son," said Harold James. "I haven't forgotten what that means."

Leaving together for the Air Base with Bartholomew and Amy, Earl sensed what Bartholomew could not. It was the ebb of despair. Together in Earl's car, they joined the increasing traffic on Highway 98. First stop, The Shelter.

Interrupting the silence, Amy said, exiting the car, "I'll be fine right here." Earl got out of the car and escorted her to the door. He hugged her and for a moment Earl thought Amy would reject his embrace. Then she flung her arms around her brother and kissed his cheek. Earl returned to the car and they set out to the Air Base. Bartholomew got out of the car and hurried to open the door for her. Her permission to allow him was a start, thought Bartholomew.

"Like to stay in touch," he said.

"Not sure about you Bartholomew. Bye," said Amy. Her tone was soft, very much a departure from herself, he thought. Earl and Bartholomew attempted to drive to their apartment. From the main road they could see the roof was ripped away. There was no way to enter the flooded parking lot. They had everything of any value already stashed in their vehicles.

The Hathaway Bridge was open and they joined the rest of the vehicles in a slow slog across the inlet. No clouds made the sky appear shocking blue. The surging inlet water was dirt brown and littered with drifting debris. Two small fishing boats weaved to avoid collision with two sections of plywood. Four two-by-fours from a new construction site that for an instant resembled a tic tack toe board were fast separated by the wakes of the two boats.

"My uncle thinks you're someone special—he means it—a Biblical kind of special."

"Tell me what you think about Earl. Damn, you know what I think about." Earl said nothing. Fifteen minutes later they crossed the bridge. Traffic showed no sign of easing. They noticed the further east they drove there were fewer buildings with visible damage. Sweaty bare chest, beer gutted men were removing sheets of plywood from window store fronts and sweeping debris from parking lots and stacking piles of debris along the sidewalks. The business of carrying on after the hurricane was well underway.

"You think about getting laid," said Earl finally, talking, as if to himself, scanning both sides of the street, observing the cleanup and damage assessment activity happening on every corner. "...As if you are controlled by that compulsion."

"Damn right. And you—you don't, I take it."

"I've thought about it. Not controlled by any means, like you," replied Earl.

"Earl, I've been chasing pussy since I was 13 years old. I got thrills at six years old waiting for my babysitter to bend over and expose her boobs."

"How long have you been a regular at strip clubs? That place where we dropped Amy off—The Shelter, that's a strip club, right? How long have you been going to those places?"

"Since Senior year in high school," said Bartholomew.

"And before you go askin', I only get the high class prostitutes. Lord knows I've paid too much for blow jobs."

"What do *you* think about Earl? I mean, what do you make of it, that you've been right there—smack in the middle of a huge tornado, in the worse hurricane to hit here in decades, and rescuing those people?"

"You were there too Bartholomew. Why doesn't your uncle think you're special?"

"*Damn* it, Earl. What do you think about?" Frustrated, Bartholomew pounded the dashboard, turning away from Earl and stared out the door window. The traffic lights were functioning approaching Springfield. As the light changed to green Earl answered,

"I think about many things—probably too many things—too many things with hard-to-find answers. I mean, look how far philosophy has gotten us since Kant."

"Oh shit, you're not really a deep thinker type, are you Earl? Not a deep philosophy-theology kind, are you? Not a 'what's it all about' thinker type? Oh no. No... Really?"

"I think about things that don't seem to have answers. I can't help it."

"You mean like, why you drove into the middle of a tornado *and* a hurricane in less than a year?"

"Something like that, yeah," said Earl.

"You ever had a girlfriend?" asked Bartholomew.

"I have one now. I think."

"What the hell you talkin' bout boy! You either do or you do not have a girlfriend."

"No. It's not that cut and dried," said Earl.

"What's her name? Where she from? Is she hot? She like sex? Is she rich? You call her? Gotta photo of her? I've never heard you call her."

"We write each other."

"You don't seem the real religious type, Earl. Are you one of those too?"

"She's Jewish. I'm a Catholic now."

"You're weird, man," said Bartholomew.

"I'm not a cock-hound, that I can say," said Earl.

"Whoopdi do!" said Bartholomew, pointing a twirling forefinger up to the roof.

Turning right into the main base entrance they found the gate open and manned with security. Earl lowered his window and held out his ID card. Bartholomew thought the airmen offered Earl a tired salute, more like a withering wave. He joined Earl in returning the airman a sharp salute. The air base seemed normal. Normal traffic flow, no posted warning signs, no debris scattered about. They drove near the flight line to see whether any jets had returned. The flight line was empty and the squadron parking lot held four cars. They finally found someone in the back of the squadron building. One of the assigned F-15 instructors, the C Flight Commander, was on the phone and taking notes. He motioned Earl and Bartholomew to come in and sit down. Hanging up the phone, the Flight Commander said, "Well guess what, you two...You're officially graduated. Congratulations. Start packing and out-processing. Get with personnel to get your orders and schedule your household goods pickup and get yourselves up to Elmendorf AFB." He went on to explain that since the squadron jets weren't coming back for another three days and Earl and Bartholomew had only three flights remaining to complete the course, the commander decided they weren't going to wait until things returned to normal ops. The hurricane wrecked their class flying training schedule for the remainder of the year. Besides, he told them, they were the two strongest pilots in their class.

"No use wasting any more sorties on you two. Check in with ops in the morning and at 1630, in case we need you for some bullshit duties. Right now, it's nothing but a cluster fuck around here. Sorry for no formal graduation. And by the way, you're both Distinguished Graduates."

Neither bothered to tell the Flight Commander there were no household goods to pick up. They filled up Earl's car at the base gas station and checked in at personnel but they were closed for the day. They stopped at the shopette and picked up jugs of water and a case of beer. Both were being rationed until further notice. The commissary was also rationing and they bought whatever was left on the shelves; crackers, canned beans and vegetables, beef jerky, and peanuts. Before leaving the base, Earl swung by the post office to check his P.O. box. Back in the car he quickly thumbed through his mail before leaning over and shoving it all in the glove box.

"Wondered why you never got any mail at the apartment," said Bartholomew.

"Habit," replied Earl.

"Secrecy?"

"No, using a P.O. box," said Earl.

"Right," said Bartholomew, scoffing to himself.

"Any from your girlfriend?"

"Helen?"

"Is that her name?"

"It's Helen."

"Helen's a Jewish name?"

"Not sure, Bartholomew. Her first name's Miriam. Maybe that's Jewish. She's Jewish I told you."

"You write poems to her, like Edgar Allan Poe did to his Helen?" Bartholomew thought sure he'd gotten to Earl this time. It's gonna show on his face, he thought. It has to, he thought, leaning forward with his head turned, staring at Earl. Earl looked straight ahead.

"I suck at poetry," deadpanned Earl, and with that they broke out in loud laughter.

"Well, I know you drink beer," continued Bartholomew.

"Catholics drink," said Earl, adding, "So do Jews."

"Well, then you're not *that* religious," said Bartholomew.

"The Pope drinks hard. Needs to—job's a bitch," said Earl, failing to keep a straight face. He burst out laughing. And he could not stop. Twenty seconds later tears streamed down his cheeks.

"Hey now, I'm just tryin' to figure you out, Earl," said Bartholomew, very relieved the tension disappeared between them.

"Here's what I'll say to you." Earl slowed to a stop, waiting for the light to change. "Know what I learned? I know more about things around me, outside of me, when I keep my mouth shut. I don't necessarily know more about what I think about when I keep my mouth shut but I know more about everything else around me. There's plenty for me to learn just watching and listening. That Bartholomew-- is what I learned. And now you know." He accelerated to pass a large slow truck.

Bartholomew thought, Earl observes reactions; I on the other hand, love to generate reactions in people, and then observe their reactions. Class clown and all, thought Bartholomew, or maybe, just a jackass.

"You like being a fighter pilot?" asked Bartholomew.

"Yeah," said Earl.

"Why do you like being a fighter pilot?" asked Bartholomew.

"And in particular, you want to know, why a single seat fighter pilot—right Bartholomew?" said Earl.

"Ok then, a single seat fighter pilot."

"Transcendence," Earl replied, knowing Bartholomew had been dying to ask this question.

Bartholomew laughed. "You went all meta-physical on me, didn't you?"

"I'm sure I'm not the only one who said that, Bartholomew."

"I'm sure you're one of the few fighter pilots who knows what the hell that really means," said Bartholomew.

"You know what it means," said Earl.

"I know what it means and I'm guessing you mean it in every possible way—ain't that right Earl?" Earl looked up and squinted momentarily--thinking, and then turned to Bartholomew.

"True enough." *I knew it*, thought Bartholomew, feeling confident he was finally figuring out what made Earl tick.

One day he entered Earl's bedroom after he left for the wood shop. Bartholomew leaned over Earl's pad-locked footlocker that he kept under the windowsill. The guitar he was making Bartholomew knew about, because Earl made no attempt to hide it. What Earl read or did in his room Bartholomew knew little, and he figured whatever Earl read must be inside his footlocker. It wasn't a Government issued item, it was old and not ornate, not an accent piece, yet made of handsome hardwood with brass brackets. It was also heavy, thought Earl, and he was very curious as to its contents. It barely fit into the trunk of Earl's car. Bartholomew figured Earl preferred to live alone and only relented because of his insistence that the money they saved could be better spent once they moved to Alaska. At least that was Bartholomew's theory.

That evening they spent the night on the floor of St. Basil's Church, along with Bartholomew's father, uncle and the rest of the volunteers and those without homes and apartments to return to. Bartholomew and his father sat close and talked in a front pew. They would pause and watch the news on a portable TV with a fuzzy screen set on top of a large cardboard box on the main step leading to the altar. Reverend James kept fiddling with the rabbit ears to get a clearer picture. Abby Westmoreland reported the latest news about the various rescues that took place during Hurricane Amy. Earl was again on TV, and was again being hailed as one of the heroes—this time the report combined footage of the survivors of the Lubbock killer tornado who talked fondly of Earl, and some were now calling him a savior. A volunteer shouted something when she saw herself on TV helping a young family get situated in the Parish hall that had been converted into a temporary sleeping facility. There was no mention of Reverend James in tonight's TV news. Earl picked up his sleeping bag and foam rest pad and went outside and tried to sleep in his car. The night was still and the humidity had returned. Earl could not get comfortable lying fully reclined in the driver's seat. He tossed the sleeping bag and foam pad over on the front passenger seat, started the car and turned east on Highway 98. The excitement of moving on kept him charged and awake as he left the Florida Panhandle and entered Mississippi. He gassed up in Gulfport and sipped his coffee with his window rolled down, soaking in the moist, salt soaked air, and observing and listening to the Mississippi coast slowly awake for another day.

Chapter 32

"She's a TV star now. It's what she always wanted, I guess. Never once mentioned it to me when we were married."

"Never in a million years would she have guessed you'd be the catalyst that launched her into being a TV news somebody. Her only son. I wonder who else knows this?" Theodore Neuhaus finished his Vodka Martini and asked Earl if he wanted another beer. It was five o'clock in downtown Houston and hot as a sweaty firecracker. The long bar felt almost cold to Earl and he welcomed it. They sat watching the TV mounted above and behind the bartender's station. Earl had driven straight through from Florida. He blocked any feeling of exhaustion. Being with his father, that's where he wanted to be.

"Congratulations Earl on your becoming an officer and a pilot." He lifted his Martini just a couple inches and placed it back down on the bar napkin. Even at close glance it was difficult to see the resemblance between them. Theo always acknowledged Earl got his mother's features, but the ears, they were all Theo's. Tiny sculpted ears affixed to the skull with craftsman precision. They were how ears should look on a man, his ex-wife once said to him. One of her most endearing compliments he ever received from his ex. Theo was a short six feet tall, according to his ex, and she was a tall six feet, according to her. Earl got the height as well as the looks. Theo's hair was shock white and thick and he kept it cut uniformly close. Made him look like a military man although he never spent a day in uniform. Earl noticed how lean his father was.

"Couldn't let myself go in prison, not after I watched some guys just let themselves go. They gave up on themselves. And most were only serving a ten-year stretch or less. It wasn't the end of the world Earl, not by a long shot. Much of it I owe to the Rabbi, and the rest I owe to you."

"I don't think so, Dad. You kept yourself going. It's not your nature to give up."

"Maybe..." mused Theo, as he remembered his failed efforts to get his wife to return. He failed on all counts and swore he'd never give up trying to get her back. It was Earl who told him to stop trying. He was right, and Theo would never forget that fact—and never would forget why his son told him what he did.

"Here they are," said Theo, looking past Earl and seeing the two men walking towards them. As they approached, Theo set his face, not of flint, but of relaxed ennui--his war paint during uncontrollable circumstances.

Paul Benson wore a grey suit and a multi-hued blue stripe tie with a standard knot. Lamar Wilkinson wore a double-breasted navy suit with faint narrow pinstripes and a maroon tie, also a standard knot. Both were taller than Theo, but not quite as tall as Earl. They dressed like they were big players in the land where everything is big.

"Theo!" said Wilkinson, in the navy double breast.

"And if it ain't Lieutenant Neuhaus, brand spankin new F-15 pilot," beamed Benson, reaching for Earl's hand as Theo stood to shake Wilkinson's hand.

"Heard an awful lot about you, Lieutenant. Now you're saving folks during hurricanes?"

"Well Colonel..." "No need for rank around here young man," Wilkinson interrupted, with apparent experience in controlling events, "Lamar is just fine."

"Two McCallans, neat," called out Benson to the bartender. Both men took note of Earl's attire; black blazer, crisp open collared white shirt, creaseless sky gray colored slacks and smart black loafers.

"And call me Paul," added Benson. Theo asked them if they wanted to find a table. Wilkinson declined and said they were only there for a quick howdy and a single malt. The small talk only covered how long Earl was going to be in Houston and how was he getting to Alaska. The two colonels in civilian suits shared a story about one of their buddies and his adventure driving the ALCAN Highway. More like mis-adventure, seeing how their buddy's truck bent an axle hitting a large rock and forced him to wait until a trucker picked him up and drove him to Whitefish. Lost his truck and everything crammed inside.

"Long story, the rest of it. Let's just say he planned poorly and paid dearly." Both Wilkinson and Benson laughed hard and loud. Wilkinson seemed to be the leader of the two. He finished his Scotch and extended his hand towards Theo.

"We're really looking forward to you being on board with us Theo," firmly shaking his hand, and patting Earl on the shoulder said, "And Earl, don't be a stranger. Stop in any time when you come to visit your Dad."

When Wilkinson and Benson left, Theo and his son took seats at a dinner table in the back of the bar. They ordered Filet Mignons and baked potatoes, Theo ordering squash and Earl opting for long green beans. They had not seen each other since Earl visited him in prison just before setting out for pilot training in Texas. They talked liked old friends rather than father and son. Their bond seemed unbreakable.

"You don't have to use my attorney's address anymore. I'm back to being your home of record. Unless of course, you use your mother's address now."

Earl shook his head.

Theo smiled.

"How did you come to know Wilkinson and Benson? They seemed to know you. Was it from the tornado in Lubbock? They recognize you from the TV news?"

"I met them at the Officer's Club on base. They flew in an F-4 a couple times and talked to me and Bartholomew at the O'club bar. They danced with Mom and Amy at our assignment night party."

"No kidding?" Theo smiled. "So, they knew you before they knew me?"

"Think that's a coincidence, Dad?"

"Absolutely not," said Theo, "Absolutely not."

"I didn't know they were Air Force."

"They're Reservists," said Earl. "I think they're tight with the Texas Governor, too. He's an Air Force Reservist too, or was. He flew F-4s with them in Vietnam."

"Bit old to be flying fighter planes, aren't they?" asked Theo.

"You don't mind them calling you Theo?" asked Earl. "Thought you hated being called Theo."

"I don't hate much anymore," said Theo, smiling. "They actually called me 'Chance' at work. Got that nickname in prison. Those two do their homework, I'll give them that."

"What exactly are you doing for them, Dad?"

"Upcoming mergers. I've been brought in to square up
any suspicious account activity. They want whatever they're
going to acquire to be 100 percent squeaky clean. Full
transparency. They told me to highlight anything questionable.
They figure I know what to look for. Haven't seen anything yet.
Just waiting."

"And I don't hate your mother either, Earl—not
anymore." What surprised Earl about his father's admission was
that he never thought his father hated his mother. Earl never
knew when they actually divorced. Six months after his mother
left, his sister demanded to go live with her. It was Earl and his
father in the house—until his father went to prison. His father's
lawyer looked after Earl until he left for college, mainly by
having a maid clean the house every week and a cook to prepare
Earl's dinner at night. This was preferable to Earl and the
lawyer, who had been married three times, never fathering
children and always demanding a pre-nuptial. His true love was
his bank accounts and said as much. Earl's neighbors said
nothing because there was nothing to say about his living as a
high school bachelor. Their distant sympathies for Earl were of
the same substance as their sympathies for a distant cousin with
stage four cancer—thank goodness it didn't happen to one of
them. As long as the lawn was kept and the long driveway was
not jammed with loud teenagers in search of a permanent drunk.
Earl mowed the lawn and kept no partying friends. They lived
in an exclusive neighborhood with deep front yards and estate
homes with too many rooms. The neighbors were not actually
neighbors in any sense of the word. They were families whose
fathers were ambitious and attempting to accumulate as much
wealth as they could get away with. They used the fate of Earl's

father as their behavioral boundary—they were fully versed on the details that led to Theodore Neuhaus's fall. His trial was one of the rare occasions people living around the Neuhaus's engaged with each other. Nothing like the trial of the richest man in the neighborhood—and a mere accountant—to generate titillating speculation and evoke schadenfreude. The Neuhaus's two next-door neighbors across the street evolved from intentional strangers to swift friends and cocktail companions as a result of sharing factoids of the trial.

It was during the trial where Earl got to know his father's lawyer, William 'Willie' Koenig. He became a regular at the house, sometimes staying in the guest room after descending into legalese incoherency at three am—usually because he was too drunk. Willie brought his own tall chrome cigarette butt can and smoked on the back steps of the Florida room. With or without a lit Gauliouse between his stubby fingers, the stench of cigarettes smoke trailed him. No one could resist not calling him 'Big Willie' behind his back. He was five foot zero and accumulated a belly that forever hid the tips of his calfskin Italian loafers from his sight. He was born into caricature, knew it to be so, and relished living within the bowels of his own myth. Earl thought him to be the happiest person he ever met.

His father continued, "Are you bothered by the fact she is using you to escape being a weather reporter? First she escaped marriage, now the weather. She's becoming quite the TV darling, connecting you to saving people in tornados and hurricanes. She thinks no one will find out her secret. Wait till the true media hounds find your scent."

Earl smiled. He grabbed the bill from the waiter and slipped in his credit card he had palmed in his hand. Theo made a mock face of irritation.

"Wait until the media tracks *you* down and starts digging in *your* trashcan—you may not be smiling then," said his father, thinking about what his own reaction will be the day the media again starts digging in his trashcan, once the parasites discover who Earl's father is. Same as before, Theodore thought, *my reaction will be the same as last time.*

"Actually, in an after-the-fact sort of way, I learned something from your mother, and I'll go as far as to give her some credit," he father mused, as they both exited the establishment and stopped short of the curb.

"I got the cab fare home," said Theo.

"Your mother knew in order to change--I mean a radical path divergence kind of change," he said with self-revelatory intensity, "she had to separate herself from what she was connected to, regardless of the consequences, regardless of how reliant others became of her. Now I don't know how reliant we all became on her predictability. I guess predictability has a quality of comfort all its own—or maybe it's all interconnected, hell I don't know that either. But I do know this--for change to sink in and stick, you have to separate from that which you feel compelled to separate from. And your mother did just that."

"Dad, that sounds more like your Rabbi buddy talking than you."

"Yeah, maybe." Earl wasn't sure yet if his father had put two and two together. His father was a concoction of thoughts at the moment. He thought maybe he was wrong, but

he didn't think so. He believed he knew why his father was re-
assigned to Houston.

Opening the door to his new apartment, Earl's father
asked, "You going to see Helen before you get up to Alaska?"

"I am," said Earl.

"Please tell her I said hello," said Theodore.

"I didn't save anyone, Dad. The tornado and hurricane, I
mean."

"In TV land, that doesn't matter does it?" said his father,
adding, "In TV land you are in fact a savior. In TV land, what
you can get away with matters, because at the end of the day,
the money behind the television, the money guys—they know
they can grab more power in the form of influence—and a
pleasant side effect to that power is all the glorious revenue they
obtain from those they influence. Narrative matters because it
generates power. Period. So this whole savior narrative that
your mother is peddling…"

"We'll just have to see how it plays out," interrupted
Earl.

"You have the power to change that narrative, son.

"I know."

Chapter 33

Susan James stepped out onto the front porch just after Bartholomew shut the door to his truck. She waved and skipped down the porch steps and wrapped her arms around her only son. She kissed him hard on the cheek. The three days beard growth scratched her lips. His body odor reminded her of his father.

"You two worried me to distraction," she said, grabbing his backpack and slinging it on her shoulder.

"I got the rest Mom," said Bartholomew, walking around to the back of his truck to get his other bags.

"Don't faint Mom—all my clothes are clean."

She beamed. "You are trainable, then." Harold was about half a day behind, having to get his driver's side window replaced in Alabama. Other than the window, the hurricane damage to his truck was mostly superficial. Bartholomew's mother returned to the kitchen to make sandwiches.

"You'll never guess who called last night," she yelled, as Bartholomew returned from dropping his bags onto his bed. This time home his bedroom seemed as if it was someone else's, as if he were a houseguest of an acquaintance. He felt odd glancing around at old high school and college photos on his wall. His small bookcase still had books he read when he was in junior high. Those memories were already fading.

"Bartholomew, you hear me?"

"Yeah, Mom," he yelled downstairs, "Who called?" His mother had a roast beef on rye with chips and a big dill pickle at his usual place at the table.

"What do you want to drink?"

"Any beer in the fridge?" he asked. She returned with an unopened bottle of beer.

"It's a twist off," she said.

"Thanks Mom." He twisted off the cap, swallowed a third of the beer in the first draw, and bit a large bite out of the thick sandwich, looking for a napkin to wipe off the deli mustard leaking from the corner of his mouth. Crumbs collected on his early beard.

"Slow down, you'll choke to death," said his mother, leaping out of her chair to fetch the forgotten napkin.

"You can eat and listen at the same time?" she said with a smile. His glare was mimicked in return.

"You know, I haven't spoken to her in I can't remember how long," his mother said. Bartholomew wiped his mouth and he bit into the crunching dill pickle.

"Who?" demanded Bartholomew.

"Laurie Tillerbrook." Bartholomew finished off the pickle and crunched on the last of the potato chips.

"Well?"

"Why'd she call?"

"She called asking about you, dummy."

"But why?"

"Maybe, just maybe, she still has feelings for you." His mother grabbed the used napkin from his hand and tossed it on the empty plate and went back into the kitchen muttering,

"Although I don't know why." From the kitchen she said, "She left her number, in case you forgot it."

"Wonder if she's still that cute little thing she was in high school?"

"I don't know Mom." His mother returned to the dining room and asked," Well, aren't you at least somewhat interested in what she's like now? When's the last time you saw her?"

"Hell, Mom, right before I left for college. Our breakup was not pretty."

"Cause you were messin' around with that other girl too, right? What was her name?"

"Jennie."

"Oh yeah, Jennie Whitten. Her Mom was real nice, a real sweetie," she said, adding, "Jennie was a sweetie too."

"They both dumped me," said Bartholomew, going into the kitchen for another beer.

"Double-timing never goes over very well, son," she said. "You can play football, and evidently fly jets real well, and if you ever really applied yourself, you could be a PhD type person. You're the most handsome boy I've ever seen—you could lose a little of that beer belly, though. But you just can't treat girls that way Bartholomew. No matter who you are."

"I really liked Jennie."

"And she really liked you too, her momma told me so."

"I wished she called instead."

"You going to give Laurie Tillerbrook a call back?"

"Where's Jennie these days, Mom?"

"Nursing school in Ohio somewhere," she said. "I see her Mom every once in a while in town. We just wave at each other now, that's pretty much all."

"Next time you see her, will you tell her I asked about Jennie?" said Bartholomew.

"I don't see her as the type to latch up with a military man—I think she's a home town girl."

"Just tell her I asked about Jennie, please."

"I will, I will." She handed him Laurie Tillerbrook's phone number.

"You never did have a steady girl in college did you? Just played the field—right?"

"I'm going to lie down for a nap, Mom," he said, kissing her cheek and thanking her for lunch. She returned to the kitchen, gently rubbing her kissed cheek, rolled up a thin slice of roast beef and ate it, and put the lunch items away. She went out to the porch and sat in her favorite chair.

Later, she was still sitting on the porch when she heard the airbrakes belch and soon after watched her husband's truck turn into the long driveway. She had dozed off earlier but now had energy back and leaped out of the chair, quickly entering the house and then on up the stairs to shower and get herself ready. She couldn't wait to see her husband. Dinner reservations for three in town were in an hour.

Chapter 34

Earl was still well charged from visiting his father. Leaving before sunrise, he kept to the Texas highways as he drove North and West. As usual, his interior life dominated, and he knew that he should spend more time outside his own ruminations. The American West vista was something he always wanted to experience, this being the first time he ventured west of Texas, but he couldn't bring himself to enjoy the vast unfolding landscape of the Edwards Plateau; the tall grasses with islands of escarpment live oak, juniper and mesquite trees that have survived the bison, the livestock ranches and urban spread in and amongst the limestone ridges and rolling hills, all giving way to the high plains of north and west Texas. He knew there was more to see than what he merely scanned, more in and around the shades of brown and beige plateau grasses and shrubs, as if propping up all the oak, juniper and mesquite. He noticed the sharp shinned hawks, not knowing their name but watching them in established orbits around their aerial domain, hungry for hares foraging within telescopic eyesight.

His thoughts returned to dinner with his father. They discussed Amy at dinner the previous night. His father didn't know what he could do for his daughter.

"Nothing you can do, Dad," said Earl.

"Tell her I want to get back in her life, not in her business, but her life."

"I promise," said Earl, knowing that, in order to fulfill his promise, he had to also stay connected with her. And, after leaving home, she never made family connections a high priority. He couldn't speak for her and his mother's relationship, although by the looks of their combined antics at his pilot graduation party, he assumed Amy and his mother kept in touch.

Earl's phone call to Helen went well, he thought, and he was beginning to look forward to seeing her. He had a longing to now be whisper near and within her scent.

Earl recalled the entire conversation with his father—as short as it was--about his mother. About his mother--as if she was declaring to the world that she discovered a new savior--and as if she was directing her message to needy pockets of populace around the world that actually were hooked on America's fixations. Well, they were soon to be transfixed again—it was a new season of nature's violent outbursts in America. From the tornados and hurricane a new savior emerges. This is how his father perceived Abby's TV coverage of Earl. She was attempting to create a kind of religious phenomenon that only America could create. And that perception was reinforced by the Righteous Reverend Delroy James, who along with a few of his followers, claimed to be witnesses during Hurricane Amy. She worked the Reverend and the rest of them into every one of her interviews. Up until his father described it this way, Earl had not taken notice. He avoided watching television.

Avoiding what his mother's ambitions may hold for him was not difficult. He locked away any and all thoughts about his mother. He chose not to recall how long it took for him to succeed in building a secure enough compartment in his mind to dump his mother—and the lingering feelings for her. His father told him that the violent rash and hives would pass; yet the

itching pain brought tears to Earl's eyes. They came on him at
night, three days after his mother left. The medication helped
somewhat, but the prayers, not so much. After almost a month,
the last remnants of the hives faded away. Looking closely he
could see the scars on his neck and chest and upper legs. He
knew his back was like a field of tiny exploded landmines. Back
then he imagined successfully tracing an impossibly navigable
path from hive to hive, and he prayed the path would end at a
place where the pain ceased. That was the time his sister Amy
was smoking two packs a day. Very soon after, she came and
went as she pleased, and there was never a time again where the
remainder of the family dined together—other than her high
school graduation, when she had the look of hate imprinted on
her face.

Earl wanted nothing more than a clear mind, free of
anything except that which he thought about, and only when he
thought about it. When he no longer desired to think about
something; that thought disappeared. Instead of filling his mind
with constant distractions in order not to think of something,
Earl practiced eliminating distractions in order to keep his mind
clear of anything. For this ability he thanked his mother. He
thanked her so as not to hate her.

Amy's mother sent an irregular sized, obnoxious and
ornate graduation card. Earl knew Amy cried as she burned the
card in the bathroom sink. The plastic and glitter glued to the
card cruelly delivered an acrid odor into the hallway and the
upstairs bedrooms. The burning saddened Theo.

Earl kept his mother in a tight compartment in his mind,
as secure as a bank vault, and it was Earl's intention to keep her
there, lest his anger seep out and corrode his mind. Earlier,

198

there was a time when he thought about his mother--before she left--when she would tell stories of her childhood in west Texas growing up with a father firm and focused on becoming an oilman of consequence. Earl loved her stories because Earl sensed his mother loved telling them. He knew he was driving the same roads his grandfather must have driven back in his day, but it meant little to Earl. He wished he could have met his grandfather. She spoke little about her mother.

Now thoughts about his visit with his father were enveloped in thoughts of the father and son inside the overturned school bus in Lubbock. Anymore, the dead father and son were never very far from his thoughts, because Earl made little attempt to suppress his recall of seeing them—and of the boy clutching both their lunch pails, a final act Earl was convinced was done as the boy lay dying. Many times Earl replayed his mind's imagining of the boy after the tornado's killing sequence—straining to see his father, crying out to him, reaching for him, unable to move, save to gather and clutch close their lunch pails. To Earl, no awe inspiring Texas vista could ever supplant his mind's picture of the father and son from Lubbock. These thoughts he let roam freely in his mind. He gave these thoughts full permission to roam about his conscious, sensing fully his unconscious was busy weaving experiences of the father and son from Lubbock into his very soul. He avoided Lubbock by staying on westbound highways.

Chapter 35

"I know all about images, all about what captures attention, and more important, holds attention for just the right length of time to sink the hooks in their minds," pitched Abby Westmoreland. The producers were easily convinced of one thing; her lush eyelashes framed blazing green eyes locking with theirs as they fought the temptation to look at her cleavage. Their attention was aroused. Abby Westmoreland swore that cleavage was leverage, and dismissed any woman as a fool who never leveraged cleavage. Low thread count white blouse and a sheer brassiere, with a hint of nipple. Convincing them why Earl Neuhaus was an American Savior was something else, however.

"He's got the height and looks..." said the quiet producer--the boss.

"Looks? Barely," interjected the short and fat producer, showing no fear of his boss.

"But he's a military man--an up and coming fighter pilot. Some mystery about him, as well."

"And gentlemen, we don't want to spoil the mystery. That's a selling point. Women love that," said Abby.

"And what else do you think women want, Abby?" asked the short fat producer. Abby thought to herself that he must know he is the classic stereotype of a producer. The double breasted wide pinstripe gray suit--consciously balding--a sheen to his forehead. Trying so hard to be a big man in stature. Surely he must see that in himself, she thought.

"Women—they're relational--big-time," she said instinctively, and just then realizing she did not say 'We'. The producers caught that as well, and were impressed.

"Then who is he related to?" asked the producer who was the boss. Abby's chest tightened and lifted. She wanted to tell them she was his mother. God, I so want to tell them, she thought.

"He's related to America through the armed forces and we have a very popular TV preacher that believes he is special. Military and religion—very compelling combination."

"That pompous rotund preacher you interviewed?" said the short fat producer.

"Pompous and rotund reverends don't sell," he said, "Unless they're entertainingly black, which he's not. And that's not the market we're trying to capture."

"What about a girlfriend, a love interest?" asked the boss producer.

"Let me commit to this project and I'll find every relational angle," Abby pitched.

"Tired of being a weather gal?" said the short, fat, wannabe boss producer.

"Ready to move on."

"Then go get me proof that women of America have so convinced themselves that they'll convince their own husbands and boyfriends why this Earl Neuhaus is the next American savior," said the boss producer.

"I would love that in writing, sir," she said, now a submissive Abby Westmoreland. She tasted sourness in her mouth, from a familiar fear. Her stomach turned. A stench of bile escaped as it burned her upper esophagus.

Chapter 36

This particular dinner was a first for Bartholomew's parents. It was their favorite town restaurant, not that there were many choices. The town was good size, but not the most prosperous part of the state. Locals tended to stay at home. But the Northern Italian Bistro caught on, for reasons more logical than unexplained. No one can remember or care to recall when the Albia family immigrated here--and most of them stayed. No locals were ever in conversations that complained about that fact. Perhaps a jealous restaurant owner wannabe—but no serious conversation ever captured a complaint about the Albia family's decision to stay in the western part of Virginia. Family sized portions suited the locals' sense of acceptable proportion—and the Albia family retained an outstanding wait staff. They were the best paid wait staff in the region. It was a first for them because this was the first time they dined out when Bartholomew was of legal drinking age.

"Remember Bartholomew, the Air Force has a fat boy program, and you don't want to be on it early in your career," said his father.

"You drinking dinner, son?" asked his mother. At Bartholomew's request, the waitress brought the second carafe of Chianti. She was endowed to his liking. Four glasses of Chianti did that to him, he thought. He was large. And large-- with his parents--in the same tired restaurant he'd been going to since his high school years. The only thing he liked about this restaurant was the owner's fondness for shapely waitresses.

"I called Laurie Tillerbrook, like you wanted me to, Mom."

"And?"

"We're coming back here tomorrow night for dinner."
His mother was well pleased.

"Beth, what's this all about?" asked his father. Excited,
Beth James explained to Harold about Laurie's phone call and
her wish to see Bartholomew again. The veal scaloppini was an
exceptional portion, and Bartholomew could offer no complaints
as he worked to clean his plate with the last of the garlic bread.
Their conversation centered on the particulars of Bartholomew's
move to Alaska. Both parents, since Bartholomew started pilot
training, had been tag-teaming their son, dispensing their own
Air Force lessons learned as to how best to move from
assignment to assignment, with minimal frustration and
household goods damage, and maximum compensation when
filing all the travel and moving vouchers. Let the Air Force pay
in full for the hassle of moving every three or four years, they
said.

Now they were repeating themselves, thought
Bartholomew, becoming nervous his mother detected his
impatience with them. Her eyes darted his as his father reached
for the salt and pepper. She darted her eyes again at
Bartholomew—he quickly looked down at his plate in
exaggerated concentration on the remaining portion of veal. He
could not look up. His mother changed subjects.

"You have a list for your trip? Maybe I can help you get
everything you need. You'd much rather get it all at the
beginning than have it distract you while you drive. I know how
annoying that can be."

"Mom, I'm a pilot—I can cut out those kinds of
distractions. Besides, there's nothing I can think of that I'd

really need that I can't get on the way up there." Bartholomew never looked up at his mother, keeping his eyes fixed on his now empty plate,

"Well, fine then," she said. Mustering the nerve to look at her, Bartholomew said, "Look Mom, thanks—really. But I think I got it all. Though, if you like, I'll make a list and give it to you."

"Oh, no need son, I'm sure you got everything." Now Harold's eyes glared at Bartholomew.

"Mom, I'm…"

"Never mind Bartholomew—never mind." The once delicious veal scaloppini now turned in Bartholomew's stomach.

Chapter 37

Helen's roommate did not mind Earl sleeping on the sofa
for a few nights. She knew Helen was as excited as she had
ever seen her. As much as Earl protested, saying he already had
a hotel room nearby; Helen would have none of it, and insisted
he stay with her. Earl's memory of Helen remained rich in
detail; she ran near fifty miles a week—the reason for her
premature lined tan face. If not for running, Helen would be
stunning, thought Earl. High and tight cheekbones, prominent
nose and a soft square chin. Seeming to eschew her own facial
beauty, Helen's lush auburn hair on the other hand was a gift
she sought to protect. Earl wished she shaped her brows a bit
and glossed her tight lips. Her clouded blue eyes did not pierce,
they lingered. Her runner's calves easily met a sculptor's high
standard. Earl had a few photographs of them standing
together—awkward poses, pushed together by their fathers,
while Helen and Earl visited them in prison.

She greeted him with a quick lip kiss and nervous hug
and offered to help him with his bags. She wore a scent—faint
but present—and Earl thought of his mother for an instant. He
liked the fragrance. A lot of little chatter about the trip, traffic,
finding her apartment—Earl answered in short statements,
careful not to give the impression that her questions were
tedious. To Earl they were not. Earl knew it was her way of
getting comfortable with him. He didn't mind at all. They were
questions of immediacy, questions he could answer and forget.
He wasn't nervous around Helen, but he was fairly certain she
was at least somewhat nervous because of that fact.

"It's still in my mind, so unbelievable that my father played matchmaker—in prison of all places. Arranging for us to meet in our fathers' special picnic bench in the prison courtyard. Can you imagine?" It then occurred to Earl that this was the second time he was unsure if Helen actually was attracted to him or her father's loving advice that Earl was a young man worth the time to get to know. But her eyes relaxed Earl's skepticism somewhat; Helen's longing gaze seemed never to let him get far away. She was very excited, darting around the apartment checking the time, showing Earl the bathroom and the Navy blue guest towels on the rack adjacent to her sea foam green terry cloth towel. A cleared off shelf above the toilet for his bathroom kit. And a quick tour of the rest of the small apartment and the limited view of not much to look at anyway from the sliding glass door that opened to a tiny terrace. The apartment had the feel that it was not lived in—merely maintained for appearance.

"A clean-aholic I'm not, I assure you," said Helen, fidgeting with an elastic black cloth hair band that she never ended up using to pull back her hair. Long enough to pin behind her delicate ears but short enough to make her look ambivalent about her appearance if she ever did use the hair band. Her ponytail would barely extend three inches, extending straight out the middle of the back of her large head. Helen *was* a clean-aholic, thought Earl, and was disappointed with her denial. But not much disappointed.

"You're apartment's fine Helen—and please tell your roommate how appreciative I am."

"Oh, she'll be stopping by," beamed Helen.

"I'd like to take a quick shower to get the road off me—let's go to your favorite restaurant," said Earl. Helen's white summer dress offset her light brown skin and wrapped tight her small waist. The hemline drew the intended attention to her athletic legs. Large eyes in a small face, eyelashes magazine models envied, Earl was very attracted to her delicate cheeks and prominent nose and chin. Delicate and prominent, thought Earl. When he appeared from the bathroom, invigorated and famished, Earl caught Helen futzing with a large portable computer in the small kitchen. Earl walked towards her.

"May I say, I find you very, very alluring." Helen was caught off guard and froze. She recovered quickly.

"Yes, you may say that," she said, and moved to kiss him—again quickly, until Earl wrapped his right arm around her waist. Just for a few moments, as he gently touched his lips to hers. Delivering a short kiss, then releasing her as if she was on fire. Earl wanted her, but now uncertainty leapt back into his mind. He was able to push the creeping fear out of his thoughts during the drive to California, but now, in the moment, the fear returned. He could not stem the fear, as much as he loved being near her, so close, touching her. Earl's heart and mind were in gridlock and he felt his heart was weak, not experienced in matters of the heart and therefore not as strong as his mind. He struggled with the impulse to believe he was losing Helen already, and Helen was oblivious.

"I'll drive," she said, her nervous excitement rushing her movements to push her slender arms through the sleeves of a thin cashmere sweater, a flash of worry she was stretching the sleeves, and then darting to grab her purse from her bedroom and emerging to swipe her set of keys off the edge of the kitchen counter. Earl trailed her out the front door and waited until she locked both locks.

The Italian restaurant was intimate and Donato had little desire not to let Helen sit in her favorite corner table. Donato's was the restaurant Helen dreamed of when dreaming of a romantic dinner. That was Donato's objective from the earliest days starting from the first location, a former peep show house that was famous simply for being the closest porn shop to the university. Donato wanted to attract students and faculty, but more important, he wanted to be known as the owner of the most romantic Italian restaurant around. Helen thought he had succeeded and never failed to tell him.

"Now you need someone to share dinner with," remarked Donato the last time she dined. Donato remembered his comment to Helen as she sat down with Earl. Helen started the table conversation, remarking how remarkable it was that they both wrote often to their father's while they were in prison. Helen wanted to talk more. She wanted to know more. She wanted to be sure of everything. She was compiling a list of whys—why she should consider selecting Earl. She yearned to have the coincidences in their lives be linked as a bond, to serve as her affirmation that wonderful karma touched her life and presented her with love.

"Your letters to your father weren't destroyed in the Hurricane?"

"They're with me, in a fireproof box along with some other things. I'm not letting them get away from me." As her approval of the letters safekeeping became slowly evident on her face, Earl slowly showed a grateful smile. He was counting on his heart to be strengthened by each smile he gave to Helen.

Earl was not giving in to his mind--a mind that no longer wished
to keep his mother locked away. His mind let Abby
Westmoreland free to roam his thoughts. Earl knew he was
powerless to stop thoughts of his mother rough stomp his
feelings for Helen.

"As I promised, I have them with me and you are
welcome to read them. I've got nothing to hide from you, but
fair warning, I did write about you and my father wrote about
what your father thought of you—and what he thought of me."

"You're not embarrassed?" Helen asked. "God, some of
my letters to my father are so embarrassing—I still don't know
if I can have you read them." Her blushing made Earl's smile
broaden.

"Some of my first letters are corny, but you be the
judge," said Earl, adding, "Remember, I never asked to read
your letters."

"It wouldn't be fair not to read mine," she said.

"It's not a fair or unfair issue to me," he said.

"Nobody writes letters anymore," she said.

"Is there anything I'll find shocking?" teased Helen. She
hadn't opened her menu yet, nor touched her first glass of Pinot
Grigio. Donato stopped by to ask if anything was wrong with
the wine and Helen blushed hard as she took two quick sips.
She apologized repeatedly to Donato, telling him the wine was
excellent. Earl wasn't drinking wine. Donato would have none
of that.

"Signori, try this Chianti—not sweet, I promise you—
and very smooth. You will like. Young people know not much
about the wine—that's ok, that is why I am here," smiled
Donato. Earl did not refuse a second time and thanked him.

Donato was right about the Chianti. After placing their orders, Helen could not wait any longer.

"I'm dying to ask you about what you think about it all." Helen's excitement spilt out of her. She seemed like a young teenager, barely able to contain herself. Earl guessed what she was dying to know all about. And Earl knew Helen might explode right in front of him if she knew everything there was to know about Earl's steady gaining notoriety on television.

"Do they know you're here? In California—here, visiting me?" Earl wasn't sure if she should have a third glass of wine. He finally finished his and attempted to order black coffee. Again Donato intervened, placing a cappuccino in front of Earl and begging him to take just one sip. Earl found the coffee excellent, and thanked Donato.

"He really likes you Earl." Now Earl wasn't sure if Helen's blushing was caused by the Pinot Grigio.

"What do you make of it all, Earl? Have you talked to your father about it? Have you talked with anyone about it?" said Helen, hoping he would say no and that she was the only one he could talk to. Helen wanted to be the only one Earl would talk to—about anything.

"I talk with him some. He's busy getting his life back on track. He can't stand any media coverage, especially TV."

"But, Earl, what do *you* think?" Earl sipped his cappuccino, unwilling to share any thoughts on the matter. For, any thoughts on the matter led to thoughts of his mother and his mother was in a place where he wanted to keep her, in a strong lock box, hidden away. But she was loose now.

"I mean Earl, you'd think your mother would contact you and say something—I mean *anything*," said Helen.

"Ok, ok, I'll tell you what I think," he said, to ensure his mother was not brought up again that evening. They both had agreed earlier not to talk about their mothers until both were ready to talk about their mothers.

"I think…" Earl delayed, sipping his coffee, testing Helen. He wanted to observe her reactions. He wanted to know why she was interested in him—because he had already formed doubts about whether any true interest in him existed. Helen cleared the dessert plate away to the side, swept clean the tablecloth with her right hand and folded the napkin from her lap and laid it carefully next to her plate. Her eyes locked with Earl's.

"I think that weather reporter is using me to get to where she thinks she wants to go—in her career—in her life. She believes she has grabbed the opportunity of a lifetime and I believe she will not let go until she wrings every single bit of opportunity out of a story of her own creation. This is her baby, her creation, and she wants to see her creation fulfilled. But, as you can hopefully see, I'm already created. And I could care less about her new designs for me."

"Oh my God!" squealed Helen, so loud, nearby patrons stopped dining to notice. Helen blushed. They squabbled for a minute about who would pay for dinner. Earl relented, and did not think about why. Donato seemed very pleased with Earl's decision, kissing Helen on both cheeks and giving Earl a vigorous double handed shake, imploring them to return soon.

As Helen opened her apartment door, Earl said, "Helen, let's talk a bit more." There was no objection from her as she slid her keys on the kitchen counter top and excused herself to go the toilet. She called out for her roommate. No response.

Earl hoped he had been effective masking his emotions because he could see no future for them together. He could not imagine how he could make her happy. By following him from assignment to assignment? By having her choose and acquiesce to only his career development? By having Helen as the dependent wife? That's what the military calls family members--dependents. Earl convinced himself that she had not thought this through. Helen didn't know anyone in the military. No one in her family served in the military. Earl's military experience was nothing. He knew no one in the military prior to pilot training. This cannot work. Thoughts of his mother blanketed his mind.

Helen returned, minus her sweater, and asked Earl if he wanted something to drink. He declined and asked her to sit next to him on the couch. Helen did so willingly, with a quiet disposition. His nearness was what mattered most. They sat side by side, a mere inches from touching-whisper close. A soft ache blanketed the room.

Chapter 38

Danny, her cameraman for the last four years, declined the opportunity to accompany Abby. She did not try to persuade him to come along, but she did offer. They were partners traveling in a windowless van and she had little trouble following Earl by herself from Houston. She wasn't used to being alone on the road. She hated being alone on long drives or long flights; her thoughts always channeled to her son and daughter, and on particular occasions--usually tipsy--her ex-husband. Nurturing was not her strong suit she continued to tell herself. Danny would remind her of that; she was convinced Danny said it to make her feel better. Sometimes it helped, for a little while. Danny was terribly smitten with Abby; she knew that to be fact. She was fond of him, like a homeowner fond of their favorite yardman.

Earl was easy to follow but a persistent anxiousness set in as she approached Barstow. Abby prayed for an opportunity to talk with Earl without his girlfriend present. She only knew of Helen, never knew who she was until Amy mentioned her on the phone. And Abby's information about her ex moving to Houston and Earl going to visit him also came from Amy. Amy knew because Earl told her their father wanted to reunite with her. That wasn't very damn likely, Amy told herself, and she told her mother. Amy knew nothing about Helen, other than Earl met her while visiting their father in prison. All very, very boring, thought Amy. But it was enough information for Abby to work with. She prepared to sleep in the van, in fact whatever else was necessary, in order not to lose her son. She guessed Earl wasn't the kind to start a road trip at 400am. Following him was easy; but she was now panicked, worrying whether he'd say any more than two words to her. She was afraid to drink coffee for fear of too frequent restroom stops. Danny's amphetamines kept her shaky but at least awake. A pinched ache above her right eye twitched the eye muscles, flickering her eyelid in asymmetric rhythms. She found a hotel a few miles from Helen's apartment, and after watching them go out to Donato's Restaurant, return, and confirming the lights in her apartment went out, she finally checked into her hotel room, grabbing a taco salad and diet soda along the way. Abby stuffed the food in her mouth and washed it down with another diet soda from the hotel vending machine. She popped two Valium, ran a hot bath in the short tub, and submersed herself until she ran out of breath. After exhaling and drawing a lungful of air she slid back down under water again. Surfacing, Abby laid her head on the back of the tub. She masturbated, finally reaching climax in violent spasms, and settled back into the lukewarm tub water, her brow beginning to perspire--her head throbbing. She awoke shivering in cooled bathwater, quickly got out and dried herself, and fell into bed.

Early the next morning Abby parked the van on the street, within eyesight of Helen's front door. She sipped a large coffee in a fancy to-go cup and munched on a blueberry muffin. She kept her light jacket zipped to her neck. The inside of the van fogged over but she still had a direct view of Helen's apartment. Dawn approached, as did the increasing flow of traffic. She listened to a cacophony of small birds announcing the start of another day in some large, thin leaved tree behind her. Abby was giving Earl until 800am to leave the apartment. Maybe solo or with Helen, maybe for an early walk or run, maybe for breakfast. She ran through all the AM and FM radio stations, first her affiliate stations, then the rest and after a half hour turned off the radio. After urinating in a plastic container, Abby returned from the back of the van and resumed her watch. Ten minutes later she observed a light go on in Helen's apartment. She checked her makeup in the rearview mirror, arranged her hair, and applied soft red lipstick. If they don't leave the apartment in fifteen minutes, she thought, she was going to knock on the door. She changed her mind, wanting Helen now present when approaching Earl, thinking he would be inclined to stay and listen rather than walk away.

Abby was no longer fearful, excited now by the challenge and once in a lifetime opportunity. To win over her own son--after what he thought she did to him--abandoning them all, years ago—this was her moment, this was her test. She had to convince him to be interviewed. She secured an eight-minute profile piece slotted for evening prime time, on the number one news show in the country. Abby quickly went to the back of the van and urinated again. It was almost 800am. Outside, everything seemed to reflect the sunlight to her eyes as she fumbled around in her large bag for sunglasses. She cursed for quitting smoking three years ago. The threat of wrinkles was just too much, and something had to give. She tossed a nicotine piece of gum in her mouth, compliments of her cameraman, whom she threatened to fire unless he quit smoking. She re-checked her mini tape recorders to make sure the batteries were fresh and the tiny cassettes were operating properly. Her standard procedure was to keep one recorder running and hidden in an outer pocket of her handbag, and produce the second one when interviewing a subject.

Abby's nostrils flared exiting the van as she filled her lungs with the cool California morning air. She felt alert and her excitement quickened her step crossing the street. Earl and Helen were walking to the parking lot. They were close but not touching. Abby noticed Helen's slight smile, maybe from something Earl said.

Abby waved at them. "Excuse me! Earl Neuhaus? Can I please have a few moments of your time?" After two steps Earl froze, holding his arm up to the side, blocking Helen from walking any further.

"Please, Earl." Earl faced Abby and waited. Helen, startled and confused, stood by Earl.

"We have an opportunity of a lifetime—an opportunity that will forever change our lives and I'm asking you to please consider what I'm about to say." Abby approached slowly, coming within arm's reach of her son. Earl raised his hand and she stopped.

"You have a car nearby?" he asked. Abby, now off guard, nodded.

"Then why don't you follow us and join us for breakfast. I'm sorry my car is fully packed and can only take two people. What are you driving? " Light headed, she turned and weakly pointed to her rental van. Earl asked Helen how far the breakfast place was. Under ten minutes, she said in a soft voice, meant only for Earl.

"Don't worry, I'll drive slow." Earl turned and escorted Helen to his car. Abby ran across the street, dropping the keys as she attempted to unlock the van.

"Do I really need to go along?" asked Helen, stopping at the front passenger door.

"I'd very much appreciate it if you would," said Earl, walking around the front of the car and opening the passenger door.

"You can now see for yourself, instead of imagining," he said with an embracing smile. Helen insisted she close her own door.

Earl drove fast enough not to irritate the morning rush. Abby's van was tucked close behind them. Helen recognized Abby as the reporter. Now her mind raced on and on about what Earl talked about last night. He was a military man now. She was accepted to law school next year. Only phone calls and letters, maybe a chance to be together during the holidays. Plus a new way to send messages over the computer--electronic mail. A very sober discussion is how her father would describe it, thought Helen. Earl was just presenting the facts. How long would a long distance relationship last? He wouldn't sleep in her bed because he didn't want it to be the only time he did so. Helen did not know the words to say after Earl told her that. Did she love him or not? There was no declaration of love by either of them the night before. That only meant she was afraid to tell him or tell herself she did not love him. Helen knew which one it was and she knew it well before Earl arrived. Helen knew why she had so much difficulty concentrating on her studies. But knowing did not relieve her fear. Knowing brought no relief whatsoever. And now, this reporter stalking Earl.

"She's going to attempt to touch my soul," said Earl, following Helen's directions and turning left onto a busy thoroughfare. The restaurant was about two miles away on the left. KK and B stood for Katrina's Kitchen and Bistro (sometimes). It was Helen's favorite place to eat and meet her girlfriends for a glass of wine.

"Meaning what?" asked Helen.

"Meaning she believes she can persuade me to believe I'm a savior and she should be the one to tell the world," said Earl.

"I've never asked you what you think about all this, have I?" said Helen.

"You can ask me anything, anytime you'd like," he said, wanting to beg her to ask him anything. Helen pointed at Katrina's. Earl glanced in the rearview mirror. The van's turn light began to blink. Abby joined them at the restaurant entrance.

"This is Helen," said Earl. Abby extended her hand and Helen's initial hesitation set an immediate tone between them. Earl asked for a corner table. They sat down in silence, Abby facing Earl, Helen to Earl's right. The waitress was chatty and friendly, serving them all coffee and ice water. The menu was on the far wall in large red print letters.

"We'd like to have a cup of coffee first before we order," said Earl. The waitress offered a broad smile and bounced to another table to clear plates. Abby hid her frustration well--she was starving and seeking a way to control the situation. It was busy but there were still tables available. The chartreuse and brown trim walls made the place barely memorable. It was filled with women—mostly students and those whose life styles did not require them to work. Abby knew why the waitress was beaming approaching their table.

"Look, this is awkward, I know, but give me twenty minutes and I'll pay for breakfast," said Abby, taking one of her recorders out and placing in the middle of the table. "It's off, until you agree to let me turn it on," she said.

"Does Helen know who I am?" asked Abby.

"You're the weather reporter," said Helen, speaking up, determined not just to be a hanger on.

"I told her you were the reporter in Texas and Florida. She recognized you from television as well," said Earl, staring directly at Abby. She had made no attempt to cover up her gray brown circles under her eyes. Earl made no attempt to convey any other information with his stare. Helen and Abby sipped coffee nervously; Helen added more half and half. Earl's coffee was untouched.

"You have an opportunity to---no wait---let me start again---we have an opportunity to tell this story to all of America. My network is giving me an eight-minute exclusive during the prime evening slot. Tens of millions will be watching."

"It's not much of a story," said Earl. "We both know that. Deceit, that's what it will turn out to be."

"Not if we don't deceive them," said Abby. "Waitress! Sorry, I've had shit to eat for two days and I'm starving," said Abby, waving down the bouncy young woman. Abby ordered like a man, with bacon and turkey sausage. Helen's egg white vegetarian frittata would take a few extra minutes and Earl ordered a bowl of oatmeal and a side of cantaloupe with a tall glass of grapefruit juice.

"I'm going to confess," declared Abby, finishing her coffee and grabbing the table coffee pot to pour another cup. She did not ask if anyone wanted a refill. Helen reached for the pot after she put it down. Abby and Helen's eyes met for an instant and Abby apologized.

"I'm going to confess on camera that you are my son," she said. Helen stared at Earl. Earl stared at his mother.

"Confess? Confessing you're my mother? What else are you going to say?" Earl asked. He appeared like flint, his voice low and monotone.

"This is your mother?" said Helen, her jaw slack and eyes squinting in pain.

"Perfect time for me to find out what you've been tellin' people about me, Earl," said Abby, ignoring Helen.

"He told me nothing about you. I know about you from Earl's father, who was a friend of my father," blurted Helen.

"Breakfast everyone!" said the bouncy waitress, both hands full of plates. She laid them out with skill, announcing each order as she placed them in front of them. Abby asked for Tabasco sauce and a fresh pot of coffee.

"Ahhh. Prison buddies?" Earl nudged Helen's foot beneath the table. Helen glanced at Earl and he closed his eyes for a few seconds. He drank half of his lukewarm coffee in one take.

"Helen's father is dead," said Earl, not waiting for Helen to take the bait.

"Sorry honey. I mean it--really," said Abby, digging into her breakfast, her West Texas twang more prevalent than Earl ever remembered. Chomping on bacon, she continued, "Anyway, I'm going to confess that I left you all before your father got all caught up in that funny business at his company— and why I ran away from you all to be a reporter..." Abby left all table manners somewhere in west Texas and ate as if she was going to miss the most important event in her life.

"Are you asking for his permission?" said Helen, incredulous.

"I am," said Abby, pouring her third cup of coffee. A bead of sweat hung from her left temple, as if waiting for official clearance to drop. Helen fixated on the sweat bead, wishing Abby would melt.

"Who are you confessing to?" asked Earl. He felt remarkably calm and did not know why. He wanted her to talk and talk.

"You, him—your father I mean, Amy, every single person in the U. S of A."

"And you're not going to try to tell anyone that I am anything other than your son?" Wiping the last drying yolk from her plate with her last piece of dry wheat toast, she said, "Of course I'm going to tell them I think you're special. America is going to see you are special because I'm going to tell them you are my good son." Helen ate in silence, as if she was eating alone, now dying to just eat alone. Finally, Earl lifted his spoon and began to eat his oatmeal. The Mexican water boy brought them a fresh pot of coffee.

"Listen to me, America is always looking for someone like you. You are exactly what America breeds...and needs! Mother leaves, father goes to prison in a high profile corporate greed scandal, daughter wanders aimlessly from lousy man to idiot man, son joins the military and starts saving people. I mean Earl, my God, it's perfect! If you aren't the quintessential American savior I don't know who the hell is!" Abby's lips quivered with excitement. She wiped her brow with her well used napkin. She was dying for a cigarette.

"What did Amy say about this?" said Earl.

"You're sister loved it! C'mon Early, Amy absolutely loved the idea!"

"And Dad?"

"That's another thing I'm countin' on you for, Earl---I know how close you are to the man." Helen excused herself and left the table, telling Earl she'd be back in a few minutes.

Abby leaned across the table. "Earl, please, I *need* this real, real bad. Regardless of what you think I am because of what I did, I need this bad. This is it for me. I can't help myself—honestly I can't."

"I am not a savior."

"Dammit Earl!" Abby's barking voice stopped most conversations in the restaurant. As if on cue from an invisible maestro, the rest of the patrons began eating and talking again.

"You *are* a savior Earl, people believe in themselves again because of you," whispered Abby. "Listen to me, I am a reporter and I talked to all kinds of people in Lubbock and Panama City—asking what they thought about what you did. They cried when they spoke to me, Earl...Dammit, they cried."

"Earl, here's what I've learned—everybody—and I do mean everyone—has desires. Some...No, in fact very few desires can actually be met. Most of their desires remain just dreams or they try to live through someone who desires the same thing. People--doesn't matter whether they know it or not--have not one single original thought in their minds. What they want is what they see that some other person already has. I'm no different from all the rest. You, I can't quite figure out yet, but I'm bettin' you're the same as everyone else. But, what you've done and how you've done it has a very, very high appeal factor to people. What I mean is…People want to be like you, and if they can't, they want to believe they can be like you. Because, seeing someone who's good and wanting to be that someone who's also good—I believe *that* to be a good thing. And the fact that most can't be good all the time--well--maybe *hoping* to be good is all they can ever achieve. Can't help them any further than that. But you *have* helped them Earl… When they see you and know your story…You understand what I'm talkin' about?" They sat in silence until Abby saw Helen returning.

"Earl, you don't hate me, do you?" whispered his mother.

"I kept you locked away—because I was afraid I'd hate you."

"Am I still locked away?"

"No. But I am not a savior. Find the widow of the bus driver. The one who died with his son in Lubbock. I want to talk to her."

"And when I do? Will you agree?" Abby's negotiation with her son tightened her heart.

Helen returned and before sitting down said, "Earl, we should go—right? To get those things done you needed to do before you leave?" Earl smiled at Helen. Abby watched Earl.

"At least let me know where you're going to be stationed next," said his mother.

"Let me know your decision real soon, please….Please Earl?"

"I'll talk to Dad about it tomorrow—how's that?"

223

"Alright, fine. Fine. But I have a very limited window of opportunity here. Here's my card with my number to my new phone." She produced a gray cellular phone from her handbag.

"Call me."

"See you soon?" said Abby, standing up, hoping for some kind of response, maybe a hug, from Earl.

"Sure," he said, and extended his hand. Abby offered hers, and he carefully shook her hand. Departing, Helen said nothing. Outside, Helen asked, "What are you going to do?"

"I'm going to think about nothing in particular, except what you and I decide to do for the rest of the day."

Chapter 39

Bartholomew noticed little change when he arrived to meet Julia Davenport. He did not visit the university library when he and his father met her for lunch last time. She insisted it was her turn to buy lunch, as it had been his father's insistence when calling on Ms. Davenport enroute to the West Coast. Bartholomew was irritated he had to visit her at all. Not because he disliked her, but because she was her father's friend, not Bartholomew's. Plus the fact his father demanded his mother not know of the visit. His father said, "It's only lunch, for God's sake. Can you do me this one favor and let her treat you to lunch?"

Making the road trip even more irritating, he had to go for an overnight visit to his uncle, Reverend Delroy. His mother said Delroy was terribly impressed with him and would be honored if he stopped by. "He'll give you the royal treatment, he promised your father. And I know he will at that." All Bartholomew wanted was to get up to Alaska and start flying.

He left early morning, knowing he'd arrive in Steubenville well before lunch and have to find something to do until then. Bartholomew could not wait to get this cross-country drive over with. He was growing to loath road trips. His mother rose early to feed him a country breakfast to start him off. He was not hungry, yet ate to please her. His father joined her as he finished packing his last suitcase in his truck. He hugged them both, and both wished him a safe journey, his mother giving him an extra hug and kiss on the cheek as he opened the truck door.

"Call us when you get to Uncle Delroy's," insisted his mother.

Arriving early as expected, Bartholomew decided to go inside the library and find a quiet corner for a snooze. He did not want Ms. Davenport to see him. Two hours later, she nudged him gently awake. A student complained someone was snoring on the second floor by the west corner windows.

"I apologize, Ma'am. I woke up early this morning and thought I'd..."

"You think you're the only boy who fell asleep here?" He remembered her warm smile and soothing voice. "Hungry?"

"Umm, yes..." he lied, "But I'd sure like to buy you lunch."

"Thanks all the same, but that's not the deal. I'll meet you at the entrance in five minutes. We'll take my car." Lunch was at her house, in an established neighborhood near the university. The day turned overcast, although rain did not appear imminent. Julia's house was old, perhaps early fifties, and Bartholomew noticed it was well kept. It had been recently painted, in an off yellow, not too bright, with sea blue window trim and eaves. The small front yard was mowed and the summer flowers on both sides of the sidewalk lined the porch. Wax Begonias, Impatiens, and Morning Glories were stuffed in their beds on either side of the porch steps, all brilliant in their colors. Julia parked short of the detached garage and Bartholomew followed her into the living room. There were photos on the mantel, but none seemed to be recent. No apparent husband or children. Photos of arm-in-arm adults, aunts and uncles maybe, maybe cousins. Bartholomew was nervous and impatient. He was out of place, as if he stepped into a complete stranger's home. She in fact was a complete stranger to him, he knew and it made no difference to Bartholomew if Ms. Davenport felt the same way or not. This stop was fulfilling an obligation, nothing more. He longed for a couple beers.

The dining table off to the left of the living room was already set for two. Julia entered with a bowl of German style potato salad and a plate of sliced cold cuts and cheese.

"Back with the condiments in a second. Iced tea alright?" Bartholomew said iced tea would be fine and offered to help her bring in the rest of lunch. She told him to pick either place at the table and make himself comfortable.

Entering the dining room with her hands full, she said, "I don't often have guests. When I do, I look forward to cooking...and to make sure they don't go away hungry. Didn't have to cook much for lunch, but I did make the potato salad."

She brought out enough food to feed Bartholomew for three days. "Help yourself, and don't make some wimpy sandwich. Build one large enough to satisfy. I'll make you a couple sandwiches for your trip afterwards. Eat your lunch and I'll tell you why your father asked you to visit me. " Bartholomew could hardly wait for her to spill her guts. The cold cuts were deli fresh and delicious. And the potato salad— Bartholomew could have eaten the entire bowl. Real ingredients, none of the low calorie shit, he thought. He forgot he wasn't hungry. Julia ate slowly, observing Bartholomew.

"Fantastic lunch, Miss Davenport."

"It's Julia." He nodded as he chomped down on the second half of the sandwich.

"Dropping your vehicle off in L.A. or Seattle?"

"Seattle."

"Commercial flight into Anchorage?" Bartholomew
nodded as he sipped his tea to wash down the remaining portion
of the sandwich. He loved salami and prosciutto.

Julia excused herself and returned to the kitchen.
Bartholomew was lost in epicurean lust. Julia soon returned
with a full glass of Chardonnay. He noticed but it did not
register. It was noon on a workday and she did not bother to
offer him a glass. She barely touched the food on her plate. She
sipped her wine.

"Bartholomew, I was your father's first wife. We
married when we were Airmen, and divorced almost two years
later." Bartholomew froze, as if numbed by an agent that left
him unable to move, but remain fully conscious. He wanted to
push himself away from the table but was unable.

"I asked for a divorce because he started an affair with
your mother. I told you I knew her. We were all stationed
together. She's a sweetheart of a woman. What's not to like?"
She finished her glass of Chardonnay and returned to the
kitchen. Bartholomew tensed and rose from the table. He
walked into the living room, looking out the front picture
window. Julia returned with a full glass and asked him to sit
down on the sofa. He did as she requested. She stood before
him. She was an attractive woman, but dressed as if she either
dismissed her beauty or was ashamed of it. Her porcelain skin
made it difficult to tell her age. Bartholomew loved the look of
women. He loved the touch of their skin. He imagined Julia in a
low cut dress.

"Your father made an unforgivable transgression and
when he confessed I demanded he leave that day. I divorced

him as soon as the system would allow. I rejected his apologies, his tears, and his anguish. We were both 22—no excuse in my mind, but we were at an age where we thought we knew everything there is to know. At least I did. I was one cocky girl back then. And I got crushed. "

"My father asked you to tell me all this?"

"Bartholomew, I am so grateful he asked me to tell you." She smiled and sat beside him.

"This makes no sense to me. I'm sorry."

"No need to be. Your only job now is to listen. And I promise not to babble."

"You're father and I became friends again, some years after he married your mother. I will tell you this; I forgave him because I thought it was the right thing to do. I did not want to carry the hurt for the rest of my life. It seemed ridiculous, and the older I get the more convinced I am that it would be ridiculous to carry that pain. He's got pain too, you know. "

"Now…the reason you're here, visiting me…." Anger began to well up inside Bartholomew.

"Don't tell me—it's because he's afraid I'm like him and he doesn't want me to be like him. I will tell you something—it's too late. I already know what kind of man I am…I'm for the present. The past has no control over me. I will not let it." He rose from the sofa and asked her to take him back to the university.

"I could have been your mother. I was pregnant and thought not to have a child under the circumstance. I could have been your mother. And your father never knew I was pregnant."

"Yes, he wanted me to talk to you about the seriousness of a man and woman. Becoming a singular essence of humanity. He wanted me to tell you about that—and forgiveness. I've never met a more gracious man than your father. I forgave him because he had the courage to seek it. And until now, I longed to talk to you."

Bartholomew froze. He reached for the sofa as if suffering from a stroke. His view of women hardened, even more so. Women simply weren't worth the extraordinary effort required to figure out what satisfied them. In the long run, satisfying a woman was beyond a desirable reach. Bartholomew was committed to the short run and his thoughts remained close to the present—thinking just far enough to avoid getting jammed into an uncomfortable circumstance. *And never, never dwell on what's already done.* Every football coach he ever knew told him that. It was sound advice for playing football, flying fighters, and going about day to day life, he thought. He was collecting and applying aphorisms because between football coaches and instructor pilots there was more than enough sound advice to do things well enough to stand out and have a say about things. He loved to convert an aphorism into an action, as he loved converting a third and five to a first down. Or, as he had just learned in F-15 training, executing a perfect air-to-air intercept to a blind conversion on a clueless adversary. But completing a first down or a perfect fighter intercept was much simpler than converting an aphorism into a desirable result. He knew this to be true. It was knowledge that was available to anyone who could apply that knowledge. With his skills, he thought, he could do just fine in this world. Bartholomew wanted more than anything to be an expert applicator of knowledge. Not to merely possess knowledge, but to convert knowledge into achieving desire. As long as it was worth it, he mused.

"I'll get my purse," said Julia, returning to the kitchen. Once inside her car, she said, "You don't have to worry about being just like your father. Strike that worry off your list." She did not bother to fix him extra sandwiches. Bartholomew guessed no amount of thank-yous would ease the tension between them. He offered his thanks anyway for her excellent lunch and hospitality. Julia said nothing. He left her and started up his truck and drove on to Kentucky.

Chapter 40

Bartholomew never visited Kentucky. His uncle moved from Virginia five years ago, seeking a new start in a new state. According to his father, in Virginia things got a bit sketchy for Delroy James. Funny name, thought Bartholomew, especially since he chose to be called by his middle name. His mother remained fond of Delroy, regardless if she knew him growing up as Billy. William D. James. Sounded upstanding, thought Bartholomew, giving no thought this time why he demanded that he not be called Bart. He wanted everyone to spend the time necessary to pronounce his name. Other than be a Reverend, Bartholomew knew nothing about him. He never met his uncle until high school—his father only mentioning that he never married and never stayed in touch with family until the past few years—where he seemed to become a regular part of his father's life. At least by telephone.

Three hundred miles to Uncle Delroy's. Bartholomew figured to get there by 730pm, late enough for dinner and late enough to beg off any small talk until the next day. The drive was uninteresting and under a light gray overcast. The weather threatened to clear, evidenced by occasional rays of sun through slivers of cloud break, but never materialized. At least it wasn't raining, he thought, fumbling through the radio dial, trying to get any college station that might offer some relief from the same whiny male vocalists whining about being so bored. He was beginning to listen only to country stations—if there was any respectable rock and roll on the airways Bartholomew failed to locate it. Nashville country was predictable and proudly so. But the voices and harmonies were outstanding and there always seemed to be a little lyrical twist to the same old story line. He much preferred the attitude of country vocalists to the whiny, emasculated singers who swore they were rockers. Stringy and skinny and whiny—that's all they offered? Their compressed guitar sound was the same for nearly every band on radio. He swore the rock music was better in his father's day, and that fact angered him. He thought about lunch with Julia Davenport and why she never remarried. He tried not to think about wanting to do her doggy style. He wondered about what Laurie Tillerbrook was doing now. He glanced in the rear view mirror and smiled. He surprised himself being able to nail her two nights ago. God, she screamed like she wanted it all night long. I needed that bad, he thought and he never wanted to see her again. Bartholomew wondered about Earl, about where he was about now. Bastard left without a goodbye. But Bartholomew cut him slack. The news people were bearing down on him, just like in Lubbock. Bartholomew could not wait to get on his way and drop his truck off in Houston and fly the rest of the way to Anchorage. He saw nothing of interest along the way.

Rising Ministries was not difficult to find. The church complex was a grey tinted glass office building that was never completed due to lack of confidence, poor market research and hasty investments. It was the spacious parking lot and adjoining three story parking garage that Reverend Delroy James keyed on. His pitch to investors was simple, "If I can't get five hundred members in one year then shut me down and do something else with the property." He and his two partners had thoroughly researched the property, the economic outlook of the neighborhood and city, and the overall health of a half dozen congregations within a twenty-five mile radius. None had the capacity or the vision to build thousand member congregations. Delroy's would be the first in the area and his aggressiveness impressed the investors to agree to pursue TV licensing. Delroy had the look, the oratory skill, and the acting talent to attract and keep a live audience. Delroy convinced the investors he could do the same with a TV audience. "Just give me a couple giant transmitting towers on the highest hills, plus a satellite deal and we're off."

Bartholomew pulled into the parking lot at 730pm. It was Friday night and Rising Ministries appeared closed, save for one white Cadillac, older, but clean and well cared for. Bartholomew got out and stretched his legs, walking around the Cadillac, peering inside. He found the double glass doors open to the building and walked towards the stairs leading up to a second floor. Bartholomew called out and up towards the light from the bottom of the stairs.

"Won't be two secs," replied his uncle, and seconds later the light went out and Bartholomew could just distinguish his uncle starting down the stairs.

"Found the place, I see," he said, and extended his hand, shaking Bartholomew's like a man wanting to be convincing.

"Good to see you, son. You must be hungry enough to eat a mule."

"I am at that."

"How was the drive?"

"Not bad. Easy enough to find your church."

"Ministry," corrected his uncle.

"Not as formal as a church, more like a gathering place. You know, like Christ intended."

"Sure." Bartholomew watched his uncle set the alarm and lock and double-check the front doors.

"Follow me to my place, we'll get you settled in real quick and then we'll go out for some supper." Afterword, Uncle Delroy drove them to a local BBQ place that played country music from a jukebox. The place was packed and full of cigarette smoke, mainly coming from the bar. They stopped by the bar first and Uncle Delroy got the bartender's attention to bring two beers. He handed one to Bartholomew and said, "Welcome to Kentucky." He clinked the neck of Bartholomew's beer bottle with his own and took a fast sip. Bartholomew finished half the bottle in one long pull. "One more, please!" barked Uncle Delroy, with excellent timing, for the bartender had just finished placing cash in the register and turned around. Bartholomew thanked his Uncle and finished off his first beer. Delroy swapped the second beer, paid, and left a two-dollar tip. He motioned Bartholomew over to an empty high-top table for two and sat on one of tall stools that offered full view of the bar. Bartholomew told his uncle he'd prefer to stand for a bit after the long drive.

"You figured maybe we were raised Baptists, your Dad and I?" asked Uncle Delroy.
Bartholomew thought no such thing. His father never mentioned anything other than being Protestant and Bartholomew never cared what denomination he was born into. He thought that by not knowing too much about how his parents were raised he would not be burdened by their past and therefore free to choose his way. He gave his parents credit for never mentioning what church their parents attended. It was not rationalizing within a sphere of conscious ignorance. It was a

realization that some knowledge is not worth knowing, and worse, knowing it would endanger his freedom of choice. And as much as he became interested in religion as a subject, it was his love of history that fed his interest in Christianity. Christianity was to him a subset of human history—that's all. He decided not to think why he was alive because that was wasted effort. He thought about what he wanted to do while he was alive, and as long as he could he wanted to obtain what his talents could obtain. If he didn't possess them outright thought Bartholomew, he'd imitate those that did possess them. He knew one of his talents was keen observation—he believed he could make time stop in order to observe the minute and subtle details of human beings—their movements, their voice inflection, their habits. Bartholomew was convinced he could almost read a person's mind if he could study them long enough. He was focused now on studying his Uncle Delroy.

"Protestant, that's all I was told," replied Bartholomew, now realizing why he asked the question.

"Humanity and alcohol are forever intertwined, not to mention some lucky species of animals too. Dogs and horses. Can't abuse the booze or become a slave to it. Same can be said for all the other things that trap humans. Well, actually, we trap ourselves and then cry like spoiled children about our miserable lot in life. Well, it ain't a miserable life at all, and to suggest beer is the devil's drink is selling us way, way too short. Don't you think so, Bartholomew?"

"I do."

"I drink beer and I drink bourbon and I am better off for it, because I know myself and my fellow man better because I drink with them."

"Sure you're not Catholic?" Delroy laughed hard. He pounded the table with his open hand.

"How long were you in the Marines?" The question reduced the smile from Delroy's face and he took another short sip of beer.

"Five years—got out shortly after the bombing in Beirut. Recall that tragedy? Too young, maybe. God, I still swell with anger thinkin' about it."

"Were you there when it happened?"

"I was sent over to help with the recovery and all the rest. Changed me, that whole experience, it surely changed me."

"Why'd you get out of the Marines?" asked Bartholomew. The bar was now packed with the Friday night regulars. Delroy leaned in close.

"I was asked to leave on less than honorable circumstance, not a dishonorable discharge, no sir, but then I didn't get an honorable discharge either. That fact changes a man's path in life and forces some tough thinkin' about yourself. Did for me anyway."

"Dad never said much about what you did after you left."

"Which is a roundabout way of askin' me how I got into this line of work," said Delroy, looking at Bartholomew straight in the eyes.

"Sales, my son, sales," Delroy laughed out loud.

"Started in the used car business, because no one asks much about your past or much cares either, as long as you can move merchandise. And I can move merchandise," bragged Delroy, sticking out his tongue and pointing at it. Now he pretended to smooth back his thick hair. He flashed a white toothy smile.

"People always want something, Bartholomew, it is a natural fact of actual nature. And most times they don't know what they want. These ain't no secrets son, they're just facts of nature. If a man or woman yearns then that's when Delroy earns."

"Plus, it pays off in all other ways when God is in the picture, because selling God is what God wants us to do. It's a win win." As if on stage, Delroy finished his beer, banged the empty on the table, and said,

"And that's my story. Let's have one more beer and get some BBQ takeout."

"I'm buyin' the beers," said Bartholomew, lifting off his stool like a rocket. Delroy watched him tapping the waitress's shoulder. She was a cute, big-bottomed brunette. Tall, maybe a jock in high school thought Delroy. He watched how Bartholomew engaged with the waitress. As hectic as the bar had become, the waitress slowed her pace, listened to whatever Bartholomew said, smiled as if in want, and then dashed off to the bar to fill her orders. Bartholomew hit the men's room, and timed his return to lift the beers from her tray and replace them with a twenty and keep-your-change wink. Beguiled, thought Delroy, and he smiled as Bartholomew returned to his stool.

"I figure I'm really here in Kentucky because you're dyin' to ask about Earl—isn't that right?"

"Well, what do you think Bartholomew—does your friend have a gift, does he possess something unique, something mysterious--something someone would desire to also have? Let me ask you this, why is he your friend? You two seem awful different from one another." Bartholomew sipped his beer, eyeing the waitress making her rounds.

"Thanks for the beer."

"Anytime, Uncle Delroy."

"You'd be excellent in my profession, you know that," said Delroy.

"I'm just fine workin' on being a fighter pilot."

"Well, for now, maybe. Your friend Earl, I'm not so sure I see him as a fighter pilot."

"What do you know about fighter pilots?" asked Bartholomew.

"Not tryin' to get you fired up at all Bartholomew, not at all."

"You think he's preacher material, is that it?"

"I think he's unique and so do other people. That reporter gal—she thinks he's something as well. And I think you believe it too."

"Believe exactly what?"

"You're fascinated by Earl, and you're maybe jealous of him too, but that doesn't matter as much to you as tryin' to figure out why he has you for a friend."

They finished their beer in silence, watching the regulars laugh and back slap and spill beer. Stepping out into the night Bartholomew felt the humidity. It seemed to tighten around him. Or was it this place? Either way, it was a clear vibe for Bartholomew to grow an itch to leave and get on the road. The BBQ aroma filled the car before leaving the parking lot. He hoped his Uncle accounted for his powerful hunger. Pulling out onto the street his Uncle continued the conversation he started in the bar, "So, deceit and desire, is that what it's all about?" The street was now busy with Friday night goings on.

"Deceit?" asked Bartholomew, not wanting to continue the conversation, but feeling obligated.

"Exactly. Deceit."

"Deceive oneself, deceive others. To satisfy the desire. Right, Bartholomew?"

"Is this a Bible lesson?"

"Not at all, my man, not at all. It's not a lesson; it's a fact staring us in the face since the beginning of man. I'm just sayin' the fact out loud—to you—here in my Cadillac." Reverend Delroy laughed. Bartholomew wanted to say nothing. He wanted nothing more than to tear into the rib and chicken combo and have his face smeared in thick BBQ sauce. My God, the smell is making me delirious. *Add that 'D' word to your subject list*, thought Bartholomew. He could eat BBQ ribs for an hour straight. Bartholomew could not stay silent. He could not sit and just listen to the Reverend Delroy James.

"Here's my confession Bartholomew—I'm trying not to deceive anymore. And the first person I'm tryin' not to deceive is myself. That's my first task, my most important task. You understand Bartholomew?" Delroy made every green light for the next two miles. He turned right into his neighborhood. Bartholomew understood deceit and wanted to spend no time contemplating any sliver of it.

"And that's why I got into the preaching profession," said the Reverend. The garage door took forever to rise. His uncle switched off the ignition and turned to look at his nephew.

"Realize we deceive and---wham!---desire suddenly fades away!" Delroy's eyes blazed.

"Ok, I get it, Uncle Delroy," said Bartholomew. His uncle didn't mind his nephew not wanting to talk about deceit and desire. His point had been made.

"I went to Bible College. I started reading different subjects. Changed my life again. And I thank the Lord Jesus for that."

"Enough of that, right Bartholomew? Let's chow down." His uncle talked nothing but football and how he followed Bartholomew and his team through all four seasons. Bartholomew added nothing to the conversation because his uncle never asked him to join in. It was a soliloquy, not a conversation. Bartholomew figured he'd been alone for some time. He knew his uncle was married when he was young, but that didn't last.

Later, Bartholomew lay on top of the guest bed, staring at the ceiling. Now he felt he was a stranger in his own flesh. Soon after, he fell asleep and dreamed of the waitress from that evening. He dreamt he was kind to her and she thought he was the most romantic man she ever met. She invited him into her bed and Bartholomew ran away. Then he woke and listened to rain pelt the roof. He fell back asleep as a smoky dawn met Kentucky.

Saturday was rainy. Gray clouds hung low on the horizon, sagging from the weight of the rain, a pregnant swelling until the clouds could no longer bear the weight. Early grocery shopping for the road trip came soon after a cereal and juice breakfast. Bartholomew called his parents and let them know all was well. The rest of the morning was spent at Rising Ministries. Reverend Delroy introduced his nephew to his staff, all women in their early thirties, with the exception of the soundman who doubled as the janitor and routine maintenance man. Dexter's tall and wide frame provided sleight-of-hand to obscure his obesity. He was not much older than Bartholomew. A friendly smile and easy disposition. The women were overweight, two cute ones and one too fat to tell if she was cute or not. Bartholomew observed all the women were attentive to everything Reverend Delroy said. He was definitely in charge and decisions came easy. Reverend Delroy disappeared into his small office to finish preparing for his weekly sermon. Bartholomew tagged along with Dexter the soundman as he made his equipment checks. They talked some about themselves. While making his rounds, Dexter provided brief technical details to Bartholomew a few times when he thought necessary. Bartholomew remained attentive, asking no questions. The sky remained thick with gray clouds and rain persisted well into the afternoon.

At three pm, Reverend Delroy emerged from his office, handing sheets of paper to one of his staff and told her he'd see them all tomorrow morning. Now that the musicians were on rehearsal break, Bartholomew soon dozed off in the back row. His uncle nudged him awake just as Bartholomew's jaw drew slack.

"Your penance is complete. Let's get something to eat," said Uncle Delroy, chuckling. His staff giggled watching him wake his nephew. "I'll make a salad and we'll order a pizza. What'd you think of the choir and band? Don't they sound absolutely inspirational?" On the way home, Uncle Delroy explained to Bartholomew about his Sunday. It is a full day of churching and preaching, and pressing the flesh of his congregation. And the Reverend loved every second of Sunday.

"Sunday is the grand finale of the week. We conduct church and I go and seek out those who are new to the congregation, greet them with a giant hug because that's what they're really looking for—some reassurance that they are indeed on the right path in life—and then see if I can persuade the ones of means to help out at Rising Ministries. With their pocket books, I mean. With God's help, I can find the shy generous ones. They're my favorites." Bartholomew told his uncle about tagging along with Dexter while he conducted all his Saturday duties and equipment checks.

"That Dexter is one giant heart of a man, but I don't think he's cut out to be a preacher, and Lord knows he's got his giant heart set on being one. And so does his fiancé." Reverend Delroy paused before saying softly, "We'll have to pray some more on that one, yes sir. More prayer required."

At home, his uncle washed up and began preparing a butter lettuce salad, giving Bartholomew instructions to call Fiore's Pizza and order a large thin crust pepperoni and mushroom plus a sausage, onion, and black olive pizza.

"No beer for me on Saturday night. I have to be runnin' on all cylinders tomorrow. Tomorrow night is different. But then, I don't suspect you'll be staying tomorrow night—that right Bartholomew?"

"I have to hit the road early tomorrow."

"And after pizza, I have to study my passages I'm going to use tomorrow. It's an early night for me. Plus, I dream after eatin' that Fiore's pizza. Must be the pepperoni."

After grace, they settled in the dining room to eat.

"Great pizza," said Bartholomew.

"How's the green salad?" asked his uncle.

"That's fine too."

"Wasn't sure if you were allergic to greens," said his uncle. Bartholomew left the table to grab his third beer from the fridge. Clearly not allergic to beer, observed Delroy, smiling to himself.

"You ever think of marrying?" asked Bartholomew.

"I was married once, long time ago—didn't last past a year," said his uncle without hesitation. He looked at Bartholomew, letting a pause catch his nephew's attention.

"I'd love to marry again. Always wanted a family. A big family. I have a few prospects here in town. "

"From your congregation?"

"Yes, and that's the conflict. A couple gals seem very interested, the way they gossip to my staff and all. They're both divorced with children. They're lookin' for some stability first, a husband second. Or so it seems to me. I'd like to find a nice widow. A new start if you will—for both of us. Young widows are kinda scarce—I guess that's a good thing. I figure I may have to settle for an older widow."

"You pray on that Uncle?" Delroy looked up quickly and stared at Bartholomew.

"I don't," he replied, revealing a small smile.

"And I don't have guests that often either. But I'm grateful for your visit. And I'm glad you asked about me. I appreciate that."

"Think you and your friend Earl would accept my offer to speak to my congregation—about your experiences in the tornado and hurricane?"

"Can't begin to say Uncle Delroy. And I'd rather not, if you don't mind. "

"I know it was tough to come upon that young boy and his father in that tipped over school bus. I know that was a hurtin' experience. I can understand why you may not want to think about that day." Bartholomew used to think why he never thought about the father and son. He could not remember when he stopped thinking about why he never thought about them.

"Will you do me the good favor then and ask Earl if I can call him soon and talk to him about it? I'd find a way to pay for his travel expenses. Tell him that too, please."

"Sure."

"You have a special friend in that young man. Something to think about."

Bartholomew teamed with Delroy to clean up after supper. Bartholomew went outside to throw the pizza boxes in the trashcan. He noticed the rain stopped and a brilliant quarter moon was on the rise, peaking in and out of dissipating clouds. It was humid, but there was a soft chill in the air. Bartholomew knew he would be on the road very early the next morning. He could not wait. He lingered outside, recalling what his high school football coach said to him when he was just a sophomore.

"You can still your mind, I can tell the way you focus on executing a play. That's a gift boy, don't you take it for granted. You can also read a teammate's mind. I can tell the way you observe the running backs and receivers. You read their face and I bet you can hear them sweat. We're countin' on you to read the opposing teams' faces when they're staring you down across the line of scrimmage. So if you need to audible then you are authorized to audible. That's also a gift Bartholomew James-

-and don't you take that for granted." He smiled at the brilliant moon.

Chapter 41

While waiting for his squadron sponsor to pick him up at the airport Bartholomew called his parents to let them know he arrived in Anchorage. His mother answered the phone. She thanked him for calling and asked about the weather.

"It's cold and dark."

"Your father's on a trip. I'll tell him when he checks in."

"Bartholomew, did you know Laura Tillerbrook is pregnant? I guess I mean, did she tell you she was pregnant when you took her out?"

"No."

"Well she says she's definitely pregnant. Why'd she call me you think?"

Chapter 42

The eight-minute profile piece was a one of a kind event. The kind of television event that was such a phenomenon the network repeated the piece twice more over a week's time to allow those who had only heard or read about it to see for themselves. For once the network had an amazing secret to reveal and for once they were true to their word. The climax was Abby's breakdown in revealing she was Earl's mother. The revelation left nothing else to say for a brief moment, and so succeeded in leaving the audience with gaping mouths and minds charged with such scintillation they called their family and best friends to see if they watched the night's news. Then for three months every pundit in print, on the pulpit, and on television had something to say about what constitutes being a savior in America today. Abby accepted the offer to host her own half hour daytime talk show on the largest cable TV network in the United States. In three months, the Abby Westmoreland Show became the best new show on TV.

Reverend Delroy James had captured almost a thousand new faces and filled Rising Ministries three weeks after the first showing of Abby's TV profile piece. The investors were ecstatic. Now Reverend Delroy was a TV star for the Lord.

THREE YEARS LATER

Chapter 43

"The night was dark and I was sweating like a man on fire. The leather palms of my flight gloves were soaked and I was more scared of getting an electrical shock than getting shot at." Bartholomew "Fiend" James seemed to never tire from starting his story the same way. *Thank God I'm not around to hear it very often,* thought Earl "Duke" Neuhaus. Karl "Tornado" Bergsten did not require Duke to say his thought aloud to also affirm the same sentiment. Now, without exception, Fiend's operatic telling of their experiences during the Kosovo War made "Duke" and "Tornado" wander off to a quiet corner of their squadron bar. Not so back in Italy where they operated out of an Italian air base on the Adriatic Coast. The hotel bar served as their watering hole in the early mornings after the night missions. The proprietor was only too happy to keep his bar open on demand for the Americans. His hotel was filled with American Air Force pilots and maintenance personnel and he could not be happier in a time of war. No Yugolsav fighter or bomber was ever going to cross the Adriatic and attack Italian bases. NATO made sure of that, thought the hotel proprietor.

Fiend was the flight lead and Tornado his wingman the night they fired on the MiG 29. In the end, they both were credited with half a kill. It was impossible to determine which of their missiles hit the MiG first. The MiG pilot ejected and survived. But neither Fiend nor Tornado saw much that night other than the white and orange flash flurry of AAA rounds piercing the darkness over the city whose homes and shops seemed to have every light on. It all played hell on their night vision. Every aircraft airborne was flying lights out and the night vision goggles weren't worth a damn with all the city lights on. Neither saw a fireball indicating missile impact of the MiG. Both had performed eight G evasive maneuvers away from their intended target since both had their radar warning receivers illuminated indicating they were being tracked by other enemy fighters stalking the skies. The mixture of fear and excitement induced such an adrenalin surge that neither could sleep for nearly thirteen hours after they landed and debriefed the mission. Fiend landed hard but caused no damage to the landing gear. Pranging onto the runway angered him. Any mistake he made flying angered him. He was having difficulty letting things go by the wayside. After Bosnia, Fiend accumulated his failures, failures only he recognized, and stacked them upon his shoulder for reasons he could not determine, which led to an escalating level of anger he found almost unable to contain within himself. Only Earl seemed to be able to keep him from regular outbursts. But Duke could do little to erase the underlying tone of anger from Fiend's outlook on just about everything. After finishing the story, Fiend joined Duke and Tornado. Duke made Fiend promise to call him by his name rather than his pilot callsign when they were by themselves.

"How come you never help me finish that story Tornado?" Bartholomew yanked Tornado's empty beer mug out of his hand and went to refill it.

"He's gotta quit doing that," said Tornado Bergsten. But all in all, he didn't mind too much. "He never refills your mug," said Tornado.

Duke said, "Mine's always near empty with warm beer. Fiend can't stand mixing warmed beer with fresh beer from the tap. Ruins the whole thing, according to him. I'll get one more beer and then I'm done." Duke waited until two other pilots filled their mugs. The squadron bar was emptying slowly, leaving the older pilots to carry on. The Majors and Lt. Cols were beginning to circle around the beer tap for their Friday night ritual of solving the world's problems while trying not to create new ones. It was a great tradition for those with the capacity to drink beer for hours on end. And most could.

Earl, Bartholomew, and Karl were new captains. The older cadre welcomed them to join in on the bullshit session. But tonight they hung out by themselves. Earl rejoined them and clinked his beer mug against theirs.

"I'm not going to Weapons School with you Bartholomew," said Earl. Karl could read the sadness in Earl's eyes. Earl took a healthy swig from his mug. Bartholomew didn't appear to be listening.

"Damn it, I know you're not goin', and that just pisses me off to no end."

"And you know why I'm not going, right?"

"Your Dad's sick."

"My Dad is dying and I'm the only one who can attend to him."

"Your sister Amy can't do it?"

"Your Mom can't go tend to him?"

Ignoring the first question, Earl then said, "Her?"

"Yeah, Earl—her."

"No."

"So you're the only one who can take care of him. How you gonna take care of him anyway?"

Karl interrupted, "Bartholomew, get a fucking grip, cut the bullshit and lay off it. You're being a douche-bag." Bartholomew flipped Karl off.

"It's *the* prize Earl! We made it Damnit! We're going to Weapons School! It's the only thing that should matter. We just gotta keep our shit straight during those six months and we're set!"

"I'm not going to make it this class. It's not that I lost a Weapons School slot. I can go in a later class."

"Bullshit!" cried Bartholomew, spitting beer as he yelled. "You're going on a non-flying humanitarian assignment. Get that—*non-flying*! How you gonna maintain any kind of proficiency—by playing fucking stupid video games?"

"I'll figure that out when the time comes." Bartholomew threw his beer mug down on tile floor, spraying glass shards everywhere.

"Fiend! What the fuck is your fucking problem?" The Ops Officer was not the kind to cross. He described his philosophy as: "Work hard, play hard—but if you go and get stupid on my watch I'll come down on you so fucking hard you'll be crying like a pussy when I'm done with you."

"We got it sir,' said Karl, directing Earl to take Bartholomew outside to settle down while he cleaned up the mess.

"No no, Tornado," barked the Ops Officer. "Fiend cleans up the mess. If you can't drink beer and bullshit without getting into some kind of hissy fit then the three of you are done for the night. Copy?"

"Copy, sir," said Karl. They cleaned up the mess together, said their goodbyes to the bar in accordance with the squadron bar exit ritual, collected their gear and walked out to the parking lot.

"At least come with me to the ABC," said Bartholomew, sulking.

"I'm going home," said Karl. Earl winced at the suggestion to go to the ABC. The Alaskan Bush Company was the last place he cared to spend time in. Bartholomew's latest girlfriend was one of the managers. The idea that Bartholomew's girlfriend was a manager at the most popular strip club in Anchorage was perhaps the only thing that offered a temporary respite from his anger.

"Two beers and we'll go," promised Bartholomew. "I'll pick you up in 45 minutes."

"No, I'm driving by myself and I'll meet you there in 45 minutes. If you're not there I'm out," warned Earl.

"See you in 45," said Bartholomew and quickened his lumbering pace towards his truck. He lived up to his Fiend callsign in Italy—not only chasing the local girls, but eating three restaurant meals a day, or the equivalent, when the eight hour combat missions forced him to eat two full meals at one sitting. Bartholomew was now a large fat ass. Gone were his sharp handsome features. The square chin had rounded out and was now accompanied by a second chin hanging like a titless utter. The crew chiefs on the flight line had a running bet when his G-suit zippers would pop off both thighs. In his full flying gear and G-suit he walked like a big fat man in a straight jacket.

The Wing Commander called their squadron commander and told him to get Fiend on the fat boy program ASAP or he wasn't going to Weapons School. The squadron commander had put off telling this to Fiend, instead giving Duke a chance to tell him first.

At the ABC Earl told Bartholomew exactly what Bartholomew pretended he did not want to hear. He wanted Earl to reach out to him. Bartholomew wanted Earl to save him. It took Earl three beers to say what he had to say. Earl stayed close to Bartholomew's ear in order not to shout over the Eighties rock-n-roll pumping out of the sound system. Bartholomew remained bowed over the bar, staring at his bottle, sometimes lifting his head to look at the dancers. He never looked at Earl. When his beer was finished, Earl laid two twenties on the bar. He grabbed Bartholomew's hand and made him shake his. Shaking his hand, Bartholomew held back the one thing he really wanted to tell Earl. That he and Amy had been talking for months and he persuaded her to come to Alaska as a surprise to attend Earl's fini-flight party tomorrow. She couldn't make it in time but was flying in the following day. Bartholomew wanted to tell Earl that he was very excited to see Amy. But Bartholomew could not tell Earl.

As Earl left, the hottest skinny blonde on stage strolled within six inches of Bartholomew's face, turned slowly around and bent over, spreading herself, licking her lips and winking at him between her big tight breasts and long thin legs. Bartholomew thought; she's just a stick with tits. He looked through her as if she wasn't there. He left the stool to find his manager girlfriend and tell her they were no longer.

Outside, Earl smelled the smoke blowing in from the encroaching forest fires up north. His eyes burned and he tasted ash. The fires made national news. That meant his mother was in Alaska, or would be soon.

Chapter 44

The summer had been unseasonably dry and careless campers were suspected. The Peters Springs fire spread south fast with the help of gusty winds and no rain. Residential areas ten miles north of Anchorage were in danger and most residents wasted no time finding somewhere else to stay, further south. The hotels were packed with summer tourists, many complaining out loud that their expensive Alaska vacation adventure had been ruined by some local campers. Turned out the campers were not local, but from Campbell, Ohio. They wanted to see bears in their native habitat. The locals called them stupid and that judgment infected their views about the rest of the tourists from the Lower 48. There was a perfectly good reason why they settled in Alaska thought many of the long timers--Sourdoughs they called themselves. And that was to get as far away from where they were from—the land of stupid people. Which is exactly what Landau Bertram, the sixty year old, no-holds barred, big mouth taxi driver, who loved nothing more than to drive and pontificate, told Abby when he dumped her and her luggage off at the entryway to the Captain Cook Hotel.

It did not take long for Abby to discover she and her team were an annoyance. Abby's small posse included a makeup and hairstylist gal as well as Danny, her long time cameraman. She also had a young, smart and ambitious personal assistant named Tiffany who led point on her interview assignments. Abby was still major league but competition is always ruthless she assessed, and the timing of the Alaskan forest fires and her son was perfect. Prior to their arrival in

Alaska, she led strategy sessions with Tiffany and Danny, with the objective of getting Earl close to the fires. And into the fire zone, if necessary. They had to act quickly she thought and she prayed for the winds to continue and the rain not to fall. Not that Abby wanted anyone hurt—only in proximity to near mortal danger. She believed God understood what she was trying to ask for. Or rather, she hoped God would understand. Abby's plan came to her showering off the eight hours sitting in airliners, next to giddy, fat tourists who could not wait to see their first bear in the wild. She wondered if the contempt was mutual. The plan was risky, and she knew the only way she could pull it off was with the full buy-in from her devoted cameraman.

Tiffany loved the deviousness of the plan. She lived for these moments, especially when observing Abby winding Danny around her finger. Tiffany knew that no matter how tight Abby wound him, she would never suffer from constricted blood flow. You can't constrict what you don't have, thought Tiffany.

Chapter 45

The helicopter pilot spotted an arm of fire reaching away from the main body of the burn area and approaching overlarge homes on acre tracts.

"I see it," shouted Abby through her headset, elbowing her cameraman.

"Can you find a place to set us down?" she asked.

"Miss Westmoreland, down there ain't a safe place to be," said the pilot.

"That's why we need to be down there, to report on the danger." The pilot turned around and Abby saw her reflection through his teardrop mirror shades. She liked what she saw, but not what she heard.

"That's a negative, Ma'am..." As the pilot returned to giving full attention to his flight path in front of him Abby turned to Danny and motioned to him they were going to drive up here and report. He quickly nodded and unfolding his map began to mark the location and familiarize himself with the roads leading to the fire. Getting around the roadblocks was going to be a problem, Danny thought, noting the intersections where he saw flashing lights from the highway patrol's cars. She reached over and kissed Danny on the cheek, squeezing his elbow, making him poke a hole through the map with his pencil. He pretended nothing happened, pretending to study the map in more detail.

Timing will be critical, as usual, sensed Abby. She thought about Tiffany's dinner with Bartholomew last night. That went well enough to get the squadron operations phone numbers. And Abby's phone call to the Ops desk asking for her son was the plan's catalyst. Earl's F-15 fini-flight was early tomorrow morning. While he was airborne she was to leave an urgent message at the Ops desk that she and her cameraman were trapped along with a number of residents and needed help. Abby prayed the fire would not spread too quickly tonight and ruin her plan. She was picking Amy up at the airport in a few hours. Abby's excitement to be with both her children was to the point of distraction. Her plan had come together, oh, so nicely.

Chapter 46

The perch, six to nine thousand feet behind and a few thousand feet above, is where Fiend positioned his Eagle in relation to the two-ship of F-15s, led by Duke, along with his wingman Tornado. Flying six to nine thousand feet apart from each other in line abreast formation with a four thousand foot altitude stack made it almost impossible to visually pickup the two fighters in a single moment's glance. Even in the age of highly sophisticated jets with advanced internal radar and sensor detection systems, fighter pilots still depended on visual mutual support. A thin blanket of comfort drapes over them when they can see their wingman in formation. It is the willing dependency, admitted Fiend, the willingness to depend on another pilot that formed his love of being a fighter pilot. And now Duke was leaving. He felt that as if Duke's departure was affecting his relationship with the beloved Eagle.

Peering over their shoulder to reconfirm their wingman's presence, they both scanned deep behind their wingman through tinted helmet visors and inch thick super plexi-glass canopies for any glint, any movement aft of their formation that may indicate the presence of a bandit. The same way Fiend and Duke looked after their wingmen and flight leads over Bosnia.

This particular training exercise was designed to practice survivability in the event the element of Eagles is surprised by a bandit behind them. The challenge for the two-ship is to survive against a simulated heat seeking missile launch from the bandit. The exercise began by a radio call from Duke.

"Fights on."

"Mojo break left, bandit high six o'clock!"

Duke and Tornado crank a nine-G defensive reaction turn into Fiend, acting as the bandit, while dispensing flares to lure Fiend's heat seeking missile off of the twin GE 110 engines. The nine-G pull collapsed Duke and Tornado into the pit of their ejection seats. The urge to react is immediate and intense. At nine-Gs, straining to remain conscious is the only priority. Their motor heat signatures cooled as Duke and Tornado slammed their throttles back to the idle stop. The defensive turn is the only way to thwart any incoming missiles by masking the heat signature of the engines with the jet's fuselage. The hard turn eased the difficulty of maintaining talley-ho of Fiend, now pulling up high into the sun attempting to hide and gain more turning room as Duke and Tornado continued a slight descending, tight radius turn. Their engines, having been powering down for ninety degrees of turn, forced their F-15s to descend, thereby giving up altitude for more airspeed in order to generate the smallest radius turn possible.

Fiend begins a commentary out loud, to himself. The cockpit voice recorder was turned on at fights on. He completes the commentary phrase by phrase; in between deep and rapid inhales for air. Prior to the fights on call he set his regulator to give him 100% oxygen. He wanted his brain fully cognizant.

"Patience is mandatory...as nine-Gs soon reduce to seven...almost twice the number of Gs felt at any high-end roller coaster." He stopped and gulped in the rich oxygen mix. "Much easier to actually begin to work your hands and fingers over the weapon and radar switches on the throttles and stick." He stopped, exhaled and took another breath. "The demands for patience are intertwined...with the absolute necessity...for accurate perceptions and correct reactions...Patience must swell...and dominate...to permit the jet to respond...to the simultaneous stick, rudder and throttle inputs...Perceptions of bandit maneuvers...must translate into accurately predicting and analyzing...the results of your unconscious hand movements...actuating flight controls in relation to the maneuvering bandit...In order to participate in this death dance...with any chance of returning for encores...eyeballs must have hands attached." He was very pleased with his soliloquy and he thought he might use it in his instructional sessions with the new pilots in the squadron.

Inside his cockpit, Duke twists and contorts, arching his head up and yanking his neck around to maintain tally-ho of the bandit (Fiend) through the top back section of the canopy.

Duke's right arm seemed petrified and welded to the control stick. His fingers remained flexible and alert for the opportunity to squeeze the Gatling gun trigger or mash down on the red missile fire button located on top of the stick. As Duke perceived Fiend's nose pulling up and away from his two-ship he slammed both throttles full forward, working to get the engines cooking again at full afterburner. Duke pulled hard against the flight control stick and his G-suit, a pair of Nomex chaps with rubber bladders sewn in the waist and legs, filled with air, inflating and tightening around his lower torso and legs. Initially under nine-Gs, his straining against the filled bladders kept the blood from pooling lower than his head-- preventing tunnel vision and loss of consciousness. When blood circulation slows in the eyes, peripheral vision goes to hell. As he strained to keep his head and helmet from sinking to his knees, a distracting thought leaked from his mind. How many times have I slammed these damned throttles against the stops over the years? It never ceases to amaze me they don't break off against the forward and aft stops of the throttle casing.

"Duke, you damn wily bastard...You are a bitch to kill and you will be missed," Fiend growled to himself, again unable to fire a simulated heat seeking missile or 'heater' as Duke hard turned his jet again. As Duke's wingman, Tornado's task is to first turn and defend himself against any bandit weapon launched his way and then not ram into Duke in the process. This requires keeping tally-ho on the bandit and visual on his wingman, Duke. Simultaneously, Duke and Tornado twisted and cranked their necks around during the high-G turn to maintain sight on the bandit's nose to determine if Fiend was following up the first simulated missile shot with another.

Today's fight was in crystal clear vodka sky, with an afternoon sun doing a stellar job of hiding Fiend. Fiend initially pointed at Duke, and as soon as the two ship cranked into a hard right turn Fiend snap pulled up into the sun to position himself directly over the turning two-ship. Fiend's grin hints that both Duke and Tornado have gone "no-joy", that is, lost sight of him. Fiend's airspeed bleeds off rapidly during his sixty-degree nose high maneuver. He shoved his fat right boot hard against the rudder pedal and pushed the stick to the forward stop causing his F-15 to pirouette right, and then relaxed the stick to dump the nose straight down, hastening the acceleration back towards Earth. Again Fiend jammed the stick forward to point directly at Duke and Tornado that have now rolled wings level attempting to make an afterburner escape out West. But the two-ship does not have necessary distance and opening velocity to escape another missile from Fiend. Fiend recognized this as well as both Tornado and Duke, who contrary to what Fiend had hoped, never lost sight of him. Duke calls for the two-ship to break back into the bandit, popping out flares from the canister in the bottom fuselage, once again to defeat any incoming heat seeking missile. Fiend was level on the horizon as Duke pulled hard and into Fiend to meet nose to nose. Five hundred feet is the minimum safety bubble around each fighter during training. Duke and Fiend pass canopy to canopy at five hundred and five feet, both pilots hearing the muted, blasting sound of their respective bow waves of air violently colliding about them. At the merge Duke jacks the nose straight vertical, like a space shuttle lifting off, forcing Fiend to choose either Duke or Tornado to engage. Being outnumbered, another option was for the bandit to attempt escape. Not likely with Fiend as the bandit.

"Into the phone booth we go, bitch," said Fiend out loud, choosing to fight Duke one-on-one, wearing a sweaty sloppy grin behind his rubber oxygen mask. Single seat fighter pilot conversations were brief bursts of guttural emotions not intended for anyone else's ears but the ones who utter them. The love of flying by oneself was matched by the occasional need to spew visceral utterances out loud and not having to answer for the outburst. And he knew his outbursts, when heard by the younger pilots, would be enough to mold them into aerial killing machines. Just as he knew he would always mark for a short fighter pilot career, those pilots, who in his mind did not possess the inner stuff to kill any enemy within weapons reach. And Fiend no longer prayed to God that he be right about his decisions. He knew he was right. He believed he could see the truth.

Fiend loved going into the phone booth and he loved calling his adversary a bastard and a bitch in the same sentence—whether it be an enemy or squadron mate. Necessary verbal visceralaties, he called them--seemingly meaningless juxtapositions. He loved the senseless wordplay. He loved everything about language. He jacked his jet into the pure vertical and entered the phone booth, following Duke's flight path towards the sun. Every aspect of this engagement was violent. Twitchy feet and tight-gripped fingers slammed rudder controls and engine throttles respectively, to maneuver and counter move, necks twisting left then quickly bending up and right to keep sight, air-filling G-suits compressing legs and torsos to prevent veins and arteries from allowing blood to pool in the lower extremities and away from the brain—the summation of aerial battle was violent motions to achieve ends that are violent by premeditation. This destructive yet social enterprise was directed by a solitary violent thought that focused only on one thought; exploding the adversary and guaranteeing a fireball the size of an antebellum mansion vomiting pieces and bits of aluminum, steel, hair, teeth and eyeballs for all within visual range to be witness of, and internalize that sight into a distinct vision of terror.

But damn, thought Fiend, the sheer pleasure of violent pursuit tastes like nothing epicurean, not even sexual, but more a hint of ecstasy only mystics' claim to experience.

"Mystics can kiss my sweet sweat soaked ass," mumbled Fiend into his foul smelling facemask as he tickled the buffeting control stick back into his crotch.

His jet was now inverted, converting the pure vertical maneuver into a skinny loop, and Fiend's neck cranked back against the aft limits of his spinal column. A strange sort of grinning wince slid across his face as he eyeballed Duke directly below. Duke made his decision. He was going into the phone booth with Fiend. It is where fighter pilots dueled in a tight space—radically maneuvering in the vertical with minimal horizontal distance between jets—very up close and very personal--an aerial knife fight. The airspeed varies from 125 to 325 knots within this deadly ballet. A classic slow speed fight evolves from both jets blasting 90 degrees towards the stars and settling to a wings level attitude with their jet nose pointing high, 70 degrees and then some, with the jets bleeding off airspeed until just above stall speed—a couple of knots above stall speed. Both Duke and Fiend's control sticks were now buffeting against their right hands as their fingers finely coaxed the flight controls to eke out some additional altitude while banking ever so slightly to drift towards each other's high 6 o'clock. Duke knew well enough to avoid over-banking his F-15 or it would begin to stall, slipping the nose towards the horizon, losing altitude and generating a predictable descending and fatal flight path. This part of the phone booth fight was referred to as 'the scissors', for the flight paths slowly converge, cross, diverge and repeat. From an angels perch above them, each time their flight paths crossed it appeared as a 'leaf' in the scissors. Both pilots felt the control stick buffet, finessing a fine hair filament away from being buried against the aft stop and causing the F-15 to stall. Nimble, life-loving fingers tickled the stick in order not to further upset the already disturbed airflow over the wings and horizontal stabilizers. From the angels perch, an observer would see two jet flight paths in a slow and gentle crossing and uncrossing maneuver. The scissors was all about staying as slow as possible while projecting an intended flight path towards each the other's high 6 o'clock position. Fiend never much cared for this part of slow speed fighting. It was the only part of aerial dog fighting where he had any scent of weakness. Duke on the other hand, loved the scissors, precisely because Fiend grew impatient in the slow crossings. Sooner or later Fiend would slip below and underneath Duke's jet, hiding from Duke's sight while descending, descending further, and building enough altitude separation between the jets for Fiend to alter the complexion of the fight to what was known as the 'egg fight.'

A lone fighter pilot low on fuel, anchored and predictable in a slow speed knife fight with an adversary always welcomed the sight of his wingman. At the merge Duke's wingman, Tornado, had blown straight through gaining airspeed and distance, while Duke took the fight in the vertical, causing Fiend to lose sight of Tornado Bergsten—which was the intention. Tornado kept sight of them while maneuvering a few miles away to setup a pitch-back rescue maneuver towards their slow vertical fight—which was precisely what Tornado did. Tornado then radioed Duke that he was visual and tally the bandit.

"Blow through," Duke commanded in reply. That command meant Tornado did not have the flight lead's permission to employ weapons against the bandit and instead, get the hell out of the fight and back out of sight. Knowing full well that Duke and Fiend intended to wrap it up some more, Tornado acknowledged by repeating his callsign and intention, "Mojo 2, blowin' through." Tornado aileron rolled 3000 feet from the two slow speed fighters going 500 knots, leveled out and then pulled his jet straight up towards the angel's perch. He elected to watch from well above their position, in the sun and in a slow and wide, shallow banked turn—very unsound tactically but then again, this mission was not all about honing tactical performance. This mission was about the final aerial duel between Duke and Fiend. If not for this, Tornado could have easily popped the bandit sixty seconds ago with a simulated heat missile shot—with or without Duke's permission. But not this engagement. The remaining 2000 pounds of fuel was going towards their last fight in the phone booth, up close and eyeball-to-eyeball. They were now in a well developed egg fight, in essence, chasing each other in a vertical loop--the loop resembled a silhouette of an egg, with the top portion narrow and the bottom of the loop wide due to the increase of airspeed on the bottom, which increased the radius of the loop. The test was to see who can go back over the top of the egg shaped loop with the slowest airspeed, use God's-G at the apogee, and not stall going over the top of the loop. If a stall occurred, the pilot did not have enough airspeed to coax his flight controls to get the nose below the horizon, and the fighter would appear to hang up on top of the loop, becoming stuck in the sky, or in fighter pilot parlance, a strafe rag. The egg fight was fought in full afterburner and the up-close witness of dueling twin tailed, raging double-after-burning engined F-15s tangling in a 3000 foot diameter egg fight was a sight reserved only for angels and fighter pilots. Hand eye coordination, the marriage of fingers and control stick, patience, feel, and perception of motion were all on test in the phone booth. Fiend would say, "In the phone booth, fuck anything up...and the last up-close person you see most likely is the one who blew you away."

Barely halfway up the side of the egg, Duke changed the fight by performing a magnificent pirouette in full grand view of Fiend's cockpit--just as Fiend tickled his stick aft, attempting to go back over the top. Fiend became entranced for a micro second--mesmerized by Duke's ailerons, horizontal and vertical stabilizers in violent flutterings working to get the 40,000 pound F-15 to appear to rotate from nose high to nose low in front of him, like an Alaskan State Fair pinwheel.

"Damn...that was sweet!" Fiend screamed inside his mask, followed up by two whoops and a holler, not only for the transcendent pirouette but because the time had arrived to begin the final ritual.

"Ahh, the dance of the sugar plum fairies," said Tornado to himself, looking down from above, releasing his oxygen mask away from his nose and his widening, slouching grin.

Fiend stomped in left full rudder to dull his upward trajectory and rotate his flight path to the new flight path Duke was beginning to carve. This forced action flopped Fiend's jet around like a toy, causing it to enter into an extreme nose low attitude. Their jets were twirling about each other nose low-- with no more than 500 feet separating them canopy-to-canopy. Both pilots were witness to each other's thoughts through the witness of each other's aircraft flight control surfaces in theatric hydraulic motion—fluttering up and down, banging back and forth, smooth, jerky--as they both fell towards Earth. These were not traditional bed-time story sugar plum fairies—they were killer fairies with fangs out and Fiend was thinking the sugar plums damn well better be fermented to satisfy and lubricate yearning taste buds or else there'd be hell to pay. He loved this fight. And he whooped again and thanked God on the spot, knowing Duke would be proud of him of thinking of God rather than his dick thinking for him. Their canopy twirl affair was loosening up, their jets sliding further away from one another as they both decreased their angle of bank.

"Floor transition," Fiend uttered to his black-faced dials, alighted multi-purpose cathode displays, and knobby aluminum toggle switches. His cockpit now reeked of pilot musk. Tightening his lips and scrunching his face into a full squint Fiend increased bank and pushed his stick forward to slip out of the gentle orbit and transitioned into a wide-arced dive outside Duke and Fiend's flight path circle.

"Ok now, time to kill the bandit and get to the bar," said Fiend to himself, thinking Tornado should be positioning for a missile shot against him at any moment.

Duke and Fiend were now at opposite ends of a horizontal turning fight, hugging the artificial floor of 5000 feet above the glacier laced, snow covered ground. Neither had gained any advantage in the phone booth or the transition to the 5000 foot floor. Both were low on airspeed and fuel, that is, predicable, and easy pickings for any other fighter thirsty for an easy kill.

"Mojo 1, say position," barked Tornado to his element mate, not wanting to shoot the wrong jet. Tornado kept track of who was who during the entire engagement but there was no need to place the wrong jet in his sights when a confirmatory radio call would settle any doubt.

"Separating east," replied Duke, as he rolled his jet wings level, accelerating and attempt to extricate himself from the fight.

"Tally'ho…Kill bandit, right hand turn through North," declared Tornado, releasing his simulated weapon the moment he perceived Duke's wings begin to roll level. He did not actually hear Duke's declaration until after he pickled the simulated missile. He estimated two and a half seconds missile time of flight before announcing his kill over the radio. It was a valid kill shot because Tornado could visually confirm his missile seeker head never wandered off Fiend's roaring engines during the missile's projected time of flight. And no flares spewed from Duke's jet.

"Copy, Kill--bandit's bingo," said Fiend, in an exaggerated drawl, saying to himself, "About damn time you shot me, Tornado."

"One knock-it-off, two knock-it-off…three knock-it-off," all acknowledging the fight was over.

Chapter 47

Tiffany remained in Anchorage, sipping coffee and checking the Internet in the hotel lobby--on phone alert. In the parking lot outside Wal-Mart in Eagle River, Abby made the fake frantic call to the Ops Desk as Earl's flight was returning to base. She introduced herself and asked to speak to the Desk officer as soon as possible. At dinner, Bartholomew told Tiffany there was a Desk officer always on hand during flying hours. Abby now was talking to Major Brady.

"Please sir, tell my son to get here as fast as he can— please do this for me. Sir, please let him know I may be trapped up here in the Wasilla fire."

"Ma'am, he's currently airborne. He'll land in about twenty minutes."

"You can contact him from the squadron can't you? Please call him and tell him to come up to Wasilla. You'll do that for me, won't you? Please? Take my number down and call me when he knows-ok?"

"I will ma'am." Danny returned from Wal-Mart with mosquito repellent, a couple of thin light rain parkas, a Coleman camping stove, two packs of Marlboro Reds, beef jerky, and two plastic jugs of drinking water. Abby watched him pack up the van, and then offered to push the cart over to the cart stand two parking slots away. Danny gave her a funny look.

"I'll take you up on that Abby. Thanks." First time she ever did something like that, he thought. Amazing what the small things in life can do for a man's outlook. As was his custom, Danny opened Abby's door for her, but let her close the door herself. She could see smoke high and in the distance. Perfect, she thought.

Traffic seemed light as they headed north up Highway 1 towards Wasilla. Soon however, the traffic started to build and they slowed to a crawl. Abby fidgeted in her seat, craning her neck to see over the cars lining up ahead of them. "How far we got to go?"

"About five or six miles."

"Where you going to pull off the highway?" Abby said, fumbling for a cigarette.

"You can't wait until we park?"

"No Danny, I cannot wait 'til we park." She lit the cigarette and blew the first exhale out her window. Abby leaned out the window straining to see a roadblock. She could make out flashing patrol car lights about a half-mile ahead.

"About a half a mile, that's where the roadblock is. We have to get off this damned highway and over there." She pointed off to the right where the smoke was dark and obscuring the Chugach Mountains.

"The fire is over *there* Danny. Over there!"

"Go and put on that mosquito repellent. Don't be shy either. Don't forget your ankles. "Abby mocked his orders in silence, making an ugly face. Danny smiled. Extinguishing her cigarette between her fingers, she then tossed the butt out the window, undid her seatbelt and reached for the Wal-Mart bag. She cursed while struggling with the tight child proof wrapping over the cap.

"Give it to me," said Danny, biting into the wrap and creating a tear.

The American Savior

"Now give it back to me," directed Abby, ripping the wrapping away from the bottle of repellent.

"Smells wonderful," she said, nose scrunched up as she squeezed a small amount into the palm of her hand.

"You're going to need more than that."

"You drive, I'll apply. And when are we going to get off this damned road and start heading that way?"

"Now." Danny flipped on his right turn signal and turned off the highway, in front of a dulled yellow, weather tortured, concrete block auto parts store and Mexican food restaurant. He appreciated the combination--auto parts and Mexican food. He knew he'd be a regular if they carried old Ford parts and served giant shredded beef Chimichangas smothered in mole or green chili sauce—either one is fine--and Dos Equis Dark. Always tough to find parts for his '71 wood paneled, deep green Ranchero. The uneven road quickly turned to packed gravel, then loose, then dirt about three hundred yards in. The smoke smell was invasive. Danny got out of the driver's seat, running around the front of the van to get to the side door, which Abby already opened. After sliding his backpack on and grabbing his camera, Abby then slammed the van door and they stepped into deep grass, and into a marsh. Danny slipped as he tried to pull up his left leg, now knee deep in the marsh, and fell on his backpack. He kept his camera on his chest as he called to Abby.

"Take my camera! Careful," Danny directed Abby to approach him very slowly. She felt her boots start to sink in muck. Danny lifted his camera behind him trying to hand it off to Abby, who froze in place unsure where to go or what to do.

"Take my camera Abby. Now!"

"I can't!" she screamed, as she lost sight of her boots in the muck.

"Fall back and lie down. Turnover on your stomach and crawl out!"

"But I'll get all grimy!"

"Do it now!" Danny paused, hearing the panic overtaking him, slowed his speech, and said in a low calm voice, "Abby, turn on your stomach and crawl out. You're only a few feet into the bog. Please go now." Whining and cursing, Abby did as Danny instructed. She was soon clear.

"I'm tossing my camera to you now," continued Danny calmly, "And you will catch it. It's heavy. Get ready now, get ready." Danny flung the camera with all he had in a high arch to give Abby enough time to prepare to catch it. Smoke was around them now, and they tasted ash. The smoke scratched their throats. Reaching out, Abby realized Danny's throw was not enough. Falling forward, she grabbed the camera twelve inches before hitting the soft ground. It was the best she could do, softening the landing. Dragging the camera backwards she then picked it up and checked for damage.

Danny struggled to remove his backpack. After, he flipped open the top and pulled out a ten foot rope. He tossed one end back towards Abby. She looked up in front of Danny and swore she saw a lick of orange flame through the trees. Smoke swirled about them.

"Grab the rope!" Danny was screaming again. His pain was now excruciating. He had fallen on his backpack and landed on the small axe he always carried for emergencies. That hurt bad enough. But twisting off the backpack from his shoulders pulled his lower back muscle, now with sharp intense pain shooting through his hips and lower back. Abby picked up the rope and wrapped it around her wrist and forearm.

"Pull Abby!" Danny screamed in agony as he tried to pull his legs from the muck. On his back Danny could see flames above him, the tops of the dry trees catching fire. The rope was too short. Abby began to sink into the marsh as she tried to pull against the rope. She saw the flames. The hot rush of wind against her face blew off her tears, as new ones formed.

"Stay back Abby-stay back I say!" screamed Danny, as he noticed her creeping forward towards him.

"I can't let you stay here!' screamed Abby.

"Go. Go now. To the van!" He reached inside his pants pocket and flung the van keys towards her. She caught them and again fell back to the soft ground. Turning back on her stomach she crawled away from Danny. The fire was to her immediate left and she soiled herself feeling the searing heat against her cheek. She ran without her short boots, just her socks. They were lost in the muck. Sticking the gearshift in reverse she floored the gas and accelerated. Hysterical now, Abby beat her hand against the steering wheel as she looked through the side view mirror to stay on the road. Cranking the steering wheel hard to the right she swerved until the back of the van slammed against a small pine. Jamming the gear into drive Abby skidded back onto the dirt road as it turned back into loose gravel. Tears streamed down Abby's face as she screamed. Passing the auto parts and Mexican food restaurant Abby turned north and drove on the highway, now empty of traffic. The fire had crossed the highway in front of her and she was now in the fire zone. The roadblock had been abandoned and was set up further south. She swerved again and roared onto the highway heading south in a hysterical, tearful rage.

The highway patrol stopped short of her van. Abby had stopped the van in the middle of the empty road and got out to see fire swallowing up everything she had just left. She collapsed on the street. The patrolman quickly exited his vehicle and attempted to lift Abby from her knees. Easing her into the backseat, they roared south, with Abby lying down, her face buried in the empty seat, screaming. What the patrolman was never to forget was Abby, on her knees, clenched fist smashing the pavement, wailing, "Save him, save Danny—please son. Save me, save me, save me!"

Chapter 48

Earl "Duke" Neuhaus slow-rolled his gleaming metal wingtips up and down, pausing momentarily at the ninety degree point, giving each wingtip light a chance to wink to the high heavens. Left wingtip green light, right wingtip red light. The wing rock signaled Fiend and Tornado to rejoin into a visual formation for the return to base. In Duke's mind, the wing rock also signaled the last time he would fight in the F-15. He wanted the wingtips never to touch the horizon because as far as he was concerned his last fight was at an end, and pangs of regret were aching his insides. He thought about seeing his father soon. He flipped up the red regulator switch and sucked in cool 100% oxygen to clear his head and soothe his heart.

Sweaty masks were all detached from the right side of their helmets and dangled from the left bayonet clip, bumping against their harnesses that connected them to the ejection seat. Tornado and Duke shoved up their clear visor covers and pulled their dark visor down for the ride home. Fiend never liked visors and never used them, instead he relied on his metal gold framed sunglasses with his 'special prescription' that enabled him to not only see a speck of a jet miles away but some say he could see thoughts and intentions of the hundreds of pilots he had trained, flown with--and against. But his magic specs needed the slimy exertions of the day's fight wiped clean, and with far too much effort required, he pulled the chamois strip from his glasses case stowed in his G-suit leg pocket. Wiping his specs he grumbled, "I'm getting too damned wide to fit in my damned jet."

Returning to base was a seventeen-minute cruise and ten minute descent to landing. The last ten minutes were busy handling descent checks and reviewing approach plates in the event an instrument approach was required. During the seventeen minutes they returned to a normal state. Adrenalin stopped activating the heart into survival mode. Quickened pulses slowed, sweat coated and cooled their skulls and upper bodies, and breathing returned to an unhurried pace. Tornado replayed the last engagement in his mind to identify areas where he could have reacted quicker or maneuvered more efficiently. Fiend slipped a pinch of tobacco behind his lower lip and waited for the nicotine to charge his brain. Earl's leaving for the Texas Air National Guard was not how Bartholomew envisioned their flying career. He had no other contemporary on the entire base, not even Tornado—hell, he thought there was no other person he could trust with his vulnerabilities. Earl stood very much alone, that was for sure, thought Bartholomew, compared to anyone he had ever met, and he felt hollow inside realizing he was leaving for Texas. For it did not matter to Earl how impenetrable your defenses were; Earl saw everything and still remained his closest friend. Bartholomew became Fiend in full view of Earl's commitment not to judge. All the bombast and excess Fiend was known for; Earl said nothing about what Bartholomew had become.

Bartholomew also started thinking about seeing Amy again. Billy D. and the Mrs. set her loose from The Shelter. It was time for her to go and start new. Listening to Amy on the phone, Bartholomew let himself become entranced with the same prospect himself. He wished she'd be on the flight ramp waiting for them right now. He could not wait to see her. I know Earl will be surprised in a good way, he thought.

Earl rested his damp flight gloves up on the glare shield to dry out. He always flew at least some part of the flight gloveless, just to have his hands feel the controls, throttles, and switches. It was his way of close connecting with the F-15. In every basic fighter maneuvering academic session to the new guys he stressed that it is indeed a fact that man and machine must become one.

Duke would lecture, "To resist this relationship with your jet is to limit your ability to place it where it needs to be when you need it to be there." He was always quick to add, "But when you're done with your post-flight walk-around, the relationship is severed. Leave the jet on the ramp. Hell, even a badass like Fiend lets the Eagle go when the mission's over. Without question, there's a time to fly and fight. But most of the time we're with each other—or if not amongst us, then with those ladies who you've somehow convinced that you're the right guy."

For Duke, the seventeen minutes returning to base were the best times to cancel all thoughts, keep minimally attuned to the air traffic controller's direction, and let the Eagle fly him home so he could gaze at the sky and landscape passing underneath. Yet today, thoughts crept into to his mind. It was a precious time, a time to soak in the joy of being able to wonder at all he could visually capture as truth. He was not searching for a type of topography so much as absorbing it, whether it be the deserts of Nevada or Iraq, or the white capped sprinkled Pacific Ocean with the Malaysian Peninsula just coming into view through the equatorial afternoon haze, or skimming the gnarly snow stained peaks of Alaska, he amassed joy at the wonderment of flying over all the Earth. Flying alone enabled intimacy with not just Earth, but the Universe. Some would say with God, but Duke did not think of God. And flying at night, intimacy was with the shimmering stars, the lusty Aurora Borealis, and the attempt to form an intimacy with the infinitesimal immenseness of the universe. He was in love with all that he could see. And he wanted to see more, from a different point of view. He was beginning to look forward to seeing his mother. He was going to tell her that father was dying and she should see him. He knew she would. Abby had also delivered on her promise. She located the bus driver's widow. Her name is Monika. She's agreed to talk to me. He planned to meet her passing through on his way to Houston. He had to meet Monika.

In order to be with his father Earl was transitioning to the Texas Air National Guard where he would fly the F-16 part time and immerse himself in the ways of one of the savviest political machines in recent memory. And by getting a humanitarian transfer to take care of his father, he also answered the call of the two colonels. The same colonels who flew in to Reese AFB, danced with his mother and sister at the O'club, and hired his father to work for them in Houston. Earl now had to know if he could reject the temptation whilst in the midst of the tempters. He had to; he knew this to be true. He had to exorcise what both his father and mother succumbed to. To prove his strength to himself rather than run away, he had to get into the black heart of power. The Texas governor political machine was the blackest of them all—one thing his father and mother could both agree.

(First prison letter from 'Chance' Neuhaus to Earl)

Dear Earl,

A prison cell is not my idea of an ideal setting to write my son a letter. But here I sit and here is where I write.

I want to write about you. Really, I want to write how I feel about you. I won't repeat what I've said before about how I regret my decisions (or non-decisions) that got me in this place. What a delusion, pretending I wasn't a fraud. Denying what I, in fact, am, and have done, is my new definition of hell. Luckily, and without too much irony, I'm only here for a short time.

Back to you. I'm not trying to convey anything other than you are a joy in my life, not because you write me, call me, and visit this glorious place. Well, OK, it is because you write, call and visit. And more. You are smart, level headed, and calm when the time calls for someone to be smart, level headed, and calm. Extraordinary for a young man. You will do great things in life. Things that mean something in life. You will. I'm sure of it.

Rabbi Benny enjoys your company. But I think he truly relishes the fact his daughter thinks you are "it." He remains excited at the prospect of a Jewish girl marrying a Catholic man. Definitely surprised me on that one—baptized. Anyway, the Rabbi is something, I tell you. Thank Yahweh he's stuck in here with me. Otherwise this place would be real. And I would not be well.

All for now.
With love,
Dad

(Earl's last letter to his Father)

Dear Dad,

Wished you were here for graduation. I wanted you to pin on my wings. Amy stood in for everyone and put them on. We are getting along ok. We don't argue as much anymore. Not much to argue about these days, a good thing. She is still a lost soul and I hope she finds a good man. She doesn't seem to attract them however. Mom showed up at the graduation party. I didn't know she was coming. We barely spoke a word to each other. Amy thought it would be a nice surprise. Well, it certainly was a surprise. I can't blame Amy. Did you by chance know Mom was coming? I assume you don't talk to her. Is that still true? It was still more painful to see her than anything. Although I was glad to see her. If that makes any sense. She's making an effort I guess. Strange way of going about it, though. I'm trying to be more patient with her but I'm not calling her anytime soon.

I hope to see you after my F-15 training. Not much opportunity for me to visit while I'm in Florida but if I can I'll try. I plan on taking some leave before I have to report to my permanent duty station and definitely visit then. I know you are counting the minutes to get out of there. Call me the moment when you are a free man!

Love, Earl

Chapter 49

From his body angle, he'd never get the best view of the mountains, thought Earl, attempting to move against his shoulder harness. No go. He said to himself, "I can stay in this position for a while--until my lower back starts tightening." For now, he felt relaxed and in no hurry to move about, much less get out of his ejection seat. With his right hand he lowered the helmet's grey tinted visor. The front instrument panel appeared powered down. The sun's reflection was sharp and bright, refracting through his canopy. The angle of the sun— something, not sure it is the sun—it's just too bright for me, he thought. Everything seemed washed out in light. Better he thought, with my visor down I can see. Now Earl began to see images sequencing across his grey tinted visor.

He saw Fiend whooping it up, waving his Cuban around as if orchestrating a choir. Fiend was in the squadron bar bouncing his head to a rockin' blues shuffle blaring out of the dusty black grilled stereo speakers mounted above and in the corners of the bar. Earl recalled a story about the bar being built in the mid-80s by eager lieutenants hoping to make their mark in the fighter world. Fiend was yelling over the music, sprinkling cigar ashes over the yet-to-be anointed lieutenant and a fledging captain--both just completing their mission ready check rides. Circled around Fiend were other pilots, a couple of brand new guys who just arrived last week. The rest were experienced squadron pilots, flight suit sleeves rolled up short of the elbows and front zipper dropped below the chest. They were engaged in a full fangled bull shit session on how best to execute a defensive break turn and get to nine Gs without over stressing the jet and losing consciousness. Everyone had an opinion, although each claimed to offer a slightly different technique. Earl smiled to himself, knowing that all techniques were in fact almost identical. Which, as Earl could plainly see, was precisely Fiend's point when throwing out the question to the group. Earl listened as Fiend said, "The secret according to Fiend is the actual timing of the defensive break turn, not necessarily the turn itself. Start earlier than later, if you catch what I'm tellin' ya."

The secret Fiend yelled was, "Your eyeballs gotta be able to go right to the wings and nose of the bandit, watching for any hint of the jet's nose trackin' 'cross the sky and at the same time watching his damn wing tips to see what he's thinkin' 'bout doin' next with his jet. You have to see this all at the same time. If you can't see all them details right-away your screwed, boys. Not Phillips screwed, just straight screwed."

Earl smiled again, observing Fiend tilt his back and pouring a shot of Jeremiah Weed down his throat, an obscure bourbon liqueur known primarily to fighter pilots and submariners. Now he winked and grinned at Earl. Pilot's call signs were burned into the thick lacquer finish, along with the years they spent in the squadron. Fiend lifted his empty shot glass to toast Earl and turned around to re-join the shouting circle of drunken fighter pilots.

Now Earl caught a glimpse of a glow of amber light in the dark corner of the bar and as he squinted to locate the source of light, the music and raucous bar talk ceased. Earl was watching a three-year-old boy mow the front lawn grass with his new orange and red plastic lawn mower. The wheels bounced

285

along the high grass activating a thick low whirring sound to replicate the mower engine. Little Travis was making engine sounds to add to the realism of the Saturday afternoon ritual. After wiping sweat from her striking brow, his wife gave him and their son, Little Travis, her trademark wide smile as she watched her precious baby following his Dad around doing the actual mowing. Earl let loose of the wide bar under the mower handle and cut the engine. Saturdays were not complete without the smell of fresh cut Bermuda.

Little Travis stopped his mower and ran over to his Dad with right arm raised. They gave each other a high hand slap for another front yard mowed. But that doesn't seem just right, thought Earl. He saw his good friend Tornado Bergston wrap his arm around her and squeeze. Standing by, Earl could see her body bend closer to Tornado as he squeezed her close. Earl "Duke" Neuhaus said to himself, "That's not Helen." Earl's confusion dissipated as he saw his old neighbor, ancient Portis Wiebalk, waving his hand out his new red Cadillac as he drove in slow motion by and into his garage, the door barely half-way up as he nudged his Caddy's nose under the door, impatient as always for the half horsepower motor to pull back the custom made teak piece of work, complete with eighteen inch square panels of South Pacific native geometric designs. Earl's confusion returned. That woman was not Helen. Then he remembered who she was. She was Tornado's wife, not Helen.

A dark shadow appeared, blocking the sunlight. Earl felt for his visor and rolled it back up into the visor cover mounted on his helmet. The darkness remained. A bloated human figure dressed in an aluminum suit bumped something against his canopy. Earl could make out a black tinted, bubble mask

286

pressing against the canopy. He heard nothing. Brilliant sunlight suddenly returned. Earl again fumbled for his visor to shield his eyes but could not find the latch to lower the visor.

The television crew was setting up as if in a rush. The short sleeved and skinny cameraman flipped off the lens cover and buried his left eye into the rubber glare protector while spreading the tripod legs apart with his left leg. He rested the camera atop the tripod and while still looking into the lens waved his right hand above his blond crew cut to get the reporter into the field of view.

She wore her hair in a brunette beehive. Her sky blue dress was tailored to accentuate her narrow waist. Through her makeup mirror she noticed Earl behind her.

"Son, be a dear and move over to the side next to Danny." Danny motioned Earl over to stand behind him while he focused on Abby. Earl took two large steps back and left and watched his mother report the latest on Hurricane Missy. He couldn't remember any hurricane named Missy. He remembered Fiend's thoughts on such storms. "All my greatest loves were hurricanes disguised as curvaceous beauties of the fairest gender. What a gloriously effective disguise. Fell for 'em every time, and they blew me away. My God in heaven--like I was nothin' but a big ol' soft ball of horny, lovey-dovey."

What confused Earl now was the sky—it was cloudless; the air was still, and the humidity hung heavy all around. Earl "Duke" Neuhaus turned his head slightly towards the ground and viewed the ocean. The surface was like glass. A summer's haze hung about the empty beach. It was Florida—all sweaty and hot. But his mother looked icy cool as she talked on and on about the potential destruction that lies ahead for this popular

Florida Panhandle destination. Danny's white collared shirt was soaked through to his thin-ribbed wife beater t-shirt. Earl noticed the brown stained collar. A red bandana was roughly stuffed in the back pocket of his stiletto khaki slacks. His crisp and shiny black shoes looked out of place. A film of dust settled on the tops of his wingtips. The heat was stultifying.

The sunlight dimmed, accompanied by the return of the firefighter in his blazing silvery protective suit. Sparks from his cutter chipping away near the canopy rail cast a strange shadow—making the fireman's silver partner appear. As Earl closed his eyes, he felt the hacking vibration of the rescue saw jar his flushed red cheeks. His jet was overturned—the canopy was part way sunk in the high soft grass between the parallel runways. The right main gear partially collapsed on touchdown. All cockpit indications displayed three wheels down and locked. Despite Earl's attempts to maintain runway alignment, the right main gear's collapse stressed and sheared off his right main wheel and his jet departed the prepared surface.

The blonde marbled plastic Ocarina. Earl's father used to play the ocarina when he was a boy. It seemed such an odd instrument to play as a big person, Earl recalled. Such pretty melodies, so simple and repetitive. He would play them over and over again until Earl Neuhaus fell asleep. He loved his father. Very much. Earl knew he would see him soon. He was excited to read Rabbi Benny's final letter to Earl.

Earl's eyes were open but only off-white flash images came into view. Distorted, cartoonish images of people he did not recognize. They moved together, as if swaying against smooth yet strong gusts of random wind. Irregular. Sweet music filled his head. Now he recognized them. They were from

Lubbock. The tornado. Yes, there they are. The bus driver and his son, standing close, holding his father's hand. Creamy Hammond organ notes back dropped a silky slide guitar, guitar licks lingering for just the right amount of tension before releasing and resting on the wavering tremolo—or was it chorus? The Leslie speaker illuminating a Hammond B3 organ--which Earl admitted to himself--was his favorite sound. The melodic hook and groove were irresistible. What was he swaying too? He knew now. Fear left him. He wondered if his big gaping grin was real or was it his mind's grin...or his soul's grin.

In that moment, a flash of clarity struck him. And the deep lock boxes of Earl's memories vanished. The contents were set free. And memories were his treasures to love. His heart slowed. The silver man touched Earl's shoulder. Earl pointed to his breast pocket twice, where his mother's letter lay. Earl's heart stopped. It was time to rest.